THE SPIRITUAL WARRIORS

BOOK ONE-WARRIORS OF THE WAY

ORLANDO SANCHEZ

Other titles by Orlando Sanchez

Blur-A John Kane ℕ

The Deepest 𝒞

The Last Danc

THE SPIRITUAL ⟍   ⟋KS

For information contact: www.nascentnovel.com

Book and Cover design by Derek Murphy
http://www.creativindiecovers.com

ISBN: 9781479100903

First Edition: August 2012

10 9 8 7 6 5 4 3 2 1

ACKNOWLEDGEMENTS:
(REVISED 2015)

Every book is a group effort. So let me take a moment to acknowledge my (very large) group:

To Dolly: my wife and biggest fan. You make all of this possible and keep me grounded, especially when I get into my writing to the exclusion of everything else. Thank you, I love you.

To my Tribe: You are the reason I have stories to tell. You cannot possibly fathom how much and how deep I love you all.

To Lee: Because you were the first audience I ever had. I love you sis.

To my editor Lorelei: This was my first book published without an editor and it showed. I decided to give it to you because it felt right going back and having it done this way(after much hand wringing). Having this book edited threw off my timeline for the other books in the series but I am grateful to your expertise and time travelling ability. You were able to meet Dante at the start of his journey and keep his voice authentic. Thank you. Your thoughts and comments made this story go from good to great. Any mistakes in the story are mine.

To you the reader: Thank you for getting on this ride with me. I truly hope you enjoy this story. You are the reason I wrote it.

<u>The Warriors Creed</u>

I will train my heart and body for an unmovable spirit.

I will pursue the true meaning of the warrior's way,

so that in time my senses may be alert.

With true vigor I will cultivate a spirit of selflessness,

I will observe the rules of courtesy,

respect my elders and refrain from violence.

I will follow my spiritual principles, never forgetting the true virtue of humility.

I will look upwards to wisdom and strength, forsaking other desires.

All my life, I will seek to fulfill the true meaning of the Warriors Way.

PROLOGUE

A portal opened and two figures stepped out. The younger of the two looked down at his master with reverence and care as they walked into the park. It was a cold winter morning and he gently adjusted the older man's scarf.

"The lake has been poisoned for a long time, Wei," said the old man as they walked down the path. The old man took slow measured steps as he held onto his student's arm. His cane tapped the stones as they walked. His wispy hair blew in the slight breeze as he stopped to admire the trees.

"I know, Samadhi. I have a stone whose ripples will impact us all." said Wei. "He will be the catalyst we need."

"Sometimes it is better to cut down the tree than to fight to straighten it, especially when the roots have been twisted and corrupted."

"The cost would be too great, Samadhi," said Wei.

"Very well, the three align with you. Cast your stone and prepare," said the old man.

CHAPTER ONE-PROMOTION

It was 11:30p.m. The special promotion began at midnight. I found the small dojo almost by accident, walking by the entrance three times before locating the right door. Despite the fact that I had the address, it was almost as if the entrance was intentionally hidden. I didn't discover until much later, that this was indeed the case. It was located in the basement of a nondescript building on Mott Street in lower Manhattan. The stairs leading to the entrance were an old steel set and creaked every time I stepped on them.

The dojo itself was the definition of minimalism. I had trained in other dojos over the years, with the mirrors, and the characters drawn on long scrolls adorning the walls. Most had modern reception areas with computers and seating areas for guests. It seemed to me that visitors were actually discouraged in this dojo, since there was no seating area for people. A large wooden wall blocked the view of the dojo floor from the entrance. There was a desk and behind it sat a young woman of mixed ancestry. Her jet black hair framed her face, which seemed to be a cross between East Asian and something else I could not identify.

She was thin and wiry, with a presence that radiated incredible strength. She was impeccably dressed in a white blouse that offset her bronze skin. She never spoke, at least not that I had heard and her face remained impassive as each person entered. What I noticed the most were her eyes. They were a deep green, which at first I figured for contacts. I didn't know her name, and I got the feeling that I wouldn't get that information anytime soon. She was stunning. I figured she was a gatekeeper of sorts and that she knew everyone who belonged or trained at the dojo.

Once past her, there was a narrow hall that led to the dojo floor. There was a door on either side of the dojo that led to small changing rooms. The dojo itself was a large room devoid of columns. There were no windows. The floor was a polished hardwood. After the repeated knuckle pushups and poundings I took on it, it was my impression that the wood was petrified. I took off my shoes at the reception area and headed to the changing room.

The changing room was as sparse as the rest of the dojo. There were no lockers, only small cubicles for your clothes. I dressed quickly; being late to a training session wasn't an option. I changed into a white dogi, or uniform, which signaled my status as a beginner. It was made of a lightweight cotton material that absorbed sweat and became increasingly heavy as the training session progressed. In total there were eight students in the class that night. We lined up according to our ranks; those of us with white uniforms in the rear, and the most senior students in black uniforms in the front line. All of us were facing an older gentleman who must have been in his sixties, dressed in black with red trim. We bowed to each other. Then we stood and began the drills. The training session began like any other. We punched, kicked and moved in stances until my body felt it couldn't move any more. Then we paired off. Those of us in white uniforms, the four of us, each faced a senior student dressed in black. It was customary to introduce ourselves prior to fighting, so we bowed to each other. The senior student extended his hand to me and I took it and we shook. It felt like gripping warm steel.

"I'm Devin," he said and smiled.

I bowed. "Dante," I said.

"Stay alert, Dante. Tonight the Master is selecting who will move to the next rank. Whatever happens, you must not give up. Understand?"

I looked at him with a question in my eyes. "Yes, I understand," I said.

Even though I had no way to prepare for what came next.

The Master took a staff and tapped it on the floor: the signal to begin.

At six feet and 210 pounds, I towered over Devin, and clearly outweighed him. I figured with my size and weight advantage, I only needed to hit him a few times, to make it easy on myself.

I figured wrong.

One of the basic principles of fighting is to hit without being hit. Devin had mastered this principle. Barely reaching five feet, he was a small, muscular shadow. Every time I punched, he evaded and peppered me with two or three punches, which I shrugged off. Initially, my kicks—which I considered to be fast—appeared to be moving in slow motion as he sidestepped them, only to fire off kicks of his own. Each time he connected, it felt like I was getting hit with an iron bar. At three minutes, I was breathing hard. After five minutes, it was all I could do to keep my head from being removed from my body by his kicks and punches, which just kept getting faster. After ten minutes, I was prepared to reconsider my decision to train at all. The Master tapped the staff signaling to stop.

"Don't quit, Dante," Devin said.

All I could do was keep breathing. My gi was soaked and clung to me like a second skin. Out of the other three white-uniformed students, it seemed only one was doing badly. Robert was his name. Streaks of blood covered his uniform. One of his eyes had been punched shut, and he was standing gingerly on one foot. I took this all in in a matter of seconds and realized that if we kept fighting, he was done. Another of the students—I think he called himself Zen—seemed to be doing about the same as I was.

There was no clock in the dojo so I couldn't tell how much time had passed. After what seemed like ten minutes, two students came out with staffs in their hands. Each of us was given a staff and faced our seniors. We all stepped back and only Robert and his senior remained. Robert looked about as bad as I felt. I didn't think he would make it through the weapons portion of our particular torture. I made a move to go over to him but Devin gave me a look that rooted me to the spot. With an almost imperceptible shake of his head, I understood that each of us would stand or fall on our own.

"Focus, Dante," Devin mouthed.

I took a moment to center myself and breathe. Forcing all my energy into my lower abdomen, my breathing slowed and I was able to focus. I felt the moisture of my uniform and the hardwood under my feet. The weight of the staff in my hand was familiar, comfortable. My awareness expanded to include the other students; I sensed each one of them around me, we were connected.

Robert stood in the center facing his senior. They bowed to each other and entered a fighting stance. Robert chose a stance that allowed him to compensate for his lack of vision in one eye. I could tell he was an accomplished fighter just from his stance. The senior facing him, I would later discover his name was Yoshiro or Yoshi as I heard him called often, stood about five-eleven. He was of average build and seemed unassuming—the type of person you would underestimate as an easy target. Yoshi assumed a neutral stance with the staff in his left hand. The master tapped the floor with his staff.

Robert yelled and attacked with an overhead strike. Yoshi stepped… no, stepped would be the wrong word. He glided to the right, which was Robert's blind side, and thrust at Robert's left side. Robert barely had time to deflect the thrust before

Yoshi moved again. This time closer, Yoshi used a thrust to distract Robert. As Robert again deflected the staff, staggering back, Yoshi smashed Robert's thigh with his shin. Robert's left leg folded and he fell to one knee. *It's over.* I thought. I moved to get Robert and felt a hand on my shoulder. I turned to look at who it was and saw it was Zen. He shook his head and pointed with his chin. It wasn't over. Yoshi was still circling and preparing for another attack. It was at that moment that I understood that this was no regular promotion. Something deeper was going on here. Robert got to his feet as Yoshi unleashed a barrage of attacks. At some point in the attack, Robert lost his staff, and still Yoshi pressed on. Robert was done. Yoshi attacked and attacked until Robert could no longer stand. He collapsed face first onto the floor, his body making a wet, thudding sound as he crashed forward. Yoshi bowed and stepped back. Two students dressed in red uniforms came in with a stretcher and carefully placed Robert on it. They carried Robert out another door that I had not noticed earlier. The Master tapped the floor again and Zen's senior student stepped into the center. Zen was a big man. He easily stood six-foot-four and weighed close to 250 pounds. His dark brown skin glistened with sweat. He wiped his bald head and smiled as he stepped into the center.

Zen's senior, Marcus, was considerably smaller. Compared to Zen, though, we all were. I had learned by this time not to assume anything about the seniors. Marcus was heavyset, although nowhere near the size of the junior student facing him. He faced Zen and began a series of deep breaths that I knew were called Ibuki. With each breath it seemed his muscles tensed more and more. They bowed to each other. The Master tapped the floor and Zen slid in. Marcus stood still, waiting. Zen lunged in with a thrust and connected squarely with Marcus' midsection. As I followed Zen's staff, I noticed that it had indeed connected and was resting against Marcus' abdomen.

Marcus flinched and sent the staff in Zen's hand back towards him, a look of surprise and admiration racing across Zen's face. He was no longer smiling, but had set his jaw. Marcus stood waiting for him.

"Tell me that is not your strongest strike," said Marcus.

"It's not," Zen answered.

Zen began striking Marcus, Zen's staff hitting Marcus time and again, hitting legs, arms and torso. One blow landed squarely on Marcus' head, and I thought Zen had killed him. Marcus merely smiled but Zen was spent. More than the actual physical exertion, it was the knowledge that his strength was useless against Marcus, who was clearly stronger and impervious to his attack.

"Now we begin, junior," said Marcus. He took a step forward and I could feel the vibration through the floor. Marcus moved slowly, but gracefully. His strikes were efficient and precise. Each time he hit Zen, I heard him grunt in pain. Zen wasn't used to being hurt. Marcus, holding the staff one-handed, brought it down in an overhead strike. Zen raised his staff to deflect Marcus, who at the last second changed direction and crashed his staff squarely into Zen's right side. I heard the crack of bone from where I stood. Zen inhaled sharply, fighting the pain. Zen took a step back and began to breathe deeply in Ibuki. His muscles began to tense like Marcus. Unlike Marcus, though, the tension rippled across his body, moving from area to area. I could see him try and concentrate the tension across his midsection, and for a few seconds it looked like he had done it. Still deflecting the attacks from Marcus, the ones he missed seemed to do little damage. Marcus smiled and then he intensified his attack. The air in the dojo was hot and had a sweet smell to it, like boiling honey. I must have been fatigued from all of the exertion because I could swear that the staff in Marcus' hands began to glow a deep gold. At that sight, the fourth junior— I never got his name—dropped his staff and ran out of the dojo. I guess that confirmed I wasn't imagining things.

There was no way to rationally explain it so I didn't try. Marcus was attacking faster now and connecting more often. Zen began to show signs of exhaustion. Frankly I was amazed he had lasted this long for such a large man. That was the moment everything shifted. Zen rolled back, recovering his balance. Then his staff began to glow as well. It wasn't really a glow, more like a flicker as if the connection wasn't entirely complete. It was the same color as Marcus' staff. The fight was now more of an intricate dance, each missing the other by fractions of an inch as they covered the dojo floor. They moved faster and faster until it was all a blur. I could see that Zen could not keep the pace for long. He was drenched in sweat, and he grimaced in pain any time Marcus connected with his midsection. Marcus, on the other hand, looked fresh and had barely broken a sweat. He was pressing the attack. As he stepped towards Zen, I saw a wave of gold energy travel from his feet, up his body, down his arms and into the staff. He placed the staff lightly against Zen's chest and the room exploded in yellow light momentarily blinding me. Zen flew across the dojo and landed in a heap on the far side of the dojo floor. I ran over to him not caring what would happen to me. Where were the students in red? I made it to Zen's body, he was unmoving. Marcus stood behind me.

"Excuse me," he said.

I stepped aside in silence. It wasn't enough he killed him, he had to gloat, too?

As he knelt towards Zen, Marcus' hands began to glow. They were a warm orange, the color of the setting sun. He placed his hands on Zen's chest and the glow travelled from his hands into Zen, who began to stir. That was when I was aware of the students in red with the stretcher.

"I'm okay, Dante," said Zen with a half-smile on his face. As the students placed him on the stretcher, he winced in pain.

"That last attack really packed a punch," said Zen. You be careful, Dante. I heard stories about your senior."

"Indeed, he is the strongest of us all," said Marcus.

I turned to see Devin waiting for me in the center of the floor. I made my way there, staff in hand. It no longer felt comfortable or familiar.

"Are you ready, junior?" asked Devin once I assumed my fighting stance. My head was screaming "No! You are not ready!" I took a deep breath, centering and grounding myself and eliminating every distraction. Only Devin and I existed.

"I'm ready," I said and bowed to my senior.

The Master stepped forward to Devin. I couldn't guess his age; he seemed made of a dark wood, hard and gnarled. He looked at me impassively, which unnerved me more than if he had dismissed me. He faced Devin and said something in a language I couldn't quite understand, and then Devin bowed to him. Once

Devin finished his bow, the Master stepped behind Devin and produced a silk sash that he tied around Devin's eyes. The sash itself was beautiful; the colors it contained seemed alive and coruscated along the material. Deep reds and blues followed by greens and yellows chased each other around the sash. The Master with an imperceptible nod called Marcus and spoke to him in that strange language again. Marcus stood next to me and spoke.

"This is the dragon's tail," he said, pointing at the sash covering Devin's eyes.

"Dragon's tail?"

"Yes, this is as much a test for him as it is for you. He will not be able to use his eyes to attack or defend."

"Why not just a regular bandana?"

"Because any other material would not have stopped the Senpai, your senior, from seeing."

It never crossed my mind that the seniors were being tested as well. I looked down at the staff that Marcus was holding and noticed it was twice as thick as the one in my hand. He looked at me and smiled knowingly.

The Master looked at me and said," You must have a strong spirit." His voice was deep and resonant.

I bowed and readied myself as the Master stepped to the front of the dojo floor. Devin stood before me; a rainbow of color covered his eyes. Once again we bowed and waited. The Master raised his staff, looked at me, and brought it down, signaling the start of our fight and the end of life as I knew it. Devin stood still, and for a moment I contemplated not attacking—after all he was blindfolded. That moment quickly passed as Devin disappeared and reappeared behind me in the same time it took for me to blink. To my own credit, I reacted instantly and attacked with a rear thrust. I succeeded in deftly hitting the space behind me. Devin, now in front of me, tapped me a few times in my chest and abdomen. I breathed through the pain. Each time I attacked I was two steps behind, hitting empty air.

"You're too slow, Dante."

I said nothing, slowly seething at my inability to hit him. How slow could I be? I tried anticipating where he would strike, which didn't work. I tried stepping back and creating distance, but nothing worked. I couldn't attack. I couldn't defend. As the seconds passed, I got angrier and angrier. I lunged in a rage, frustrated at fighting a wisp, humiliated by my lack of skill.

Devin stepped back and gave me a moment's respite.

"I may be blindfolded, but you are the one who is blind."

"What?!" I said, frustration and anger overwhelming me.

"Why are you angry? You can't attack? So what? You can't defend? So what? Let it go and things will slow down. It's your anger that blinds you, Dante."

Just what I needed, more fortune-cookie speak. Yet somewhere in the back of my brain, a small voice asked, "What if he is right?" I took a deep breath and re-centered. I let go of my attachment to the outcome of this fight. It didn't matter if I won or lost. It didn't matter if I could attack or defend. All that mattered was that I was here in this moment, now. I saw Devin smile as he began his attack. Everything was fluid, grace and power flowed and joined. I saw it all. He was no longer moving too fast, everything had slowed down. He thrust at my midsection, which I sidestepped, bringing my own lower attack at his right leg, which he easily avoided. He feinted at my leg and brought up the staff to my right shoulder with a spinning attack that caught me. The staff crashed into the nerve cluster in my deltoid, rendering my right arm dead weight. One handed, the staff was useless to me now, as it was too heavy and cumbersome. Holding the staff in my left hand and pressing down on it at an angle with my right foot, I stomped its midsection, creating a much smaller staff or jo. I parried Devin's attack, mindful not to let him touch me. With a smaller weapon, I had to close the distance. No small feat when facing a skilled opponent. I feinted left and stepped right. Devin moved too slowly, or so I thought. It was a trap and I rushed right into it. As I brought my jo to crash into his ribs, he spun into my attack and smashed his elbow into my solar plexus. The air rushed out of my lungs and I doubled over. I knew enough not to stay there for more than a split second.

I barely avoided Devin's staff and I stumbled back, forcing my body to breathe again. I re-centered myself, running down options in my head as I circled him. My right arm throbbed, Devin, eyes blindfolded, turned to face my position and attacked. His staff glowed a deep blue. What I couldn't deflect, I avoided. I couldn't close the distance to effectively use my weapon.

How was he "seeing" me? It wasn't sight, so it had to be hearing. I stepped back and stopped moving. Devin stopped as well. He moved his staff as if searching. I had him. I slowly and quietly moved to his left side. I lunged with all the speed I could create. If I connected, this fight would be over. I watched in awe as he avoided my strike. He whirled his staff low, while I stood transfixed. His staff connected—more like crashed—into my calves. For a moment, I was briefly horizontal, and then I saw his leg coming at me. I barely got my arm down in time. He kicked through my jo and into my midsection. The impact sent me flying. I landed on the dojo floor, hard, certain I had broken something, but a quick assessment told me everything was intact. I looked around, noticing I was the only junior left on the floor. Weaponless, I racked my brain on how to attack. If it wasn't hearing, could he sense my movement? It was crazy. It would mean he could sense the displacement of air as I moved around. How was I going to move without disturbing the air? It just couldn't be done. I had seen enough tonight to know we had left the realm of what I thought possible a long time ago. I focused my breath and concentrated. I focused on all those months, years of training into this one moment. I moved without thinking, my only intention to strike Devin. Time slowed and I saw a surprised expression cross Devin's face. I raced in and sent a side thrust kick to his ribs, fully expecting to hit air as he dodged. My foot struck him squarely in the side. My brain noted a few shared inhales of breath from the other seniors. I felt I had hit a steel beam. Devin turned towards me. Too late, I realized my error. For a moment, he couldn't sense me. Rather than utilize that advantage and strike with a head blow, I kicked him instead. It was the last technique I recall. Then everything went black. I awoke with a splitting headache, lying down on a cot in a room that was sparsely decorated. For a moment I had no sense of time or location. There were other cots in the room, most of which were empty.

The students in the red uniforms walked around the room tending to cots that were occupied. I thought I recognized Robert. His face—and come to think of it, most of him—was a mess. I looked on the left side of the room, and had to close my eyes while the room resettled and stopped swaying. I saw Zen, who appeared to be sleeping. After a moment,

I realized he wasn't sleeping. His eyes had swollen shut.

"How do you like my new look?" he said. Most of his upper body was bandaged. One of the students in a red uniform stood next to his cot. He looked like he had been hit by a truck, repeatedly. I tried to sit up; my body immediately vetoed that idea. As I lay there, the room spun on a lazy axis, slowly swaying to and fro. I got the uneasy sensation of being on a ship at sea.

"What kind of promotion was that, Zen?"

Zen laughed or at least attempted to, before the pain brought him up short.

"I heard you actually kicked Devin."

It came back, flooding in. I remembered the kick and then he turned and hit me with something that shut my body down instantly.

"Yeah, it was a setup though. I kicked him and he put my lights out."

"You don't get it Dante. No one has ever laid a technique on him as a senior."

"Well, he was blindfolded, Zen. He had that dragon's tail thing over his eyes." This time Zen did laugh. I liked him more by the minute.

"What you did hasn't been done in a long time, Dante. I'm sure they will want to speak to you."

"Who are they?"

"You'd better get some rest, D." I have a feeling we are going to need it."

"Okay fine, tell me one thing, though."

"What do you want to know?"

"What were you doing with the staff? How did you make it glow like Marcus?"

Zen sat up and opened his eyes as much as he could. It looked like he was squinting against a noon sun, searching my face as if looking for something.

"Holy shit, you really don't know? You were right to ask what kind of promotion this was."

"What do you mean?" I asked.

"Let me ask you first, Dante, How long have you been training, not here, but in total?"

I thought back. No easy feat considering the throbbing in my head. I remembered my training in the various martial branches. I remembered the years, the sweat, the tears and the blood. Friends found and brothers lost.

"A long time, Zen. So long, I don't remember when it wasn't a part of my life," I said.

"In all that time, you have never heard of a group called the Warriors of the Way?"

I stared at him blankly.

"Damn," he whispered. The student in the red uniform moved closer to Zen, effectively stopping our conversation. He whispered something I couldn't catch.

"He has to know, I can tell him," was Zen's response.

"It is not your place to tell him," the student answered. His hands were glowing a deep blue.

"But he doesn't even—" The red uniformed student had placed his hands gently on Zen's chest. Within seconds Zen was sleeping deeply. The student turned to me, his hands still glowing.

"Hey, really, I'm okay. No need for the sleep assist, really." I wasn't in any condition to stop him; a two-year old could have had his way with me in my condition.

"You need your rest, warrior." He placed his hands on my chest and the deepest sense of calm and bliss suffused my being. I floated on that ocean of peace, until I left consciousness.

CHAPTER TWO-THE MIRROR

I opened my eyes and lay still. I half expected the room to pitch and shift, but it remained motionless. I was in a different room; it was small and furnished simply. In one corner of the room was a small desk, and some books were neatly placed in one corner. I couldn't make out the titles from the bed. The walls were bare with the exception of one scroll that read, "Ren Ma-keep polishing" in an older style of calligraphy. There was one window, which let in a soft light. It seemed to be just after dawn. I sat up, testing my body. I marveled at what a good night's sleep could do. Someone, I figured the red gi student, changed my clothes in the night. I was now wearing a dark grey uniform, the color of slate. It was heavy weight cotton that felt surprisingly soft against my skin. There was a chair at the desk, and a small wooden chest at the foot of the bed. I wondered if I was still in the dojo. If I was, it was much larger than I thought. The hardwood floors were bare and felt cool against my feet. As I was getting my bearings, one of the red gi students entered silently. He saw I was awake and stepped out before I could say anything. Moments later my door swung wide open and the doorway was completely filled by a mountain of a man. I quickly realized it was Zen with a huge grin on his face.

"Dante!" he yelled as he gave me a bear hug. With the air rapidly escaping my lungs and my ribs creaking under the pressure of his hug, I barely managed to answer him.

"Zen," I managed to gasp. He looked down at me and let me go. "Sorry about that, D."

"Zen, what is all the fuss? I just saw you yesterday." Zen looked at me and then looked off to the side a gesture I would become familiar with, whenever he had to say something difficult.

"Dante, you've been gone for five days."

"Five days?" I asked not quite believing him.

"C'mon Zen, stop playing, that's not funny." One look at his face told me he was serious.

"They were real concerned, D. Even the Master came in to look at you." I could tell he was holding something back.

"What else, Zen. Just tell me." I looked him straight in the face.

"Dante, when they brought you in, I could tell you were banged up bad. They just kept saying you were healing in the mirror. Funny thing is, if you notice, no mirrors anywhere in this whole building. Do you remember anything?"

"Zen, I have no idea what this 'mirror' is. Who was saying this?"

"I overheard the seniors talking." I tried to remember the last five days. All I remembered was the night of promotion, my last conversation with Zen, the red gi student placing his hands on my chest and the feeling of bliss. Nothing else surfaced.

"They said no junior had ever done that before," said Zen. "You sure you don't remember anything?"

"Nothing Zen. Maybe it will come back later?" I was unsettled by the five day gap in my memory.

"Anyway D. This—" and Zen spread his arms around to indicate the room— "is now your room."

"My room?" I asked. What about my place in Queens?"

"Oh you mean that hole in the wall you called an apartment?" Zen looked around and laughed. "I would call this a considerable upgrade. All your belongings will be shipped to the school. Besides, it's too dangerous out there for you right now."

"Why? What do you mean?"

"You remember when I made mention of the Warriors of the Way?"

I vaguely recalled the very short conversation. "Yeah, briefly before we were cut off."

"All I can tell you is that they are real and this is one of their schools."

"Excuse me? Look, all I came here for was my promotion, not any of this 'Warriors of the Way' mysterious secret society, Zen."

"Well, that's all I'm allowed to share with you. Actually I don't know if to pity you or congratulate you. Remember Marcus?"

"Yes, wasn't he the senior that put you out?"

Zen chuckled. "Yeah, well he is now my senior."

"What do you mean?"

"Each senior is paired to a junior – indefinitely. I'll give you three guesses who your senior is." It was just a tickle at first, and then the sense of dread quickly blossomed into a full-fledged gut check.

"Devin?"

"Got it in one. Don't feel too bad. I hear some of his students even survive his training!"

"Not funny, Zen." I wasn't looking forward to this except that a small, very small part of me did look forward to it.

A moment later a shadow crossed the doorway. Zen turned around to see Devin looking at him with the hint of a smile on his face.

"I believe your senior is looking for you, Zen."

Zen bowed, shot me a wink and made his way to the door.

"Thank you Senpai," said Zen as he jogged down the corridor, moving with effortless grace for someone so large.

Devin turned to look at me.

"I see you seem to be feeling better."

In truth I felt great. Somehow though, volunteering that information seemed dangerous.

"I'm feeling better," I said.

Devin smiled and then turned serious.

"Do you remember anything from the time you were unconscious?"

Memories like wisps of smoke hovered in my head, but nothing was clear.

"No, Senpai. Nothing." He looked directly at me as if willing me to remember.

"The moment you recall anything, let me know."

"What happened? Where did I go? What is the mirror?" Devin looked at me as if assessing if I was ready to hear what he had to say.

"Let's go for a walk." And he turned and headed out the door with me following him. As we walked down the corridor, I began to realize the immense size of the school. It seemed we were another level underground. The corridor stretched on for about three hundred feet with corridors leading off the main one. It was a veritable maze and as I followed Devin, I realized that without him I would be lost inside five minutes wandering down here. The corridors were well lit with sconces that appeared to be ancient lanterns. The walls and floor were the color of a warm cherry wood. It gave the impression and presence of solidity. Every ten or so feet, there were circles with symbols carved into the ceiling that glowed faintly. After a series of turns that left me completely disoriented, we came to a large courtyard that had a large reflecting pool in the center. In the center of the pool was a wooden structure, with a bridge leading to it. Around the pool grew trees. In short, the scene was idyllic.

"What is this place?" I marveled because I thought we were underground.

"Before I tell you what this place is, I want you to look in the water and tell me what you see."

I looked into the water. I saw what I usually saw when I looked into water. The water reflected the image around it.

"I see a reflection," I said.

"Look again, this time, look closer."

I figured this was some kind of 'exercise', so I looked again, fully expecting to see the same thing, a reflection of all that was around me.

Initially that was what I saw: the trees, the bridge, the small house in the center. Then the scene shifted, a sense of vertigo rocked me as I looked at Devin in amazement.

"It's – it's not the same? The reflection is different?"

"Keep looking," I was instructed. As I looked, the reflection shimmered and shifted, showing me countryside, with rolling hills. Then it shifted and changed into a city, very much like my own New York. I looked directly into the water, but didn't see my reflection. The scene shifted again to some type of caverns. I was about to reach out and touch the water when Devin pulled me back sharply.

"I don't think that is a good idea, considering what has happened to you recently."

"What is this place, what is that?" The shock crept into my voice.

"This place, Devin said, sweeping his hand around, is called a nexus. Think of it as the hub of a wheel, and each spoke leads to many other places."

"Like the places I'm seeing in the water?"

Devin nodded.

"If I jumped into the water…"

"I would imagine you would get wet? To answer your question, no, you can't get there from diving in."

"Where is there?"

"It has been given many names. We simply refer to it as the Mirror."

"I know what your next question is. Why the mirror? As far as we have been able to determine, every place you see 'reflected' is a representation of our world."

"You mean—?"

"Yes, what you are seeing is another version of this reality. There is only one exception. In the mirror, time flows differently.

"What do you mean differently?"

"In the mirror, there are areas of time that are accelerated or decelerated compared to our time here."

"You mean time is not constant."

Devin smiled at me.

"Dante, time, our time at least our construct of time, is never constant. We just choose not to see that."

"I don't understand," I said, truly perplexed.

Devin began walking to the bridge that led to the structure at the center of the lake.

"Let me see if I can explain. We both agree that a minute is sixty seconds, correct?

I nodded.

"If I was to say let's sit down for exactly a minute, it wouldn't feel very long, would it?"

"No, it wouldn't." We walked on in silence for a few moments. After what felt like five minutes, Devin spoke again.

"How long were we silent?"

"It felt like five minutes."

"But I only counted to sixty."

We had reached the structure, it was a training hall. I looked over the edge of the railing into the water where images played themselves like out of a movie. It was disconcerting, but mesmerizing at the same time.

"Now to the reason we are here, Dante. I know you have a lot of questions, and I promise to answer them all at some point. Right now I just need you to listen and accept what I am going to share with you. "Throughout the world there are schools like this one. Some larger, some smaller, the one thing they have in common is that they select and train spiritual warriors. Every few years, a promotion is held, to select those who will replace the fallen or those who have, because of age, retired from service. Sadly there are very few elders. Each school is unto itself a neutral area for the spiritual warriors. It's quite a paradox that no deadly combat can occur where we train to be deadly." As he spoke I looked around the training hall. To say it was sparsely furnished would be an understatement. The walls and hardwood floor were worn with age and use. It was the simplest of structures, but it contained strength, permanence.

Devin continued. "Each school is responsible for a designated area, and has a specific name. Not every school is fortunate enough to have an elder presiding as we do. Most schools are being run by senior students. Not every school has access to a hub. In fact we are the only school in this area that is directly linked to this hub." He stopped speaking and looked at me as if expecting a response.

"Seems to me," I said, "that would make this school coveted as a target."

"Correct, Dante. The 'promotions' that were most recently held, were for the purpose of filling our ranks. We have lost many of our own in the last year."

I was about to ask a question, well, several actually— but he raised his hand to stop me.

"I promise all your questions will have answers. Let me finish." I remained silent.

"Right now, a war is brewing. Some of the smaller schools have been attacked, and it's only a matter of time before we are attacked here."

"Who would attack us?" I wondered.

"Those who want more power, who want chaos. Those who we are sworn to fight against. It's the monsters of your nightmares and those who would control them. It is those who would destroy us all, simply because they can. Take your pick. The reason you are here" – as he swept his hand around to mean the training hall – "was your performance at the test and after it. Although you feel you failed, no junior has had the skill to touch me with or without a weapon, in many years. More importantly no one has been able to cross to the mirror untrained and unassisted, since I can remember."

"What does that mean?" I couldn't resist asking.

"It means you have a very rare ability. It also means you are a spiritual warrior, one of the Warriors of the Way."

I sat there silently, trying to take in all that Devin had just said. I shook my head. There was no way I could wrap my brain around all of this.

"With all due respect, I think you have the wrong person," I said.

Devin smiled.

"That's what we are here to find out today. You are here because I accepted the responsibility of being your senior. It is also my duty to find out if you truly belong here. Having a rare ability is meaningless if you cannot use it. Let's begin."

He walked over to one of the corners of the structure and reached down into the floor. A panel slid on the wall above, revealing dozens of weapons, swords, staffs, a multitude of bladed and blunt edged weapons. He handed me a bo, —a long wooden staff.

"You just need to repeat what you did at the test. Touch me."

"No blindfold?" I asked half-jokingly.

"I have something better than the blindfold." He laughed as he walked over to another section of the floor. As he pulled on a lever, every open section of the training hall was covered by wooden panels about a half inch thick. The training hall was in complete darkness.

"Now, hit me." I couldn't see my hand in front of my face.

"Understand that a spiritual warrior is all about balance." The acoustics of the hall gave his voice an eerie quality. 'When you complete this stage of your training, you will be balanced with another warrior who will complement your strengths and weaknesses. As brothers, you will sharpen each other, always striving for perfection. Right now though, all I want you to do is to hit me."

I held the bo in my hands, my palms all of a sudden, sweaty.

How was I supposed to hit him a second time when I didn't know how I did it the first time?

"We are all connected. Everything is one and everything touches and affects everything else." The acoustics of the space made his voice bounce in strange ways. I looked quickly from side to side to allow the rods of my eyes to adjust to the darkness. Focusing on my breath, I stilled it to almost nothing. Remembering my training, I sought to find him by his displacement in the hall. It was as if he didn't exist. He left no wake, no footprint. Sight was out of the question. A sudden pain flared up my right side, causing me to gasp for breath.

"Thinking too much, Dante." He was right of course. I started moving around the floor, careful not to make any sound as I stepped. Another sharp pain raced up my left leg starting at my thigh and radiating up and down my leg. I limped quietly to a wall, minimizing the angles of attack. That was when it happened. I don't know how. All I knew is that I wasn't going to get hit again. I began to sense him, no not him, but his intention. It was as if I knew he was coming to my right side. I moved to the left, swinging the bo to intercept his strike. The clash of wood reverberated in the hall.

"Good. You are finally learning to 'see'." At that moment, the window shutters flew open, the immediate blast of light blinding me for a few seconds. In the center of the floor stood a figure dressed in a dark blue uniform. The uniform was unlike any I had seen at the school. The trim and border were done with ornate gold embroidery. The color itself, which appeared dark blue at first, was interlaced with flecks of gold. The material appeared to be fine silk on the cuffs and in the material there were owls in flight. Devin walked over to the figure. I had no way of telling if it was a female or male, since the other interesting feature of the garment was a large hood. In its gloved hand, the figure held a scroll.

"Welcome, Meja. This must be urgent, for you to interrupt a training session."

"It is," said the woman. Devin looked over to where I was standing and motioned me over.

"Dante, this is Meja. Meja, this is—"

"I know who he is, Devin."

Devin smiled. "Of course you do. Meja is one of the senior monitors, Dante. Her job is to know just about everything."

She pushed back the hood revealing her piercing green eyes. It was the woman from the front desk. She gave me a slight bow and turned back to Devin, handing him the scroll. Devin opened the scroll and read. His face darkened.

"Are you certain as to the truth of this?" he asked. She said nothing in return, only stared back, hard.

"Very well. Where?"

"The South Watch."

A look of incredulousness briefly crossed Devin's face. "This happened at a Watch?"

Once again she remained silent.

"Meja, gather the others. We will need to meet at once."

"They have already been summoned," she said.

"I see, let's go. There is no time to waste. Dante, come with me. It seems your training will have to be on the field."

Meja looked at Devin.

"He will be fine, Meja. I won't leave him alone, I promise."

CHAPTER THREE-RITUAL OF TWO

The main meeting room was on a lower level. I felt like I was in a maze. This place felt endless, like a never ending rabbit warren. We traveled down corridors, which after ten minutes all began to look alike. Devin looked back at me and smiled.

"If you look carefully, you will see that each hallway is carefully marked," he said.

I stopped for a moment to see if I could read some kind of marking on the wall. It looked like every other corridor we had walked down. We finally came to a polished wooden door. For a moment I thought I saw a wave of deep violet energy coruscate across the face of the wood. The center of the door bore a symbol I did not recognize. It looked vaguely familiar and alien all at once. Devin must have picked up on my confusion and answered my unasked question.

"It's the symbol of our school. It means Warriors of the Way."

He placed his hand on the symbol which caused the surface of the door to ripple once. The door instantly slid downward, disappearing from view. Devin walked in and as I followed him, I noticed Meja stayed behind. Once we entered, she put her hand on a matching symbol and the door slid back into place with a resounding thud. No one was going to break into this room. The room was circular with the largest round table I had ever seen. The table seemed immensely heavy and ancient. On its surface, symbols were inscribed. Around the table must have been forty chairs and in each chair a person was seated except one. To the right of the Master of the school, one chair was empty. Behind each of the seated seniors stood a junior. Along the wall of the room, what I first took for statues were actually more people dressed like Meja. It was then that I noticed the thin lines that ran from the center of the table, down the stone floor and into the wall. Straddling each line stood a monitor. I saw Zen standing behind his senior and he gave no indication of having seen me, until I saw a barely perceptible nod. Several of the seniors were speaking at once.

"This is an outrage! They attacked a watch! We should hunt them down and erase them!" yelled one senior.

Several of the seniors around the table agreed. Devin took his seat and I was careful enough to stand the same distance behind as the other juniors.

Another senior stood and I recognized him from the promotion. His name was Darius.

"And what do you propose we do, Michael? Go in guns blazing? Kill everyone in sight?"

"Hell yes, Darius, it would be a welcome change from the way we normally operate!"

"Where exactly should we strike, Michael? Do you know where they are? Do you have a line on Sylk's whereabouts?"

At the mention of Sylk's name, I saw Meja's jaw clench.

"Darius, that's what monitors are for, to provide us this information. This is why we are in the state we are in: because we focus so much on the Way, that we have forgotten that we are warriors!"

"Extermination is not the answer to everything, Michael."

"When it comes to Sylk, I don't think having a conversation is going to work. Ask those around this table who have faced him, Darius. How many wounded? How many dead? How many here bear scars from our 'conversations' with him?"

Darius remained silent. It seemed that whoever this Sylk person was, he was dangerous. The seniors had gone silent, each thinking of their own personal battle with Sylk and his allies. The master placed his hands on the table. using the simple gesture to silence any senior that was about to speak.

"It would seem," the Master said in a quiet voice, "that this is a situation that merits our undivided attention."

His voice although quiet was crisp. He spoke with a conviction that lent weight to his words.

"The problem of Sylk and his allies must be confronted. It has been a year since our last direct encounter with him," —some of the seniors stole glances at Meja— "and we nearly lost a senior monitor. The difficulty we face is that Sylk was one of us. He knows how we operate. He knows how we think. We must then do something he would not anticipate." He paused as if giving his next statement thought. "Begin the ritual of two."

I didn't know what the ritual of two was, but I could tell many of the seniors thought this was a bad idea.

"Master," said Darius, "they aren't ready for the ritual. Many are still recovering from the promotions."

Devin looked at me, the hint of a smile crossing his lips. It wasn't exactly comforting.

"Darius, we have been waiting too long," said Michael. "This last attack on a Watch demands that we act."

Many of the seniors nodded their heads while others still looked concerned.

Devin stood. "I understand all of your concerns. The fact of the matter is that we must act swiftly and decisively. How long before Sylk attempts an attack here? No, he must be stopped. We will enact the ritual and create a group of warriors that can face this threat."

I had a feeling I didn't want to know what this ritual was.

The master stood. "It is decided, then. Let us prepare those who are able in every location."

Everyone around the table stood and bowed. The master turned to Devin. "You have two months to get them ready."

Devin bowed. "Yes, Master."

The Master turned and headed to another door in the room and half of the monitors followed him out. I was pleased to see that Meja had remained in the room. The remaining monitors spread out around the room to re-establish the balance of the ones that had left with the Master.

Once the Master left the hall, the seniors began to argue in earnest. The only one that remained silent was Devin. I realized at this point it wasn't about the ritual being carried out. That was established. This was more about who needed to be heard and who was aligned with whom. It seemed like Michael and those of the same mind were about half the group. Roughly the other half supported Darius. After about ten minutes, the discussion began to lose steam and Devin stood and turned to Michael. "Get me the names of those who are ready and nearly ready." He then turned to Darius and said, "Darius, you have two weeks to get the ritual in place. Whatever resources you need, they're yours." Darius didn't look pleased but nodded.

Devin made his way back to the door we had came in through. As he passed Marcus and Zen, he stopped and whispered something into Marcus' ear. I wasn't close enough to hear but I thought Zen was. Marcus nodded but remained seated. As we arrived at the door, I noticed Meja was behind us. She touched the same wall panel and the door slid from view. I looked back into the room as we entered the hallway and saw Zen standing behind Marcus. The room had once again fallen into a heated discussion. Zen gave me another nod and then I turned to follow Devin.

CHAPTER FOUR-DIVIDED FALLEN

"Your assessment Meja?" Devin asked as we walked the winding corridors.

"It looks like the factions are more pronounced and entrenched than earlier thought."

"Yes, I noticed."

"We believe that there is a traitor in our midst," said Meja.

"Within the monitors?"

"I use the term 'our' rather broadly."

"Ah, you mean within the warriors."

"Obviously."

"Couldn't there be a traitor among the monitors?" I asked.

Meja gave me a look that dropped the temperature of the corridor we were standing in by several degrees.

"That would be impossible for several reasons, Dante, but mostly because of the readers," said Devin.

"Readers?"

Meja turned to me. "Readers are monitors that can 'read' auras but more importantly they can sense intention."

I looked at her. "Are you a reader?"

"Even if she were, she wouldn't and couldn't tell you, Dante. No one but the most senior monitors know who the readers are—they and the Master of the school."

It seemed like a flawed system to me but I didn't say anything.

"Do you know who it is yet?" asked Devin.

"Not yet, but we are getting close."

We continued down the corridor.

Devin rubbed the bridge of his nose.

"We must find a way to unify these two camps," said Devin. "Perhaps with the ritual of two we can create some common ground."

"Or cause a greater rift," said Meja.

"Have I ever told you how cheery and uplifting it is to speak with you?"

"I'm not the one you come to when you want cheery and uplifting, we both know that."

Devin laughed and then grew serious.

"You are right, Meja. I'd better get this junior ready"

Meja took an appraising look at me.

"Do you think he is ready, Devin? You know what you condemn him to if he isn't."

Devin looked at me. "I would stake my life on it, Meja"

"I hope you are prepared, if it comes to that, Devin." We walked together, the silence embracing us like a warm blanket. She turned off at the next junction without a word.

"She seems a bit… serious" The word I was thinking of was 'depressing'.

"She has reason to be. I think the word you're looking for is dour, by the way."

Not really, I thought.

"Why is she that way?" I asked.

Devin led me down another corridor and into a small room. This warren seemed endless or I was just hopelessly lost. I was leaning towards lost. The room seemed to be a small sitting library. The walls were lined with books, none of which I recognized. Devin looked around the shelves.

"The monitors are as old as the Warriors of the Way. At any given time there are seven senior monitors," Devin paused, "but these are not normal times Dante. Right now we only have five and two of those are MIA, which effectively leaves three senior monitors to oversee over two thousand. Out of those three, Meja is clearly the strongest and most capable. The other two lean closer to Michael's point of view and want to launch a counter attack. You see not only are we divided, but the monitors as well, which leads me to believe there is an outside influence."

"The traitor?"

Devin nodded. He stopped in front of an old book. The cover was deep amber and the pages were yellowed with age.

"This is it, the book on the ritual of two." He dusted it off as he set it on the table.

"If the monitors are divided," he continued, "then it makes all of us weaker. Meja is the only one of the remaining three to have faced Sylk and is still here to talk about it."

"Is she that skilled?" I asked.

I had a hard time picturing her going up against Sylk, whom it seemed everyone either feared or at least respected.

"When she met him, she barely escaped with her life. I was the first to find her and I thought she was dead… so much blood." Devin looked into space for a moment as if reliving the scene.

"Now, even I wouldn't want to face her in combat."

CHAPTER FIVE-GUARDIAN AND WARRIOR

Devin opened the book and took some notes while I thought about Meja and Sylk.

"Why is everyone so scared of Sylk?" I asked. "Who is he?"

Devin stopped writing for a moment and then looked at me. "Sylk," he began, "was one of the most skilled warriors —one of the first to go through the ritual of two. In fact he was so naturally talented and inherently powerful, he was one of the few given the rank of Karashihan, which meant that he did not require a guardian. In essence, he was a sword and shield, and a devastating one at that."

"Does every warrior need a guardian or vice versa?"

"I wouldn't say it's a matter of need but more of complements of each other. Each warrior is considered as such because their talent deems it so. The guardians exist to make sure the warrior fulfills his duty and the same goes from the other side. In the pairing, the roles blend into each other."

"So the guardian becomes the warrior and the warrior the guardian?" I asked.

"Something like that," he said.

I still didn't see why this ritual was so dangerous and said as much.

"A pairing is the forming of a bond. If either of the two being paired is not ready mentally or physically, the outcome can be quite disastrous. Usually it ends in some kind of psychotic break and is almost always fatal."

"How long does it usually take to get a person ready?" I asked, realizing we had two months.

"Usually a year." Devin looked at me, as if assessing what he should say next. "You don't have to do this, Dante. You can always help in another capacity. You know we always need good instructors."

I sat there for a few moments in silence, giving it thought.

"I feel like this is what I'm supposed to do," I said.

Devin sighed. "I'm glad that was your answer."

"Why?" I looked at him.

"Maybe one day I'll tell you, but right now we have to cram a year's worth of training into two months, so we have no time to waste!" Devin said with a smile.

CHAPTER SIX-TRAINING

The training was grueling. Each day we awoke at five in the morning, regardless of how late we were training the day before. The first week we drilled basics, relentlessly, and when I thought I could go no further, Devin would find a way to push me even more. The second week, Devin began introducing training partners.

"I know you are used to having partners to spar against," Devin said. "That is not what we are trying to achieve here. You will learn to use your guardian as a shield, so that together you can be a devastating force." Together with my partner, Devin would put us through drills. The first was a sense drill, where I had to know where my partner was at all times, especially in the heat of battle. Needless to say I failed this drill repeatedly.

"You can't just focus on what's going on in front of you, Dante." I turned to see my guardian getting swarmed by opponents. Once again I had gone off to fight my own battle, leaving my training partner alone.

"You do this out there and you get to see him die, right before you do," said Devin. I ran over to my current partner only to find that he had been 'killed' by his opponents. "You never leave your guardian alone, Dante. That is the first tactic that will be used on the both of you. It's the reason for more deaths in the first year of being a warrior, than anything else. Remember, it's not divide and conquer. It's divide and destroy."

After three days of that, I had gone through six training partners and was pretty disgusted with myself. Devin must have seen my look of disgust and woke me extra early on the fourth day.

"Let's go, Dante. I know you think you are doing horribly, but I hear your fellow students aren't doing too much better."

"Where are we going?" I asked.

"We are going to the guardians' training arena. Marcus will be heading the training. Now you will see the other side, where the guardian tries to position him or herself so that the warrior can do what he or she does best."

We entered a large training arena, very similar to the one I had been training in for the last week and a half. The wooden floors gleamed with sweat.

"You see, Dante. Their job is to keep you alive. If they fail, they know that death is certain. Even though they can withstand immense amounts of damage, they are not invincible. Sooner or later, every guardian falls without a warrior."

The guardians were being drilled in protecting their respective warriors. At some point, each guardian was making a fatal error, which left their warrior exposed and eventually dead as a result.

I saw Zen fighting off a group of five opponents while his warrior ran off to meet another threat. It was the same trap I fell for several times. While the warrior met the 'threat', another group was working its way towards Zen. I looked at Devin, "That guardian is going to get swarmed and killed."

"You're probably right —if only he had a warrior who could help him—." He looked at me. "You know anyone?"

"Yes, I do," I said as I ran towards Zen.

I noticed Marcus looked towards Devin. Devin's nod was almost imperceptible.

I fought my way to Zen, dodging blows as best I could and "dispatching" my enemies by attacking the vital points that registered on our uniforms. When we received enough attacks, our uniform would switch color to indicate death. White was undamaged, blue was slightly injured, yellow was moderately injured, and red was dead. If you 'died', you were instructed to remain where you fell to create a sense of realism and an obstacle for the remaining fighters. My uniform was white, because I had not trained yet this morning. Zen's uniform was a light blue indicating he had taken some damage. He saw me and grinned as he evaded one strike and sent another student flying with a side kick.

I stood out like a white splash of paint in a rainbow. This made me an immediate target. I sidestepped a kick aimed for my chest and responded with three rapid short fist strikes, which effectively disabled my attacker.

Zen sidled up beside me. We were one of the few remaining pairs left.

"Think sword and shield, Dante. Remember I'm here to make sure you stay in one piece."

"If you fall then we both die, right?"

"Yeah, that's what I've seen so far. I can take more damage than you pretty-boy warriors." He laughed.

I couldn't help but smile.

"Okay big guy. What's the objective?"

"Take a look over there." He motioned with his head. I turned in the direction only to see a lone monitor dressed in blue. She was surrounded by an impressive group of students. It looked more like a wall than a group of students.

"You mean the great wall of students around the monitor?"

"Yep, we are to liberate and deliver the monitor over there." He pointed to an archway and a circle on the far side of the arena. In the doorway, stood one figure, waiting.

"Who's that?" Somehow the one figure seemed more intimidating than the human wall guarding the monitor. He was dressed in black looked like a shadow.

"Oh, that's just Michael." He grinned. Knowing the answer before I asked, I asked anyway.

"Are we delivering to Michael, or through him?"

"Look around and tell me what you think."

"I'm guessing through. It's through, right?

"Got it in one, D."

We were getting more attention as we dispatched several more groups. Two pairs had made a run at the 'wall' only to be crushed mercilessly. There were only eight to ten pairs left. A group of five attackers came at us. I stood in front of Zen.

"Let's change this up Zen, you be the sword. I'll be the shield."

"Are you sure? I don't want to pick your body up from the ground, cold and lifeless."

I laughed. "They won't kill me if they can't touch me. Besides I'm the one protecting you."

"Okay, I'm with you, this should be fun."

"We use them to get through the wall. Follow me!" We both ran towards the protected monitor with five attackers behind us. Two of the other pairs were free and were running ahead of us. As I got closer to the wall, I stopped in my tracks and dropped into pushup position, creating a horizontal obstacle. Two of the attackers tripped over me and because I was so close to the wall, into the students protecting the monitor. This created the opening we needed. Zen rushed in and kicked one student into another causing a confusion, which I was able to exploit. I leapfrogged over another student and reached the monitor. Getting her out would be much harder.

Zen grabbed another student and flung him away from us.

"Over here!" he yelled. I ran for the opening he created with the monitor in tow. The good thing was that she was fighting alongside us, the bad was that we would soon be overrun by the other attackers. I needed time and a distraction.

"Zen we need a diversion! Get me one of the women from the other teams!" Zen whistled a high piercing sound that filled the arena. I thought, *Great, so he can whistle. How is that going to help us?*

No sooner did I have that thought did I hear a commotion in front of us on my right. Attackers were dropping at a rapid pace. In the center of it all were two diminutive women who looked like dancers. One had jet black hair, the other shockingly white, so much so that her hair almost glowed. They stood barely five feet tall; their thin bodies barely filling their uniforms which I noticed were white as well. What really made me pause was their speed. I could barely follow their hands and legs as they struck. One moment they were in front of an attacker, the next, the attacker went flying or crumpled to the ground. They ran over to Zen, who towered over the two.

"This is Kalysta and Valeria. I call them Kal and Val," said Zen. They both smiled at me, and it was then I saw that they were indeed twins. Aside from the hair, they had the same tan skin and subtle Asian features, though it was apparent they weren't entirely Asian. I took off the monitor's blue robe and gave it to Kal or Val – I wasn't sure. "I need you to go in any direction that isn't near us."

They both laughed. "We can do that," said Kal.

"This will be fun," said Val.

The monitor stood in a white uniform and blended in with the rest of us. Kal and Val ran away from us, drawing a large group with them, including most of the wall. Zen and I headed towards Michael. The monitor was a young woman with piercing blue eyes and long blonde hair, tied into a ponytail. She was about my height and I could tell from her physique she trained often. She had a strong jaw line and high cheekbones.

"What's your name?" I didn't want to keep referring to her as the victim or monitor.

"My name is Anna," she answered as we ran to where Michael stood. I thought I caught a slight Russian or Eastern European accent.

"Okay Anna, I'm Dante and this is Zen. Can you tell us anything about this Michael?"

"Very dangerous warrior. It's a good thing he is alone." Then she cursed under her breath, in a language I didn't need to understand, to get the sentiment. In the archway where Michael stood, a figure emerged. I stopped short. This figure loomed over Michael and stood behind him. He had to be around seven feet tall and he filled most of the archway.

"Who or what is that?" I asked incredulously.

"That is Mouro. He is Michael's guardian," Zen answered.

"Can he even move? The guy is so huge."

As if to answer my question, a pair of the surviving "Liberators" made it to the archway. Before I could blink, Mouro was on them, having had produced a staff as if from thin air and batted away the pair with what seemed little or no effort.

"This mission just became much harder, Dante," Zen said.

"As long as I make it through the archway alive and to the circle, your mission is a success," said Anna.

"What we need are weapons," I said.

"Conventional weapons will not work for long against those two," said Anna. "Both their weapons are chi weapons."

My face must have held a look of "What?" I was about to say as much when Zen spoke.

"If I create a chi shield can we get close enough to get you through?"

Chi weapons and chi shields, I felt like I had stepped into some kind of martial arts fantasy.

"How long can you hold it intact?" Anna asked.

"On a good day, about ten seconds. This is not a good day, so I'm going to say five seconds max."

"Will this shield stop every attack?" I needed to know how effective it would be.

"Yeah, it will. But once it's down so am I, D. You will be on your own."

"Can you guarantee me five seconds, Zen?"

"Yeah, no more though. I just learned this technique."

"Fine, we can do this." I turned to Anna. "Our only criteria is to get you through the archway and to the circle alive, right?"

"Correct."

"Okay, let's go. Zen, when Mouro attacks, you hit the shield, got it?"

"Then what?"

"I'll take care of the rest. Anna, you stay close to me, got it?"

"Got it."

My plan was simple. We would rush Michael and Mouro, use Zen's shield to get us to the end of the archway and make sure Anna got through somehow. Hell of a plan. As we approached Michael and Mouro it seemed as if we had crossed a threshold. The other students were no longer intent on attacking us. I felt we had a breather.

"Be wary of Michael, he is the more dangerous of the two," Anna whispered as we made our way towards the archway. In the distance, I could see Devin and Marcus standing side by side focused on us. I took a deep breath and signaled to Zen and Anna.

"Go!"

We broke into a dead run, moving fast, faster than I had ever moved. Adrenaline coursing through my veins made my vision tight. Zen ran beside me, his face drawn in concentration. Anna kept pace with us. It felt like we were flying. The archway loomed ahead. Mouro, standing in it and filling the space, faced us. A smile crossed his lips. He readied his staff, as it slowly hummed with his chi. An orange glow faintly enveloped the staff and travelled up his arms, as if connected to him. In a strict sense it was, since it was a weapon created of chi energy. I wondered what would happen if that circuit was broken. As we got closer I could hear them speaking to each other.

"These are mine, Michael," Mouro rumbled.

"I don't know Mo." Michael used the nickname that usually resulted in something being broken for anyone else but him. "They got past everyone and they have the monitor." Mouro's eyes narrowed, as realization crept in.

He laughed and it filled the arena.

"Yes they do. I didn't recognize her."

"It doesn't matter, Michael. They may be clever, but now they are mine."

"Are you ready, Zen?" I asked as we headed straight for Mouro. "They know we have the monitor."

Realizing the greater threat came from Michael. We would create a diversion with Mouro and use the ensuing chaos to get Anna across. Like I said, hell of a plan and the best I could come up with on the fly. We were ten feet from Mouro when I signaled Zen.

"Now!" I yelled.

Zen uttered a word under his breath and time shifted into slow motion. There was an audible whoosh and it felt as if the air had been sucked out and away from us. We were surrounded by a violet blue sphere as we slammed into Mouro. Despite his size, he was not prepared for the sudden impact of the chi shield.

"What the—a chi shield? He said as he was launched to the side by the impact. His smile was gone. I looked at Zen, who was drenched in sweat. There was a collective gasp from the bystanders as they saw Mouro flying sideways. He recovered quickly, landing on his feet on the far side of the floor, without a sound, which surprised me considering his size. I turned to Michael who was now smiling. "Very clever: separating us." I nodded, conscious of the fact that Mouro was heading back. Then I realized he couldn't cross the threshold without the monitor; now that she had passed the designated area, it was sealed off. I sighed a breath of relief, which was short lived when Zen collapsed to one knee.

"Zen!"

"I… think… I'm about done, D," he panted. Each step he took, harder than the last. Michael simply stepped back, giving the shield a wide berth. I don't know why it had launched Mouro as if he were a feather but I sort of wished it would do the same to Michael. Michael, clearly impressed, examined the dwindling chi shield…

"Not only a chi shield," he said admiringly, "but one with a repulsor component interlaced? Quite advanced." Michael gave the shield some extra space.

Zen had stopped walking, falling to the floor. "Who is your senior, Guardian?" Zen almost unconscious, muttered, "Marcus" then passed out. We were about four feet from where we needed to be. I cursed silently under my breath. "Well, that makes sense," said Michael.

"Don't be disappointed, Dante, is it?" He knew my name? "No one has gotten this far, ever. And no junior has ever passed the archway with the monitor to complete the objective."

That's when it hit me, like a rush.

"You may be right, Michael," I said, checking my anger at being spoken down to. I felt the adrenaline surge mix with my anger. It coalesced in my hands and when I looked down I held a short staff. It looked and felt real enough. When I moved it, it felt unnaturally light. I didn't know how I was doing it, only that I needed some kind of weapon.

"You are full of surprises." He smiled but his eyes were serious.

I really didn't like where this was going. I had no extensive experience using a short staff or jo. The last time I held one I ended up unconscious myself.

"How long do you think you can keep it intact, I wonder?" He was goading me.

"Long enough," I hissed. Even as I said the words, I felt my strength ebbing from me. I had only one chance. Anna was next to me as I inched closer to Michael, a new respect in his eyes as the staff gleamed a dark red. I had no clue what I was doing, I only knew Anna had to get across and to the circle, and Michael was in the way. This was falling apart fast and the floor began to tilt beneath me.

"Let's go, Anna," I said.

"I don't think so." He stood to block our path just as I expected.

With my remaining strength, I lunged at him, which he parried effortlessly. The clash of our weapons sent jolts of electricity up my arm. Almost dropping my short staff, I brought my right leg up in a circular round house kick, but as I kicked in an effort to remove his head, he simply ducked. I smiled. Since I had not connected, I kept my leg going, which increased my momentum. I continued turning into a back kick. My foot landed squarely on Anna's back. She had anticipated the kick and was moving forward, my kick adding the push she needed to cross the threshold. She flew the remaining two feet past Michael. Michael yelled as he slashed at me. His blow broke through my staff and into my side. The pain was excruciating as I crashed to the floor, momentarily losing consciousness. As I lay on the floor, I turned my head to see Anna safe on the other side in the circle. The room was in an uproar as students ran towards us, now that the threshold barrier had dropped. Michael, sword now gone, looked down at me with a smile that held something more— respect, maybe?

"Well done, warrior." He turned and left the arena, Mouro joining him. It was the last thing I saw as the world turned on its side and became black.

CHAPTER SEVEN-THE PAIRING

After the training event, Devin took measures to keep me focused. The fact that I had accessed the mirror and now manifested my chi meant my training became specialized. I rarely saw any of the other students since my training was almost exclusively with Devin. The sessions were getting increasingly frustrating. Apparently my focusing my chi was not supposed to happen for another few years. The fact that I did it without training meant I was more of a danger to myself and my fellow students.

Devin was also being sensitive to the "mole" problem. He felt I could be attacked or worse, for having these abilities, and had me moved to a different wing every week for my safety. It was getting aggravating. The only constant was the upcoming pairing. I wondered who my guardian would be. I knew Zen and I were a good team, but Devin kept telling me that it wasn't that simple. The pairing linked the chi of the people involved. It created a bond that was only broken by death. And so the remaining month had been brutal in terms of my training. The only respite came at night, when I could have an hour to myself and then fall asleep. As each day passed, I became better at controlling my chi. By the third week of the second month, I was able to create my staff again without the anger. It felt different.

"When you manifest your chi from a point of calm, it will not drain you," Devin explained. "Acute negative emotions like anger, hatred, and fear will also facilitate chi manifestation, but the downside is that it will siphon off your own chi." As he spoke, a blue-white orb of energy began to take shape in front of him, floating in midair. I could feel the pressure in the center of my forehead and temples.

"Catch," he said and smiled. I mentally "caught" the orb of energy and held it in space before me by creating a barrier of my will.

"Careful, I laced a detonation component into it. If you mishandle it, it will explode and there will be little bits of you all over." He smiled. He was bluffing, wasn't he? Sweat began to form on my brow as fear crept in. The sphere began to rotate a little faster, the blue becoming darker.

"Calm down, Dante, take deep breaths." I did as he suggested and the sphere became light blue, almost white.

"There you go, see? Wasn't that easy?" It was taking all I had just to keep the orb centered. My full focus was on the sphere of energy. I didn't realize what Devin was doing until he said, with a malicious smile, "Catch." We were sitting cross-legged from each other about twenty feet away. He smiled as another blue-white orb came floating towards me. Its muted glow illuminated the training floor as it floated towards me, a promise of destruction wrapped in warm light.

"Don't let them touch," he said. I willed the second orb to stop short of the first one by pushing my chi in between them, acting as a cushion.

"Catch," he said once again, but this time he was serious. The third orb was coming slowly towards the other two.

"Dante, do not let them touch," he said pointedly. It was like watching a train wreck. You knew what was going to happen but you couldn't tear your eyes away. At the last moment I sent a strand of chi to stop it but it was too little, too late. The third orb came to a stop. I thought I had caught it in time, but it was still sliding forward and gently kissed the other two orbs. My ears popped as the pressure of the impact sent me flying across the floor, on my rear. I stopped sliding on the hardwood floor thirty feet away. Devin stood over me as I tried to regain my composure and hearing.

"At the pairing, they will be live, Dante." His tone held every implication of what the outcome would be if I didn't exercise the control and focus needed.

"Let's start again," he said as I took my place cross-legged away from him. I lost track of time as we practiced over and over. Each time I thought I had them under control, he would send one more orb and I would end up a human projectile, careening across the floor. I was at the point of exhaustion with four orbs in front of me when I saw him begin to form the fifth. I couldn't move the four in front of me as part of the exercise, but I was tired and fed up with being sent across the floor like some oversized rag doll.

He sent the fifth orb over and in my head I saw myself flying back after the impact.

"No," I said to myself, "no more." Something in me snapped. I don't know if it was from the exhaustion or just not wanting to be airborne again. I stopped the fifth orb midway in its trajectory. Devin arched an eyebrow but remained still. I sent the other four orbs at the one in the middle. Just before they touched, I drained them of their chi. As I drained them they became one large orb about the size of a beach ball. I was trembling with the exertion.

"Catch," I said as I shoved it back at him. He merely sat and watched the orb glide toward him. He lifted a hand and the orb crashed into it. Once again my ears popped. His uniform fluttered but he remained where he was as the orb slowly vanished into his palm. I looked, dumbfounded and he just smiled. "You are almost ready, Dante. Let's take a break."

I was still silent, not finding the words to express my frustration or the unfairness of it all. What I wanted was to lie down and sleep but I knew that was hours away. "The pairing is in a few days," he said as if reading my mind. "You will be rested for it, don't worry."

Anna came into the training area and approached Devin and bowed. Devin bowed.

"Yes, Anna?" Devin asked.

"Senpai Michael would like to speak to you privately, Senpai." Monitors rarely used the honorific of senior, meaning this was a delicate matter of importance. Devin allowed a moment of concern to cross his face.

"Where is he?"

"He is with Senpai Mouro in the West Hall." It would take Devin twenty minutes to get there and that was using the shortcuts.

As he turned to leave, he looked at Anna again.

"Did he say what this was about?" She bowed again.

"No Senpai, only that it was urgent and it concerned him."

Devin pressed his lips together and looked at the both of us.

"Guard him with your life, Anna."

She bowed, but said nothing. Satisfied, Devin left the training area.

"Hi there, Anna, how have you been?"

"Pretty good. I haven't seen you around much."

"Yeah, you know Devin's pretty insane with the training, pairing coming up and all."

Anna had walked over to take a protective stance near me and kept looking around as if someone might attack me.

"Really, Anna, that isn't necessary. Who is going to attack us in here?"

She stood her ground to my right and just behind me. It was starting to creep me out.

"Anna, really. No need, okay?" As I turned, I saw the knife in her hand and then in my abdomen. The knife burned as it slid effortlessly into my midsection. She grabbed me, knife at my neck as the voice came through the door.

"Anna, I ran into Michael—" Devin stopped mid-sentence as he saw the scene. The air around him began to shimmer.

"You won't get very far, Anna. Let him go and I promise you mercy."

"Mercy!" she spat. "Where was your mercy when my sister begged for her life?" The look of confusion on Devin's face was too authentic to fake.

"Your sister?" he asked.

"Sylk said you wouldn't remember. He said to ask Owl. He would help you remember." At the mention of Sylk's name, Devin's face darkened.

"Anna, you don't want to do this."

"Oh, but I do, S*enpai*," the last word dripping with scorn and hate.

Devin took a step. Anna pulled me back, the blade of the knife biting into my neck, leaving a thin trail of blood. *The knife is incredibly sharp,* I caught myself thinking over the hum of noise in my ears.

"Where are you going to go? There is no way out Anna."

"I think he and I will make a wonderful pair." Anna smiled. She pushed her hand into the small of my back and I felt a small pinch. The training area started to go grey, and I thought it was an effect of the knife wound until I saw the look on Devin's face. It was a mix of surprise, rage and disbelief.

"Retrievers?" I heard him yell as he sped to us faster than I had ever seen anyone move. It wasn't fast enough. He moved right through us as if we were ghosts. Anna laughed at the look of rage and helplessness in his face and then we were gone.

CHAPTER EIGHT-PROPOSITION

"Are you certain you used the sequence correctly?" The voice was low and slightly accented, though I couldn't place it.

"Yes sir," a female voice responded.

"Excellent," said the male voice. "Look, he's waking up." I opened my eyes. I guessed they meant me. As I turned and swung my legs off the bed to take in my surroundings, a wave of nausea and vertigo slammed into me, making me pause. I remained still until the room slowly righted itself.

"It's the effect of multiple retriever use. I'm afraid it was unavoidable, Dante." My midsection lurched and burned simultaneously but no wound was evident. "Devin is a clever adversary so I had to take precautions. How is the old alma mater, by the way?"

I was in no condition to answer as the room slipped slightly off axis.

"Annika, bring something to settle his, um stomach." And the man smiled.

Annika? I thought. Then it all came back in a flood. Anna stabbing me, becoming ghost-like, Devin trying to grab us and the hopping – we moved so many times until I was completely disoriented and nauseous.

When he saw that the realization was on my face, he smiled.

"Welcome Dante. My name is Sylk."

He was a tall man with elegant features. His face was chiseled with a prominent jaw line that held strength. His eyes were a pale grey that burned with intelligence. He had a swimmer's body, tall and thin. Wearing a pale white dress shirt and black slacks, he looked like a male model. His hair was a shocking white and was cut close and cropped on the sides. What caught my attention were his hands —they emanated power, it was the only way I could describe it. As I shifted to take in my surroundings, my midsection screamed at me. I winced and he noticed.

"What you are feeling is the effect of being stabbed or cut with a weapon of manifested chi." He smiled.

I looked around, careful not to move too suddenly. I was in a loft space. The walls were exposed brick, painted white. The ceiling was a series of skylights that let in the natural light. In the center of the space was a raised training area, equipped with heavy bags, lifelike training dummies with pressure points delineated with red circles. A weapons rack stood on a far wall holding some weapons I recognized and many I didn't. In the center of the area on the floor were circles etched into the wood. They were concentric and were of metal. The largest must have been at least thirty feet across. I saw that the living space and training area were clearly separated by a series of screens. He saw me take it all in and waited patiently for me to recognize the obvious. It took a while for me to notice, and then I realized there was no door. I saw no way to enter the space and — more importantly— to exit. I tried to stand and paused.

"I wouldn't do that if I were you." Disregarding him, I tried to stand anyway. The room shifted on its axis again and I felt the floor tilt away from me. I sat down again, sweat forming on my brow, my stomach doing somersaults. Anna or Annika came from the kitchen with a damp rag and went to place it on my forehead. I flinched. She smiled and placed the rag on my forehead then went to the other end of the floor.

Sylk sat in one of the lounges opposite the bed, and crossed his legs as he took me in.

"Being stabbed by a chi weapon disrupts the natural flow of chi in your body."

"So my chi is what, blocked?"

He stood with an economy of motion that demonstrated grace, power and strength as he walked over to me. It was like watching a tiger stalk prey —beautiful and deadly.

"In simple terms, yes. Chi weapons introduce disruption to your chi field or flow. While the wound itself leaves no physical trace, the blockage or interruption can cause a multitude of physical ailments. Some are fatal. Of course all it needs is to be released and the flow is reestablished." He grabbed my right elbow and pressed hard in my forearm, causing blinding pain. I tried to pull away but his grip was like steel. I felt like I was caught in a vise. After about thirty seconds of agony, he let go.

"Stand up."

I hesitated, not wanting my world to twist and flip again.

"Go ahead, it should be fine."

As I stood, I suddenly felt much better.

"There," he said. "Good as new."

"What do you want?"

"I want to make you an offer —a proposition of sorts."

"What sort of offer?"

"What would you say if I could prove to you that I'm not the villain I'm being portrayed as by your teachers at the school?"

"I would say why do you need to prove anything to me?"

He appraised me with his grey eyes and remained silent as if considering what to say next.

"You are correct, I have nothing to prove to you nor do I need to, except for one thing."

"What?"

"I want you to join me in my mission."

"And what mission is that?"

"We need to prepare for a greater enemy than we have ever faced."

"You mean greater than you?"

He laughed then. "I am not the enemy, Dante. I am merely the catalyst for greater transformation. The enemy I speak of has immeasurable power, enough to wipe out every warrior from this and every other plane of existence."

"From what I understand, you are public enemy number one, the reason every warrior is preparing and training."

He looked at me expectantly.

It dawned on me slowly. "That is what you want?"

"Yes, by becoming the common enemy, there is a slim chance they will be ready when the real threat emerges."

"That is quite the long game you are playing and you are killing warriors," I said slowly.

He walked over to the kitchen area and brought back two mugs. "Dante, this is a war. I regret the lives that have been lost, but when you get to my age, all you see is the long game," he said, handing me a mug. The tea was a combination of ginger, lemon and some ingredient I couldn't place, giving it a distinct sweetness followed by the sharp bite of ginger and calmed by the tartness of the lemon. It was delicious. He must have seen my reaction.

"It is my own creation and it is a medicinal remedy as well." He lifted his mug and took a sip, basking in the steam."

"It is very good," I said, meaning it.

"Thank you."

"How are you justifying killing warriors and monitors?"

He looked away for a moment, pensive. He turned to me, his grey eyes piercing me.

"Let me tell you a story, Dante." He rose and walked/glided over to a far wall covered entirely in books. I followed him and saw that many of the books were classics, and if they were authentic, the collection was priceless. I walked over to where he stood, facing a section of books whose spines I couldn't decipher. He ran his finger along a few of them almost caressing them. I looked at him and wondered how old he was. There was no real way to tell just by looking.

"About three hundred years ago, a group of warriors joined together to form a society dedicated to protecting the planes from evil. When we started, there were twenty-six of us. We were still in Europe then, England to be precise."

"We?" I looked incredulously at him.

"Are you saying you're three hundred years old?"

"I'll be four hundred and ten this December." So I was standing here with a man, if he was a man, that was over four centuries old.

"My age is irrelevant, Dante."

Like hell it was.

"Pay attention." The way he uttered those words snapped me out of my reverie. Either he was over four centuries old or he was insane. I wasn't sure which yet, so I listened.

"What you know as the Warriors of the Way was known by a different name back then. Throughout history we have been in every group and so-called secret society. We were Templars, Free Masons, Rosicrucian. We belonged to every religion practiced in the world. We were part of these groups and yet transcended them. Our calling knew no race, religion, creed, or belief system. I won't be so cliché as to say we shaped history."

"What calling was that?" I was beginning to lean towards the insane side of my evaluation. I sipped some more of the delicious tea.

"We were tasked with preventing the destruction of the planes of existence."

"Meaning there are others?"

He looked at me as if I were a simple child.

"Yes, Dante, there are others. I'm sure by now even you have been exposed to the Mirror?"

I debated telling him of my short and unremembered journey there, but figured I had nothing to lose and said, "They told me I went there when I was injured."

"Really?" He looked genuinely interested.

"Do you have any recollection of your time there?"

I shook my head and he nodded. "The first time is usually like that, especially if injury was the catalyst."

"So the different planes are just different versions of us?"

"That would be a simple and arrogant assumption, but for now let's use that."

My face reddened and he smiled at my discomfort.

"Consider that all these planes coexist. No one knows which the original is or if there even was an original. These planes or worlds or dimensions, whichever helps you understand it, never interact directly. They are like parallel lines going into infinity."

"So no crossing over, ever?"

"Except by a select few, throughout our history, gurus or enlightened masters."

"So how do the warriors…"

"I'm getting to that," he said after he finished his tea.

"Imagine that these planes were accessible and that you didn't need a state of enlightenment or any other transcendental state."

"Wouldn't everyone be crossing over, then?"

"The path we discovered was through our martial training, perfected to such a level that we were able to achieve zanshin at will."

I had heard of zanshin as being in the state of mind where everything and anything was possible. It wasn't nothingness, empty and void, but pure potentiality.

"So by achieving zanshin, you cross over?"

"Not exactly. By achieving the desired state, the doorway becomes available to you. You can choose to use the door or not, but there is a choice."

"Why wouldn't you take the door?"

"Eventually you will find out and then you get to make the choice. One thing I can assure you, no one is going to find you," and he extended his arm to take in the loft," in this place."

"Why not?" I had to ask since my noticing the lack of a door.

"I know you think there is no form of egress but you would be wrong."

I looked around again. He beckoned to me to search further. The space was expansive with hardwood floors tying the living areas together. I discovered an actual bedroom off to the side which must have been the master bedroom judging from the king size bed. All the furniture was done in an old wood so brown it was almost black. Everything looked solid and sturdy. I looked everywhere and saw no door. I walked back to the common area and it was then that I noticed the mirror. It stood at least ten feet tall and I missed it initially because I thought it was a window. As I stood before it, I recognized the view. It was the training hall on the lake, at the school. Sylk stood beside me admiring the view.

"I spent many hours training on that lake."

"We're in...?"

"The Mirror? Yes, in more ways than one I would say."

"But I wasn't in a zanshin state, how did I?"

"No, but before travelling, Annika injured your chi, setting for your automatic response to trauma and injury. The rest was a matter of sequential jumps using retrievers."

"How long have I been here?" My world, the world I was used to, born in, was on the other side of that mirror. My stomach lurched.

"Time is not a linear concept here, Dante. Here there are eddies and whorls. It may only feel linear because you perceive it that way."

Annika was in the kitchen area preparing food for what I assumed was going to be dinner. My body took over, informing me that I was starving.

"You mean you can travel in time?"

"No, Dante, time travel as far as I know is not possible. What I meant by nonlinear is in relation to the plane you originate from."

"Excuse me?"

"Think of it this way – the Mirror is a plane that is like a very long river. Parts of this river flows slowly, other parts though, flow quickly. There are rapids and falls, whirlpools and the like. If you enter the mirror from your plane without knowing exactly where you intend to go, you can find that upon returning to your plane much time has passed 'or none'."

"What about here, this place?"

He smiled then and looked at what passed as a watch, but was unlike any watch I had ever seen. "Well, according to this you have been gone exactly one hour of your time to two days of our time here." The smell wafting in from the kitchen sent my stomach into overdrive, making it growl.

"Anna is a fantastic chef, among other things." As he looked at her I could see that there was a deeper dimension to their relationship. "And before you get any ideas, he walked over and kissed her on the forehead, "she is my daughter and one of my personal guards."

I looked at Anna, wondering how old she was, if her father was over four hundred years old.

"I'm twenty-eight," she said as if reading my mind.

"The longevity factor won't become apparent until her fortieth birthday, and even then it can skip a generation or two from what I have seen."

So far he hadn't tried to kill me, even though I knew he was capable of it.

"So, my proposition. Stay here, train, and allow me to teach you to become the warrior you are meant to be. When you are ready to leave, I will not stop you."

"But why me?" There are many at the school better than me."

"Anna tells me that you have the skills I am looking for."

"Why not one of the seniors?"

"Those you call seniors, blindly follow their master and would not be open to what I have to say."

"It may be because you have killed some of them?" I answered.

"You do have a point." He crossed his arms and waited.

I thought over my situation. The only way to get back was to go through the doorway/Mirror. There was no way I could take on Sylk on my own, much less him and Anna. It didn't appear like I had much of a choice and he knew it. Somehow I knew I would regret this.

"Fine," I said. "It's not like I have much of a choice here."

"Of course you do."

"I do?"

"Certainly, you could have refused my invitation."

"Sure I could have and then?"

"And then I would have killed you." It wasn't a threat. He said it so matter of fact that the words chilled me to my core.

"I see," I said slowly.

"Not yet you don't but you will," he said as he smiled.

CHAPTER NINE-SEARCH

Devin was livid. The traitor was a monitor? How did she get ahold of retrievers? This had Sylk's hand in it, he was certain of it. He also knew that recovering Dante would not be the priority. Weeding out any other potential moles would take precedence, as would the ritual of pairing. The Master would not stop or delay the ritual no matter how talented one student was. He would have to find Dante on his own.

"Are we going to find him?" Devin turned to see Meja flanked by the twins Kalysta and Valeria, and behind them stood Zen. Devin looked at them, his face serious, inwardly he admired their courage.

"It's very likely Sylk has him."

Meja's face became hard.

"Are they ready for something like this?" said Devin as he looked at the trio.

"I wouldn't have chosen them if I didn't think they were capable," Meja answered with an edge to her voice.

Devin smiled at Meja but it was without mirth.

"I found your mole, by the way."

"She knew we were onto her, which is why she acted when she did," said Meja.

"If we do this, it's very likely we will have monitors after us. I want to know that you are doing this out of your free will," said Devin.

Meja narrowed her eyes at Devin, clearly displeased. Devin didn't care; he was not going to have them on his conscience.

"We are here because we want Dante back, it's that simple," said Zen. The twins nodded in agreement.

"Very well, then. Let's go find us a warrior."

CHAPTER TEN-TRANSFORMATION

The training was unlike any other I had ever endured. I took solace in the fact that I was training for my escape but it comforted me very little. Sylk made my time at the school feel like a vacation. We awoke each day at six a.m. Every day was the same.

"Let's begin," were his first words to me every morning. And we would start. Dressed in a loose fitting shirt and pants, standing barefoot on the training floor, he would drill me over and over on the most rudimentary techniques and forms. The days blurred into each other until I had no track of how long I had been in that place. It was another morning when he woke me—*Doesn't he ever sleep?*

"Good morning, Dante," Sylk said, looking at me over a cup of his golden tea. The pleasant aroma filled the space. I was wary. We never started our days this way.

"Uh – good morning," I said, still a bit groggy.

"Today will very likely be the most difficult of your life." He sipped some more of his tea. I knew better than to ask why and remained silent as I dressed into my training clothes, which were very similar to Sylk's. I wore a very loose fitting top that resembled a gi top. but it was much thinner and more resilient. It felt like silk but it allowed me to breathe, dealing well with the copious amounts of sweat I produced in my training. My pants, made of the same material, were also loose fitting, but not so much that it was a hindrance. It felt like training in very comfortable underwear. I stood in the center of the training circles. Something was different today. The circles hummed with power and were glowing faintly.

"In your time here, Dante, I have stripped away all your incorrect techniques and bad habits," Sylk said evenly. "It has not been easy," he continued.

I remained silent, knowing it was the correct thing to do.

"Today you will determine if you progress to the next level in your training."

It can't be! I thought. I'm going to have to fight him? There was no way I could face him and win. As he spoke, three women approached the circle. "These are women from my personal guard and they are here to kill you."

They stood outside the outer circle. The surprise evident on my face, I said nothing. I had no doubt that they would make good on their instruction. Each of them wore tight fitting pants and a top similar to mine. They wore soft sandals on their feet that made a soft shushing sound as they side stepped the tré. Each of them had their black hair in a braid that ended in a metal pin, which led me to consider that even the hair may be a weapon. Their faces, expressionless, were dangerous and beautiful. Asian features which betrayed no emotion, their almond shaped eyes looked not at me but through me. I thought it couldn't get any worse when swords materialized in two of the three women's hands.

"I have some business to attend to," he said as he approached the mirror. If you are still among the living when I return then we will continue your training. If not, well then…" he nodded towards me and stepped through.

"Watch the one that is unarmed, Dante. She is the most dangerous of the three." His voice faded away as I stood facing imminent death. She looked at me and smiled. "I am Mara, and I will be your assassin today."

I gathered my chi and kept it stored in my lower abdomen. I knew I would need it if I was to survive this. Whatever happened I would do this without taking a life. I would not become Sylk. The outer circle stopped glowing and all three stepped in as one. Once inside, it began glowing again. I realized that I was sealed in with them. I put my foot on the glowing circle and felt a jolt of energy shoot up my leg followed by excruciating pain. It felt like someone had reached in and pulled out every bone in my leg. "Ahh!" I screamed in agony. As if that were the starting signal, they moved in to attack.

CHAPTER ELEVEN-TAPPING DARKNESS

The two with swords began to move to flank me. A subdued turquoise glow emanated from the swords. They stepped slowly to my sides, while the third —remaining motionless— looked at me. My leg still throbbed but the pain was quickly subsiding. Now it just felt as if it had been asleep, complete with the pins and needles. I moved into the center of the tré, as the three circles were called. The two with swords were now equidistant from me, almost anxious to attack. I realized that it was the third unarmed one that was controlling them. I looked closer at their faces and realized that they weren't similar —they were identical, down to the clothes and facial features. I was either facing triplets or something else was going on. Mara smiled at my dawning awareness.

"We are all the same but I am the original." I remained silent, hoping to find a gap in her offense. "Finish him," she said so softly I almost missed it. The one on my left ran in, sword trailing behind her. The one on my right mirrored her. If I didn't do something within the next two seconds, I had no doubt they would slice me in two. I felt the chi in my lower abdomen and expanded it to encompass the inner circle, which was five feet in diameter. I felt it expand from my body and solidify around me like a cylinder. Lefty slammed into it first and I felt the impact across my left side as if I had gotten kicked in the ribs. Righty, seeing what happened, stopped short and prodded my chi field with her sword. Her sword was instantly absorbed into my cylinder. Mara raised an eyebrow. She gave them an unspoken instruction and they stood just outside my circle, waiting. I knew I couldn't keep this up indefinitely. Fatigue was already creeping into the edges of my awareness. Mara stood in front of me and placed a palm on my energy field. She drew her arm back and slammed her palm into the field. It was a devastating strike that would have broken several of my ribs had the field not been there. It felt like I had been gut checked. She looked at me and said,

"It would seem that this manifestation of your chi is still very much connected to you."

I looked at her darkly, too winded to reply. It was taking all I had just to keep the cylinder intact.

"Foolish neophyte, you are supposed to disconnect the chi from yourself, or fall prey to the consequences."

Disconnect my chi? I had no way of doing that. It was something alien to me.

She laughed then.

Her doppelgangers began attacking the cylinder around me. At first tentatively, then with greater intensity. I knew I had moments left. It was then when I felt the tug of power. It was hard to describe, like that feeling you get, a bass sound rocking your abdomen. It was a rumbling, pulling at my midsection. At first it felt off, like something was wrong, tainted, but considering my options, I didn't have much choice. I drew on it. I opened myself to this strange power filling me. The cylinder around me grew reddish black at the edges. I no longer felt tired, in fact a surge of energy coursed through me. I touched the cylinder and it vibrated under my hand. I concentrated, pushing it out. It expanded almost immediately. I stopped at the second circle of the tré. The twins began striking it but I felt nothing. Mara had moved back to appraise the situation, her face serious. The anger in me, which had been a constant companion, took over. It was a rage that infused my entire being. I didn't ask for any of this. My life as I knew it was over. The rage and frustration that I had kept under control shook off my restraints as if they didn't exist. How dare these women threaten me? I looked down to see a small staff, a Jo, in my hands, about four feet long, covered in ornate markings. I knew it was a manifested weapon, at the same time I knew it was real and independent of me. It felt solid. Around an inch and a half in diameter, capped at each end with what looked like steel. In each cap, designs were etched into the metal. Along the shaft of what appeared to be ebony wood were characters and markings I could not decipher, etched in a deep red. The staff thrummed as if it had a life of its own.

"I am called Maelstrom, for I come from your inner chaos to unleash destruction on your foes," a voice said. For a moment I thought it was me, but I knew I had not said a word. It was then that I laughed. I didn't even recognize my voice, my laugh. It wasn't me, yet it was.

"Impossible," said Mara. "It is a foci."

"Oh no, bitch, very possible," not-my-voice answered.

I slammed my staff on the floor and the protective field around me was sucked into the staff with an audible whoosh. The twins stood perplexed for a moment then lunged at me with swords newly drawn.

"No!" screamed Mara.

Too late they realized that instead of rushing to cut short my existence, they were ending their own. It was moving in slow motion and at an accelerated pace all at once. The twin on my right brought her sword down with a cut designed to cleave me in two. I sidestepped the attack as the twin on my left lunged with her sword at my mid-section, which I parried with Maelstrom or it parried using me. It was as if the staff was using me and not the other way around. The staff whirled in my hands as if alive. I slammed the twin on the right in the chest with the broad end of the staff. She skidded to the edge of the tré. With grim satisfaction, I knew I had broken at least four ribs. She didn't move. The left twin yelled and redoubled her efforts, cutting and slicing at me. Every time she thought she had me, she only cut air. I was everywhere and nowhere.

"Enough of this," I said in not-my-voice. "*Corrompio*," I whispered and the end caps of the staff began to glow a sickly green. As she attacked again, slashing at my legs, I blocked with my staff and lightly touched her arm with the other end. Immediately the area touched by the staff began turning black and decomposing. She moved back, fear in her eyes. In moments her arm was black and lifeless. I could see the death spreading across her shoulder to the rest of her body. She would be dead within minutes. I turned my attention to Mara.

"Come, Mara. Let us see who the foolish one is."

Mara stepped back to the edge, knowing the agony that awaited her if she attempted to cross the threshold of the tré. She looked at the edge of the circle and decided that she could defeat me.

Her hands began to glow a deep purple.

"I smell your fear, bitch. Don't worry, your suffering will be different from your sisters'. I will make sure yours is longer and infinitely more painful."

She came at me then, hands blurring. She attacked my face only to miss by a fraction of an inch. She would kick only to find me in another location. I was toying with her—or rather Maelstrom was. I had to stop this or lose myself completely. The only thing was I didn't know how. It was like a hurricane. You let it run its course and marveled at the devastation left in its wake. I began to attack. At first it was a feint here and there, and then the attacks escalated. I lunged at her head when she parried. I shifted position mid strike and brought the staff crashing on her left thigh. To her credit she didn't cry out but I was going to remedy that. I would make her scream before I was done. I kept pressing the attack until she was at the edge of the tré. I had struck her several times. She could barely stand and was unable to put weight on her left leg. Still she fought. That was when I pushed her over the threshold.

She screamed then.

I walked through the threshold of the tré and felt a slight buzzing in my body. Her eyes grew wide as she backed away. "*Infierno*," I whispered as the staff grew hot in my hands.

"No, this can't be." And she crumpled to the ground, defeated.

The large mirror showed my plane. As I looked down at Mara, Maelstrom jumped in my hands, hungry for destruction, for death. I raised Maelstrom to deliver the killing blow. It whistled as it cut through the air, only to be stopped inches from Mara's head. It was Meja. In her hand she held a sword that seemed to be forged from ice, cool and blue, covered in symbols like Maelstrom. It held Maelstrom from crushing Mara's head. "Now, Zen!" Meja yelled. I briefly registered that Zen was behind me, before I was pushed into the large pane of glass that led back to my plane of existence.

CHAPTER TWELVE-SUSPICION

When I arrived on the other side, I was surrounded by monitors, weapons drawn. Maelstrom was nowhere to be seen. To be honest, I could barely remember what had occurred. It came back to me in pieces, nothing coherent.

"Take him to the detention area," I heard one of the monitors say. A pair of bracelets was placed on my wrists and I immediately felt suppression on my chi. No matter how much I tried to gather it, it was like trying to grab smoke.

As I was led to the detention area, the monitors around me cast sidelong glances at me. No one spoke. I could see Meja up ahead of the procession and as I counted the monitors, seven in all, excluding Meja and Zen, I wondered if I was that much of a threat. Zen looked back at me and I held his gaze, knowing that things looked bad for me. How could I explain it? It wasn't me, yet it was? Would Sylk come and speak to my innocence? Somehow I didn't think so. We walked down several corridors, our footsteps echoing against the walls. The lamps cast their golden glow against the roughly hewn walls and I realized that this part of the underground facility was not meant for guests, students or luxury. After what seemed twenty minutes, we arrived at a door that looked like it would take five or six people to open. As I counted the latches, I realized why there were seven monitors. Each of them grabbed a latch on the huge door. It opened slowly at first. I had no doubt as to its weight. The seven monitors opened it enough to create space for two people walking abreast. Meja and Zen walked in first. She turned and looked at me. I got the message and followed them in. The seven monitors began closing the door once again. Now I was confused. How would Meja and Zen get out? Why were they being locked in here with me? I turned to see the immense door gliding to a close, sealing us in.

I looked around the cell. As cells went, this one was on the large side. Maybe it was a cell for a giant at one time. It was lit with a subdued glow coming from some of the stones. I calculated that it was roughly thirty by thirty and the only way out was just closed behind me. With the exception of a stone slab that protruded from the wall, the room was bare.

"What the –"

"Silence," said Meja. The tone in her voice meant she was all business. I looked at Zen, but his face was a stone mask.

From the corner, a figure emerged. It was Devin. "You have no idea what we went through to get you."

"What you went through? What took so long? Are you telling me it took months before you could find me?"

The sarcasm was heavy in my voice. Devin, Meja and Zen looked at me oddly, so I decided to ask the obvious question.

"How long have I been gone?"

"From the moment Anna took you until this moment has been four days and a half."

I sat on the stone slab. It had been months with Sylk – at least six if not more. I had no real way to tell. The days had blurred into each other. One thing I knew for sure —it had not been four and a half days.

"It was at least six months. I thought you had all given up on me."

Zen came over to me and put a hand on my shoulder.

"We were told to forget you, D., that no one student is worth risking the entire school. You were considered a casualty of war."

"It was Devin who organized a group and had us violate every rule to search for you," Meja said. It was clear Meja didn't approve of what Devin had them do.

Zen smiled. "We broke a lot of rules, but we figured if someone wanted you bad enough to snatch you, then we should get you back."

"Who was it?" asked Devin.

"Anna is a personal guard to Sylk."

Devin turned away, pensive.

"His aura is tainted, Devin. He could be under Sylk's control and we wouldn't know it. Look at what he did with Anna. She was a monitor and we weren't aware of her until it was too late."

"Well, there is that, Meja," said Devin.

"It may be simpler if we just kill him now," Meja, my fan, said. I could tell from the look on Zen's face that this was a real consideration, so I remained quiet. With the bracelets I had on, I wasn't going to focus my chi into anything but an idea. Even if I could, I doubt I could summon Maelstrom again and stand against both Devin and Meja.

"I'm going to take your advice into consideration, Meja, and keep him alive for now. We may actually need him."

Meja looked away, clearly upset, then she turned to me, anger in her eyes. She stepped close to me and spoke: "If I so much as suspect that you are a traitor, I promise you, your death will not be swift. Devin may think that you are with us but I can see the taint that permeates your aura and being. I will be waiting and watching." With that she stepped off to one side.

Devin drew closer.

"Meja tells me that you were able to manifest your chi weapon?"

"Yes and I also told you it was malevolent and radiated death. Ask Zen," she said.

Devin stayed focused on me.

"You mean Maelstrom?" I answered.

"Maelstrom, hmm? Did you name it or did the name pop into your head? Did it speak to you? Think carefully before you answer, Dante."

Did it speak to me? Had I imagined the entire thing? There was no way I could have; even Meja and Zen saw it.

"It spoke to me and told me its name was Maelstrom."

Meja looked disgusted. Zen was surprised. Devin was pensive still and looked at me, his stare unnerving me. "Were you controlling Maelstrom or was it controlling you?"

"I tried to control it, but I couldn't. It wanted to kill and destroy. If Meja hadn't shown up when she did, I would have killed—"

"It's a good thing you haven't killed anyone with it yet."

"But the twins?"

"Fortunately for you," Meja turned to me, "those were projections of Mara's chi. Had you killed Mara, Maelstrom would be bonded to you

110

and your dark aura and every time you used it, it would get worse until one day, no more you. Only Maelstrom, only the weapon." She turned to Devin, her intention clear.

"I still say we kill him and save ourselves the grief, Devin."

"Enough, Meja. No one is dying here today."

"That weapon jeopardizes every—" Devin gave her a look.

"His life is preserved —swear it, on your word."

Meja clenched her jaw and remained silent.

"Swear it." Devin's face grew hard.

Meja, not flinching from Devin faced him, "On my word, I swear his life is preserved." A palpable tension left the cell.

"Good, now that the situation of Meja trying to kill you is resolved, let's see what we can do to get you out of here."

CHAPTER THIRTEEN-ESCAPE

I had no idea what Devin meant. I saw no exit out of the cell. He went over to one corner to discuss details with Meja, who still looked like a sword in my stomach was a good idea, leaving me alone to speak to Zen.

"You don't have to worry about her, ever," Zen said as he got close.

"Why? It looks like she wants to erase me first chance she gets."

Zen laughed. "That may be true, but she swore an oath on her word, so she would die before letting harm come to you."

Now I looked back at Meja, having a hard time believing she would defend me at the cost of her life. "Why would she do that, swear that oath?"

"Because Devin asked her. She owes him her life. Also he is her big brother."

Now that Zen said it, I noticed the resemblance.

"Still, Zen, just because he asked? Come on."

"Dante, a life debt is no light thing among the warriors. Even if he weren't her brother— which by the way would have been enough— the life debt is serious business."

"So what does this mean?"

"It means you have your own personal bodyguard. Hey, you could do worse."

He laughed then, I didn't join him.

Devin walked over to where we stood.

"It's been established that you can't stay here. If someone were to see you, specifically a gatekeeper, they will kill you on sight."

"What about the monitors that brought me in?"

"They can be trusted."

"Can they?"

Meja stared daggers at me with her gaze. "I'm just saying, after Anna, can you trust any of your monitors? Or anyone in the school? How was Sylk able to put one of his people in the monitors?"

Devin looked pensive.

"You have a point, but that's for me to worry about," he said.

I looked around the cell noticing the lack of exit.

"So how do we get out of here and where am I going?"

Devin walked over to one corner of the room.

"In a moment a portal will appear, right here." I examined the wall, surprise on my face.

"This cell was for the last giant rogue we had. They have long since left this plane. The doorway was a way to circumvent opening that massive door, and its existence was only known to a few."

"That handles the how. What about the where?"

"That's a little trickier. The moment you leave, you will be fugitives from the school."

"And that means?"

Devin paused a moment and turned to Zen.

"You have a choice, Zen. You can go back to your room and you won't be implicated in any of this. I can keep your involvement away from the attention of the monitors."

"Can't do that, with all due respect, Senpai," Zen said, bowing. "It's not who I am —besides he is going to need a guardian." He said the last with a smirk. "No offense meant," he said as he bowed to Meja.

"I can't ask them to place themselves at risk, Senpai," I began.

Devin raised his hand silencing me. "Do not dishonor what they are doing. It is out of their free will that they choose this path. Meja is bound to you by her word and Zen has chosen to go with you. Honor him."

I couldn't understand why they would risk it all to be with me. Zen would be cast out of the school and Meja would be turning on the monitors, the group she led. As if reading my mind, Devin spoke. "Sometimes the paths we choose seem like the wrong one or the most difficult. Many times it is the only path that can take us where we need to go."

At that moment a low rumble followed by a deafening crash slammed against the door. Devin calmly walked over to the door. "That will be Darius and the monitors. Move over to the side so they won't see you." I moved to the corner of the room where the doorway would appear. A small section of the door slid back and a face appeared.

"I can't say I'm surprised, Devin." It was Darius. Behind him, it appeared there were twenty to thirty monitors. "Open it," he said to the monitors. The monitors grabbed the handles and began to pull and the door began to open. This was not looking good. Devin closed the section in the door and locked it in place.

"Meja knows where to go. In that bag, you have enough money to keep you moving for a while. You will have monitors and Sylk's people after you. Trust no one."

The doorway appeared in the wall as he said those last words.

"Go!" he yelled as the monitors began opening the door even further. "I will keep them busy." The monitors began pouring in. Zen grabbed my arm as I saw Devin flinging monitors back out into the hallway.

"Let's go. They cannot harm him," said Meja. "I cannot say the same for you." She pushed me through the portal.

CHAPTER FOURTEEN-FUGITIVES

The doorway led to a tunnel that was dimly lit. After a brief moment, my eyes adjusted to the darkness. Meja set off at a dead run and I followed her while Zen brought up the rear. The tunnel itself was of carved stone. It felt like we were still in the school, in some unused portion, long abandoned. The tunnel quickly veered left and Meja quickened her pace. I looked behind us to see if anyone was in pursuit. Apparently she wasn't taking chances. I matched her pace and Zen, for all his size, kept up with us. We ran this way for about five minutes. If it had not been for all my recent training, I would have been exhausted by now. It felt like we had run a mile or more. As we reached the end of the tunnel, a large door loomed before us. The door looked ancient, the wood stained with age in several places, and the hinges were as long as my arm and made of iron. The door itself was etched with markings I didn't understand with the exception of one. In the center of the door was the symbol of the monitors: an owl in flight, backed by a crescent moon. Meja approached the door. She was breathing as normally as if she had just taken a stroll and not run more than a mile in five minutes. My respect for her physical fitness went up a notch.

"Stay back. This door is keyed for monitors," she said.

As she drew close to the door, a shimmering wall of blue light coalesced about ten feet behind Zen. He turned around to look at the wall that effectively trapped us here.

"What happens if you can't open the door?" I asked.

Her attention focused on the door, she answered, "See that wall of energy back there?" Like I could miss it?

"In about three minutes, it will start closing in on us – its sole purpose to destroy anything between it and this door. Seeing as how this is a complicated lock, you may want to let me focus." I bit my tongue to cut off my answer I was about to give. Zen took a few steps away from the wall, a concerned look on his face.

Meja placed her hands together in what looked like the universal gesture of prayer. She began taking a few deep breaths. I thought that prayer was a fantastic idea if it would get us out of there. I wisely kept my suggestion to myself. Meja's hands began to glow a deep magenta. She touched the monitor symbol and it seemed as if the symbol absorbed the energy. For a few seconds, the symbol glowed with the same color and then I heard the bolts slide back and the door opened inward. As she pushed the door I noticed it was at least six inches thick. No one was going to knock that door in any time soon. The door led to a kind of circular chamber with many other doors. The chamber had six doorways in it including the one we entered through. Above each doorway was a plaque with symbols.

"What do they say?"

"They are destinations to other places."

Something about the way she said places set off alarms in my head.

"What do you mean places? Like where Sylk took me?" She looked at me calmly.

"This room is called a hub. Each of these doors leads to a place in this plane."

"What do the plaques say?" It was Zen, who up to that moment had been silent.

"Two of the doors lead to watches, the Eastern and Northern," she said as she pointed. "I suggest we avoid those. These two," she said, pointing again, "lead to other schools, again not a good idea."

"This one," she said pointing to the remaining door, leads us to the street in New York, where Sylk will have his followers and where teams of monitors will be hunting you." She turned to me as she said the last word. "Are you ready?"

Zen and I both nodded. She placed her hand on the symbol and pushed. The door opened and much to the shock of pedestrians, we stepped into a warm summer night in New York City, the city that never slept.

CHAPTER FIFTEEN-BLACK LOTUS

"We need to get off the street." I couldn't have agreed more.

"If you see a mirror, don't linger and stay close."

It suddenly dawned on me that every mirror was a 'window' for monitors or Sylk. We were going to be extremely vulnerable.

"Where are we going?" I asked.

"I'd rather not say, considering that we may have monitors who can overhear us around us even now." We made our way down Fifty Seventh Street, crossing Eighth Avenue. I turned to see we had exited the newly redone Hearst Building. Half a block away was Columbus Circle and beyond that Central Park. The street was vibrant with activity as only New York can be. People going to and fro, some at a pace just short of a run, others were languishing in an evening stroll. It was why I love New York; it's alive, warm and unforgiving at the same time. No other city could compare, now that night held another menace: hunters.

"This way," Meja said, as she led us to Central Park.

"When they begin tracking us, we will lose them in the park, without bringing danger to innocents."

"Central Park at night?" Not a good idea as every New Yorker knew. As we crossed Columbus Circle, I noticed a man following us. He was tall, and stood out somehow. His blonde hair cut short to his head, he wore worn out jeans, what looked like construction boots and a plain white oxford shirt. There was something about the way he moved that set him apart from the throng of people on the sidewalk.

"Umm, Meja—" I began.

"I saw him, Dante. The one behind us is called Rory, leader of the Monitors Wolf Pack."

"Wolf Pack?"

"It's the group of monitors that is not openly acknowledged: think of them as black ops. They don't exist and they are here to make sure we don't either."

Zen grunted and turned back to look at Rory.

"Can we take him?" Zen asked.

"Meja kept speaking as we stopped before the Maine monument at the Merchants gate.

"If it was just him, yes but the wolves always travel in threes and his team is the best."

"The best at what?" Zen just had to ask.

"They are the best at extermination. The reason I know this is because I was the one who trained them."

"So what do we do now?" I asked.

Meja turned to me. "You keep that tainted weapon of yours sheathed. You let me do the talking and fighting. Whatever happens, do not separate from each other, guardian and warrior, split up, you die. Got it?"

Zen and I both nodded.

"Let's go." And we headed into the park. Being summer in the city meant that there was still activity in the park, even at night. As we progressed further into the park, the amount of people thinned until finally we were alone. Or so I thought.

"When the fighting starts, you take him where we discussed. Give Owl this." She handed a silver coin to Zen. "He will know what to do."

"Hello, Meja, I see you have been keeping yourself well." The female voice came from behind a nearby tree.

Meja turned to face the woman, surprise, shock and anger, all fighting for expression on her face.

"Diana, it has been a while." Meja's voice could have cut stone.

"Yes it has. I normally wouldn't accept these types of assignments, but seeing as how it was you, well how could I resist?" Diana smiled. She stood under a street lamp with her hands on her hips. Her long black hair was done in a long braid that hung down to her waist. Dressed in a body length dark blue body suit, she looked alluring and deadly.

"Who is she?" I whispered to Meja.

"Remember when I said that the Wolf Pack was after us because I saw Rory?"

"Yeah. Is she part of his pack?"

"Not quite. Sometimes, very rarely, they take the leaders of the three shadow groups to form one more group. Rory from the Wolves, Andres who I'm sure is close by, from the Ravens and Diana, here, from the Widows."

Diana bowed and semi curtsied. Her bodysuit, which was open backed, revealed a tattoo of an Asian dragon crushing a tiger across her entire back, in vivid detail.

Zen whistled. "We must have really pissed them off."

"That and more," said Meja. "They are sending a message. Not even Sylk would think of going up against these three: the Black Lotus."

"I don't get it. Meja you trained Rory. Isn't Diana just another student of yours?"

Meja looked at me and I saw fear in her eyes for the first time.

"No, child," said Diana, "I'm afraid you have it backwards, she is my pupil. She was good but still a pupil."

Meja stepped back to stand next to Zen. "You two need to run, now." Zen grabbed my arm.

"We won't be having any of that," another voice with a slight Latin accent said from behind us.

"Andres, I'm flattered," Meja said calmly.

"Senorita," he said as he nodded his head slightly.

"Andres, make sure those two don't run off while I deal with my pupil," said Diana.

"Of course madam." Andres stood behind us and placed a hand on each of our shoulders, holding us in place.

"Meja, I give you my word to end their lives swiftly, right after I have taken yours," said Diana

"That is what it will take for you to touch them."

"It doesn't have to come to this, Meja. You can walk away." It was Rory.

"No, I can't. I gave my word no harm would come to him."

"That was always your weakness, child," said Diana. "Very well, then, let us begin."

Rory stepped back, a grim look on his face as if he disapproved of the turn of events. Diana walked slowly over to Meja.

"I must say that I'm disappointed. All those years of training and you can't evade a simple triad."

Meja, her jaw set in anger, turned to angle slightly away from Diana.

"This is no simple hunting triad, Diana. The Master set the Lotus on us." Diana waved dismissively in the air while shaking her head.

"How many times have I told you, shown you, that it is all the same? Where it really matters, there is no difference."

I looked over to Zen and whispered, "What is with all the talking?"

"You have much to learn and precious little life to learn it in," Andres answered.

His melodious voice reminded me of an old ad that described Corinthian leather.

"What do you mean?" I asked.

"Look closely and you will see two masters waging a battle."

I couldn't see anything except Meja slowly stepping in a circle, mimicking Diana as they spoke.

"Do not look with your eyes." Andres said.

It was not the first time I had heard that. It brought back memories of Devin and I wondered how he was. I took a deep breath and focused my inner sight on Meja. Her aura was blazing, extending at least three feet from her in every direction. Streaked with red and gold, she looked like a phoenix reborn. Diana's aura was equally active, the colors a more subdued blue and violet. I turned and looked at Zen and realized he saw it too, from the look on his face.

"Meja, our mission is to bring him back," Rory said, pointing at me, "alive or dead. Let us do what we need to do." He was almost pleading with her.

"Don't waste your breath, Rory. Her mind is set. You cannot reason with her and tonight she will forfeit her life to protect his," Diana answered.

Meja stopped circling and I could see her draw her energy inward. Her aura grew tight, almost like a second skin. I looked around with my inner sight and I saw the flow of energies around me. The trees, leaves, even the grass gave off energy signatures. The air itself held a kind of energy that ebbed and flowed. When I turned back to Meja, a gleaming sword was in her hand. I recognized it as the sword that stopped Maelstrom from killing Mara. It was about three feet long and straight. The double edges glowed in the night and the energy flowed from Meja to its point. Meja moved the sword through the air with amazing speed and dexterity. Diana's aura had drawn close to her as well. In her hands she held two sai or short swords that were a little longer than usual. They emanated a violet energy that flowed from Diana. She stood with a sai in each hand, points down.

"Come, pupil, let us end this."

Meja moved so fast I could barely follow. She lunged for Diana's midsection. Diana sidestepped and parried easily. As Diana parried, Meja turned,

127

bringing her sword in an arc, slicing down at Diana's knees. Diana back flipped to avoid the slice, landing gracefully four feet away. Again, Meja attacked —thrusting, lunging, whirling around us. It felt like being in the center of a hurricane. Each time, Diana either blocked or stepped away just in time to have Meja's blade miss her by a fraction of an inch. At this rate, it seemed Meja would tire herself out before Diana would attack.

"Enough, child. I tire of this game. I see you have not improved much since my tutelage," Diana said as she ducked under Meja's blade, in a slice meant to decapitate.

"Your moves are slow, predictable and lacking intention. I can assure you I will not show such mercy Meja."

"I am aware of this, Diana, no quarter given, none taken. I know I can't beat you in a fair fight which is why I did this!" At that moment, Meja slammed her sword into the ground almost to the hilt.

Diana's eyes opened in recognition. "It can't be. I never taught you the –"Diana froze along with Rory and Andres.

"No Diana, you never taught me the Widow Skein, but I wasn't just good, I was your best student. Did you think I would be unprepared for you?"

As I looked with my Inner Sight, all around us more lines of red and gold energy formed what seemed to be a giant web. Everywhere Meja and Diana had stepped created a part of the web. What Meja did with her sword was complete the web, making it a whole and trapping the Black Lotus.

Diana, with great effort of will, turned to Meja.

"Well played, child," she said and smiled. "I won't underestimate you the next time we meet."

"I look forward to it, Diana," Meja said and bowed slightly.

"We need to go now. This won't hold them long. Anyone else would not have been able to speak much less move," Meja said. My head was still spinning. We were facing certain death and now we were free.

"Why aren't we stuck as well?" I asked as we ran out of the park and back to Columbus Circle.

"The widow skein is the most complex of all the black widows' kata. I had to disguise it or she would know what I was doing. The skein allows you to trap enemies while leaving allies free, once you master it."

"How does it know the difference?"

"It doesn't, I do." One miscalculation and we all would have been trapped or worse, dismembered," she said calmly. I sighed realizing that while I had learned so much, it was the proverbial tip of the iceberg. The wave of heat that greeted me as we descended into the subway brought me back to my present situation. We paid our fares and made it to the platform.

"We need to go into the tunnel. Walk to the front of the platform." The platform itself was sparsely populated. As we walked down, a train came into the station, sending a blast of warm air into us, as it screeched to a stop. We waited for it to pull out of the station and the station to clear out before we jumped down to the tracks and headed into the darkness.

CHAPTER SIXTEEN-SAFEHOUSE

We walked for a good twenty minutes before Meja signaled us to stop.

"Whatever you do, no sudden moves."

I looked around. Who were we going to threaten? The only people around us were homeless men and women who had made the subway tunnels their home. As we moved off the main tracks, we began to venture into an unused part of the subway. The rats, which were the size of Chihuahuas, and much more dangerous, looked at us with their impassive eyes. The air was stale and warm. It felt like a summer afternoon, without the sun.

A stumbling figure walked towards us. Something about him set me on edge. He stopped about ten feet from Meja.

"Hold, monitor," the figure in rags and old clothing said. As if on cue, several other figures emerged from the shadows. I looked around to see that we were surrounded by a good ten to fifteen 'homeless'.

"We need an audience with Owl." The first sentry paused as if to consider Meja's words.

"You are pursued by the monitors of your school, the servants of Karashihan and the Black Lotus. Our master has taught us that a warrior's power is measured by the strength of his enemies."

"Truly your master speaks wisdom," said Meja. "It is also said that the warrior's true power lies in the hands of allies."

"Well spoken, monitor. Proceed along the tracks, please do not stray from them left or right. They will take you to our master's meeting chamber."

We walked on as the sentries faded back into the shadows. I could sense they were still there, watching, ready to act. I drew a little closer to Meja, as we walked, careful to stay in the center of the track.

"That's it? It seemed pretty simple to get past them."

"If I had answered out of protocol, we wouldn't be having this conversation."

"After what I saw you do, I think you can take ten homeless guards."

"Ten?" Meja stopped and turned to face me and Zen.

"Listen carefully. At any given moment there are anywhere from forty to fifty of these homeless guards around us." I opened my mouth to speak and then decided against it.

"Finally, you are learning that silence is often more valuable than a witless retort. This is Owl's territory and he is a leader among the Samadhi. Anyone of these 'homeless' would give me a hard time after the skein I just executed. They would easily defeat you and him." The last she said pointing her chin at Zen. From my studies I knew that the Samadhi were the strongest and fiercest of the Warriors of the Way. I also knew that each discipline had three Samadhi so that the information would never be lost to next generations. It also meant that Owl was powerful, but whether he would help us remained to be seen.

"Do you think he will help us? Or at least hide us until we can figure this all out?"

Meja looked pensive as she walked.

"I don't know, honestly. His discipline is chi manifestation, which is why we are going to him, to see if he can help with that thing you call a weapon."

"You mean Maelstrom?" I asked, not liking how she said 'thing' in reference to it.

"Yes I mean Maelstrom, your tainted weapon. You would do well not to share its name so easily. Names have power."

It seemed like every time I opened my mouth, it was so I could shove my foot in it.

"I'll remember that, thank you."

"Make sure you do." She turned to Zen.

"Have you manifested your weapon yet?"

"No not yet," he answered quietly.

"If Owl decides to help us, then he can help with that as well. In the meantime, think about what it might be."

We reached two large doors. that appeared to be rusted shut. They reminded me of huge furnace doors or blast doors with tracks leading directly to them. As we drew closer, they swung in silently. The track kept on for a few more yards and then came to an abrupt stop. We stood in a room that reminded me vaguely of Grand Central Terminal. It felt cavernous and because of the lack of lighting the ceiling was obscured, which only made the room feel more spacious. Spaced at even intervals along the walls were doorways. In the center of the room was a large circular area that was sunken in and was covered with what appeared to be expensive rugs. Pillows were arranged all throughout the area and I took these to be the seating arrangements. As I continued to look around, I did get the impression we were being watched. Meja stepped forward into the circle and Zen and I followed. In the center of the circle was a statue of a man in simple robes. The statue seemed carved of a very dark wood.

"I will do the speaking," Meja whispered.

"Fine. Who will you be speaking to?"

Meja shot me and icy glare and that was when the statue began to laugh. Meja, her hands in prayer position, bowed.

"Greetings, Samadhi."

The statue/man stood up and walked towards us.

"Greetings, Meja, of the House of Aumera." He bowed, his hands mirroring Meja's. His dark skin glistened and I could sense the power beneath the poise and grace. "I see he is as impertinent as I have been told."

He turned to face Zen. "You are the Guardian. We will have to coax your weapon out if your charge is to survive this ordeal." Zen bowed.

He turned to face me with the hint of a smile in his eyes.

"Are you Owl?" I wasn't taking anything for granted anymore.

Meja gave me a withering look and was about to speak but he raised his hand. He outstretched his hand and I took it. It felt like old solid wood laced with steel and he gripped my hand tight in a handshake that felt more like a vise. Meja was in shock. "Hello warrior, I am Owl. Welcome to my house."

CHAPTER SEVENTEEN-OWL

Meja was still in a state of surprise, so I asked Owl the only question on my mind. "Can you help us?" Meja recovered quickly, then gave me a look that suggested I keep all questions to myself. Owl chuckled at Meja's discomfort.

"Come now, surely I am not that stuffy that every question must be trapped in protocol? We can speak freely here," he said as his arm swept the circle. It seemed that Meja relaxed a bit.

"Samadhi, as you know we are being pursued."

He nodded his head. "Pursued would be stating the matter lightly, no? Let's call it what it is. You are being hunted. While you focus on the small triad, monitor, you are losing sight of the larger triad."

Meja looked pensive as Owl waited for her to answer.

"Monitors, the Black Lotus and Sylk's followers."

Owl's smile was grim as he nodded at Meja.

"I can't believe I missed that," said Meja.

"Well, when staying alive becomes a priority, occasionally our vision narrows," said Owl.

"So what does this mean that we have three groups after us? Why is that so important?" asked Zen.

Meja remained silent, fuming.

Owl turned to Zen, "For the Warriors of the Way, the triad is the number of power. The fact that you have three groups hunting you means that this is being orchestrated by someone who can influence all three groups."

"Sylk," spat Meja.

"You let anger cloud your perception. You must see without seeing," he said as he tapped the center of her chest.

"Who else could it be, Samadhi? We are in this because of him. It was he who took Dante, who forced a taint on him. Because of him, Dante now has a dark weapon and a tainted aura!" Her voice echoed in the room. Meja stood outraged.

"Please, sit," he asked but somehow it didn't come across as a request. Meja sat down slowly, the pillow making a fluffing sound as she sat.

"It is true, that the Karashihan took the warrior, but how did he know to take this particular warrior? It is also true that the warrior has a taint but aren't we all tainted in some way? And while he may possess a dark weapon, even darkness serves a purpose, does it not?"

Meja remained silent, still angry.

Feeling awkward at the silence, I coughed to clear my throat.

"Sir, so what you are saying is that it may not be Sylk behind this?" I looked from Owl to Meja.

"What I am saying is that the Karashihan is being guided into certain actions, by someone who knows him well."

"When I was with him, I mean trapped by him, he made mention a few times of a larger threat, something we are not ready for."

"He is not mistaken. I am aware of a threat on the fringes of this plane. As soon as I try to pinpoint it, it eludes me."

"Eludes you?" Meja said, surprised.

"Yes, even I have my limits, monitor."

"But if it can elude you this means—"

"That means that whoever or whatever it is, is immensely skilled, at my level or above."

"How can that be, you are Samadhi?"

"It is true, we Samadhi are skilled and some would say powerful but we are not all powerful, and while many of us are long lived, all of us are human and someday must perish."

"Of course, Samadhi," Meja said, "I meant no disrespect."

"I know, but in regards to this entity, it may be we have one of the keys to its discovery here."

"A key here? How?" I asked.

"Your dark weapon, warrior, is it sentient? Does it speak to you, do you hear a voice?" I looked at Meja and she nodded at me.

"Yes," I said, "it sounds like me, only deeper."

"Hmm, does it have a name?"

"Yes, his name is—"

Owl held up his hand. "Do not tell me, warrior. I will discover it in time."

Meja turned to me. "It speaks to you?"

"Yes, almost like speaking with me and through me. It's difficult to explain."

Meja looked at Owl. "Samadhi, I don't trust this weapon. How is it a key?"

"Tell me, monitor, have you noticed how everything in the Way is based on the triad? Monitors are sent in triads. The Samadhi are always three for each discipline. It is always a Master and two seniors. And yet in the pairing, we join only guardian and warrior?"

"Yes, it has, Samadhi. It has always struck me as odd but I thought considering the conflicts, it was a matter of using resources wisely."

"Yes, that is what we tell each other now."

"You mean that isn't true?"

"Not entirely. Long ago even before the time of Samadhi, it was always the triad, two guardians and a warrior." Then he paused and looked at us. It took a moment to sink in, then it dawned on me that even though Meja was a monitor, she had also given her word to protect me, give up her life, if need be to keep me safe. We were two guardians, one warrior.

"In that time," Owl continued, "a warrior arose who was the first Karashihan, but rather than take the title of Karashihan, he accepted the status of warrior, which meant he would be paired with two guardians. His name was Lucius."

"Lucius, as in Lucius the Destroyer?" said Meja.

"He wasn't known as the Destroyer in those times, just Lucius the First. Do you know the House he came from?"

"Yes, I do but only because my brother shared this with me. He came from the House of Iman."

Owl nodded in agreement.

"But wasn't the House of Iman cut off and extinguished?"

"If you mean, weren't all of the relatives of Lucius hunted down and killed, then yes. We could not risk another Karashihan from the same bloodline."

"Why?"

"Their discipline was twofold; they were chi amplifiers and wavedancers."

Meja looked stunned. "No it can't be—no."

"What's a wavedancer? I'm guessing we aren't we talking surfing here?" Zen looked serious.

Owl smiled. "Of a sort guardian. You are aware of the mirror, yes?" Zen nodded. "Well, a wavedancer can use almost any highly reflective surface to enter and exit the mirror."

"You mean a pane of glass?"

"A pane of glass, a mirror, a clear lake, a still puddle, anything that reflects an image can be used by a wavedancer."

"That's an amazing ability," I said.

"It was and we deliberated for days before eradicating it. In the end it was decided the threat outweighed the benefits and the bloodline of Lucius was destroyed. Or so we thought."

"Sylk," Meja said. The name carried a weight all its own.

Owl nodded. "Some of us believe that he may be the last of Lucius' bloodline. It would certainly explain how elusive he has been and it also explains the warrior's weapon."

"Chi amplification, of course, if he can amplify chi he could accelerate Dante's ability into manifesting his weapon before he was ready," Meja said as she looked at me.

"Why destroy the bloodline? What did Lucius do?" I asked.

"Lucius amplified the chi abilities of his guardians to the point that they were for all intents and purposes, invincible," said Meja. "Then he began to kill the warriors, saying that they were weak and unskilled. His guardians, corrupted by his abilities and their own lust for power defended him and he slaughtered thousands of warriors." "His true crime was much worse," Owl said. Meja turned, questions in her eyes.

"It is true he killed many on this plane. What is not shared any longer is that he went across planes to eliminate entire populations in his bid for power and dominance over the planes connected to this one."

"I've never heard of this," said Meja.

"And after today you never will. The order of the warriors will never admit their moment of weakness. They still call that act the great betrayal, rather than what it really was the great complacency."

"Wait a minute sir." I said.

I shuffled around on my pillow. As large as it was, my ass was still beginning to hurt.

"You said all the planes connected to this one. How many is that?"

Owl looked at me and smiled.

"How many planes of existence do you think there are, including this one?"

"I don't know. I'm not even going to guess."

He turned to Zen.

"How about you?"

"I would say ten?"

"You will make a good guardian, willing to risk even when you do not know the outcome."

"After the great betrayal, it was decided that warriors would never be part of a triad. It took an untold number of warriors to stop Lucius and his followers. Some of us believe that he managed to escape somehow. His body was never found." Owl stood up, his pillow barely holding an impression. "My old bones are tired and we have a long day before us tomorrow. One of my sentinels will take you to your quarters, where you can rest and bathe. There is also food if you are hungry. Tomorrow we will meet your dark weapon." We all stood and bowed as he bowed to us. He stepped out of the circle, which I noticed had three levels. As we stepped out, a sentinel silently approached us.

"This way, please." It was the 'homeless' man from the subway. Except that now he was wearing a silk robe that barely contained his muscular torso.

His head, shaved bald, glistened in the low light. His hands were large and powerful, his wrists were wide as my forearms. For all his size, he moved silently towards one of the doors.

"Hey," I said, "he never answered my question about the planes."

Meja was walking beside me, deep in thought. I looked at Zen.

"I can't even guess, at least we know it's not ten, right?"

Meja, snapped out of her reverie, answered. "It's the most important number in our Way, Dante. The answer is three."

CHAPTER EIGHTEEN-MAELSTROM

Our quarters were sparse but very comfortable. I had not realized how hungry or tired I was until the aroma of food wafted by me. I was ravenous. It seemed Zen was as hungry as I was, matching my mouthfuls. Meja looked at us and announced she was going to bathe.

"And I expect there to be food when I get out of the bathroom." I looked around at all of the food.

"Don't worry, I don't think Zen and I can eat all of this," I said as I pointed to the fruits, breads and carefully cut portions of meat.

She entered the bathroom and closed the door. Once I heard the water running, I turned to Zen.

"You think she's okay?"

"What do you mean? She seems okay."

"Zen, she just faced her teacher, which we barely escaped. And she has monitors after her."

"Dante, I think she will be fine. She gave her word to protect you. And you heard Owl; something is going on behind the scenes."

"Yeah, I really hope it's not that Lucius character. He sounded like a nasty piece of work."

Zen nodded, his mouth full of food. I looked around the room and noticed that it seemed to be part of a larger room that was divided.

"Who knew this place was down here?"

"From what I understand, there are a lot of places like this: old abandoned stations or hotels, even some bunkers that no one remembers."

"True, like that whole setup under the Waldorf that Roosevelt used."

Zen was looking at me, staring, actually.

146

"What? I have food on my face?"

"Hey D., are you ready for tomorrow?"

I stopped to think about how I would have to manifest Maelstrom, and my appetite quickly left.

"I don't know, Zen. I don't know if I can manifest it again. Don't know if I want to."

Zen grunted in assent.

"I get you. When I saw you at Sylk's place, I barely recognized you. I knew it was you but it was also not you."

"It's hard to explain, one thing I can tell you, it feels wrong."

"Good, it should feel wrong." It was Meja who had stepped out of the bathroom noiselessly.

"It should always feel wrong. The moment it feels good, you are lost." She wore a white robe laced with flecks of blue, which complemented her bronze skin. Her hair, which was usually in a ponytail or bun, was loose and flowed around her face, framing it. It dawned on me that she was exceptionally attractive. Zen bumped into me when he caught me staring.

"Shouldn't you go shower, long day and all that?" He looked at me and smiled mischievously pointing at the bathroom with his head as Meja busied herself with the food, oblivious to us. Or so I thought.

"Yes you should bathe. The stench is starting to become intolerable," she said as she placed some portions of food on her plate.

Zen laughed. Meja turned to face me, her face all business.

"I'm going, I'm going." I entered the bathroom, which was immense. As I ran the water for a shower, I could hear Meja speaking to Zen, but I couldn't make out her words. I guessed it had something to do with my dark weapon and the threat it posed. The water crashed to the floor further drowning out the voices. I made it as hot as I could take it and then a little hotter. It felt good on my aching muscles. I was exhausted and it was finally catching up to me. I had no idea if I could manifest Maelstrom or if I could control it if I did. And how was Maelstrom a key to stopping whatever was coming? My thoughts wandering, I let the hot water wash away the soreness. When I stepped out of the bathroom, Meja was fast asleep. Zen headed to the bath.

"Try not to make too much noise. I get the feeling she is a very light sleeper."

I nodded as I walked over to my bed. The robe felt cool against my skin and sleep was overtaking me.

"What were you guys talking about?" I asked Zen.

"Contingency plans in case something happens, to one of us."

I lay down on my bed, barely able to keep my eyes open.

"Contingency plans?" I yawned.

"Nothing to be worried about right now, so get some sleep. I'll see you in the morning."

"Hey, Zen," I said, "Thanks for everything."

He faced me, placed his right fist in his left hand, and bowed.

"You're welcome. See you in the morning."

My last image was of him entering the bathroom as I feel asleep. I dreamt in fits and starts. At one point, I found myself in a vast desert. The sun was blazing and the heat was oppressive. Everywhere I looked I saw sand. I knew this was a dream. I had the surreal sensation of being outside looking at myself, knowing it wasn't real.

"Hello, Dante," a voice behind me said. I turned to stare into myself, albeit an older, scarred and noticeably stronger version of myself.

"Who are you?" But I knew the answer even before I asked the question.

"I am you and I am not. I am the chaos, the anger, the power that resides in the deep dark places."

"Maelstrom."

"Yes, and we have much to discuss, you and I."

"What can we possibly need to talk about?"

"You know, Dante, as far as vessels go, you can prove to be one of the strongest."

"Excuse me?"

"Let me explain. I am you or rather a manifestation of you. I am also beyond you and all mortal life. I have always been in one form or another. After you perish, I will continue."

"That's encouraging. What are you?"

"I thought I told you. I am the chaos—"

"No, what are you – are you alive? Are you a being, a spirit, what?"

He looked at me a moment, pensive. "I apologize, this form of communication, words, is so limiting. Permit me." He drew close to me and placed a hand on my heart and another on my forehead. A flood of images cascaded into me, war, strife, death, anger, hatred; vision after vision of battles, duels, power plays, murders flooded my mind. I fell to my knees, overwhelmed, holding my head. It felt as if it were about to burst.

"Do you understand now?"

"I do, but using you would kill me."

"What is the death of one when an entire plane of existence hangs in the balance?"

I always hated that argument. It always sounded like the right argument, unless of course you were the one called to make the sacrifice.

"Is there any other way that doesn't involve you completely taking over?"

"It has always been so. The moment you take a life with me, and I am bonded to you, it is your life's energy that directly gives me my manifestation."

"That is the only way?"

"Well, there is another way that you can wield me but the cost is higher and none accepted the burden for very long."

I figured it couldn't be worse than being possessed by some ancient weapon. I was wrong.

Maelstrom/Dante looked at me as if assessing if I could handle what he was about to offer.

"Very well, my vessel, I will tell you. In order for you to wield me, I must absorb life. If I bond to you and your essence is closed off to me, I take the essence of your adversary." It didn't sound too horrible but it felt like there was a catch.

"What happens to the person?"

"The physical being perishes." He stood quietly as if waiting for my next obvious question.

"And their spiritual being?"

"Becomes a part of me and therefore you."

This sounded bad.

"You mean I you— absorb who they are?"

"Yes, it means your life is prolonged in a considerable fashion."

"Stop talking in circles. What does it mean? What happens when you absorb an essence?"

Maelstrom smiled at me but it was a cold, empty smile, haunted and alone.

"It means everything that person is, good or evil becomes part of you. You acquire their knowledge, their desires and dreams. You are given access to their innermost being. It is an opportunity to achieve great power."

"Stop it," I said, knowing full well that I was having a conversation with myself, but not with me.

"What happened to the last person who agreed to this arrangement?"

"After several years of dispatching his enemies, he went quite mad, not being able to distinguish who he was amidst the accumulated essences. In the end, he killed himself. It was actually for the best."

"Is there another option?" I had a feeling there wasn't but it didn't hurt to try.

"Well, yes, but no one accepts it."

"What is it?" I asked, hope in my voice.

"Well, you simply surrender your will and I take control of your body and mind."

"I become a puppet?"

"You become a very powerful puppet."

"Is there any way to rid myself of you? You know, make it so you are never a part of me?"

"No, once I am manifest, I am with that vessel until he or she dies." He cocked his head as if an idea struck him.

"I would imagine that is one way to get 'rid of me', as you say."

"Not an option," I said.

"You did manifest *me*, not the other way around." He crossed his arms as he looked at me.

"I know."

"When do I have to decide how you do this, my life or my enemies?"

"When you take your first life, you will have to make the choice and I never said enemy."

A strong wind began to kick up sand, obscuring him from view.

"The choice will be in your heart and then I will act. You cannot lie to me for I am you as much as you are me."

It was only his voice now, the sand blocking my view in every direction.

When I opened my eyes, I was alone in the room.

CHAPTER NINETEEN-
MANIFESTATION

It was morning. Zen and Meja were nowhere to be seen. I got out of bed, stretched and got dressed. I helped myself to some of the fresh fruit and bread that was prepared for us. Last night's dream had me shaken. Did I imagine it all?

Somehow I knew that what Maelstrom had said was true. This meant that all I had to do was avoid killing anyone with it, ever.

I really doubted that was going to happen. I knew that today Owl was going to try and have me manifest Maelstrom. I just didn't think I would be able to do it. It wasn't like I could just think about it and summon it up. Or was it really that easy? The last time it appeared, I was in a fight for my life. Maybe it only appeared when I was in danger? I had no way of knowing how this was going to work. I was lost in thought when a shadow crossed before me. It was Zen.

"Hey there D., sleep well?"

"Not really, had the craziest dream."

"Hmm. I guessed as much. Who did you see in your dream?"

How did he know I saw someone?" I hesitated. "Why do you ask?"

"Dante, this is me, okay? I'm here to make sure you stay safe."

He was right of course and I was being wary for no reason. Even though the events of the last few weeks left me with little desire to trust anyone.

"You're right, Zen, sorry. I had a dream or vision, I don't know. I was speaking with Mael- my weapon."

"You mean the dark staff? You were talking to the staff?"

"No, he, it looked like me, an older more dangerous me."

"So you were talking to yourself?" A hint of smile crossed his face.

"This isn't funny, Zen. That weapon is dangerous."

"I know, D. It's just you know what they say— one of the signs of insanity, having conversations with yourself." He chuckled.

"Okay. Okay. Dante," he said when I didn't join in the laughter. "What did it say?"

"The bottom line is that I'm stuck with it."

"Meaning?"

"That unless I'm dead, it's going to be a part of me."

"Kind of a harsh deal there."

"Yes I know. Hey, where's Meja?"

"Owl sent me to see if you were awake and to 'collect you' as he says. They are in the main training areas."

"Areas?"

"Yeah, this place is extensive. I don't know how they have been able to stay down here and not be discovered. They have extended the abandoned station into living quarters, training areas, an armory and some other areas I didn't get to see."

After using the bathroom which was interesting without a mirror – it made shaving an adventure – "Okay, let's go do this," I said.

Zen walked ahead of me through the corridors. He was right; the place was a labyrinth of corridors. He led me down several passageways which as I followed the pattern seemed to lead ever inward. Don't ask me how I knew that, it was the impression I felt from the space, like we were going ever deeper and in. We finally arrived at a large door. It seemed that everything was done in extra-large down here.

"Here you are, Dante."

"You're not coming in?"

"Not this way, no. Owl said that this was your way in and your path to walk, only you."

"I see."

"I trust him, Dante. I don't know why but I do."

"I wish I shared your conviction."

He stood back as if deciding something then stepped forward, encasing me in his arms with a tremendous bear hug. "Zen, I need air." He laughed then turned serious as he released me and my ribs sighed in relief.

"Dante, do what you need to do but don't allow them to force you into anything."

"Thanks, Zen."

He turned and walked down the corridor. Pulling open the door revealed a large training area. Around every wall were racks containing weapons of every type. In the center of the room was a large tré. It was easily twice the size of the one Sylk had. Around the outer ring were symbols inscribed into the floor. Each symbol had a faint golden glow to it. Each ring of the tré was a deep red material that looked like ruby. I couldn't imagine how difficult or costly it would be to create three ruby circles of that size. And in the center of the tré stood Owl. He was the only other person in the training area. He beckoned to me to enter the tré, of which I was wary, since the last time I entered a tré, my life was in danger shortly thereafter. I crossed the threshold of the outer circle and felt the rush of energy close around me. I looked back and saw that the symbols now flared a brighter gold. I turned to look at Owl, my stomach clenching.

"Let's begin," he said.

I stepped into the innermost circle of the tré, facing Owl.

"In the past, you needed to feel threatened or in mortal danger in order to manifest your weapon."

"How did you know?"

"Fear is one of the most powerful emotions involved in chi manipulation. It is also the most dangerous."

"Why is it so dangerous? Not that I'm disagreeing." The memory of what I almost did to Mara flashed in my mind.

"When a weapon is manifested out of fear, it becomes almost impossible to control." That sounded about right as I thought back to the control Maelstrom exerted when present.

"So rather than threaten you with death, let's pursue a different method," said Owl.

Anything that didn't involve my death — perceived or otherwise—was great in my opinion. I looked around for Meja or Zen or anyone else for that matter. Owl must have sensed my apprehension.

"We are alone here, and the tré is sequenced to obstruct any curious eyes."

I nodded.

"Now focus, control your breath."

I did as he said. "Now, carefully look. You will see that your weapon lies just beneath the surface, in this case, in your fear or anger. Take a look."

It felt like forever before I sensed the energy that was Maelstrom. Once I touched on it, it recoiled at first. Then it embraced me like a lover. I was completely enveloped by this presence that was me and not me.

"There, Dante, that's it. Surrender to it, let it fully manifest."

I dove headlong into the sensation; it was raw with power, primal, feral. It coursed through my body. I gave myself over to it, but this was different than the last time, I had control. I looked down to my hands as the short staff materialized, a slice of ebony covered in blood red symbols. My voice however was deeper, raspier. Two voices, one overlaid the other. Maelstrom was fully present but I retained control. How was this possible? Then I looked at Owl and saw that sweat covered his brow and I knew he was making it possible. He smiled and spoke with some effort.

"It is quite the formidable weapon you possess, Dante."

He was going to get himself killed! For what? As if reading, my mind, he said. "I'm in no danger from you or your weapon. Dante, banish your fear, it has no place here." He swept his left arm in a semi-circle in front of his body. As he finished his arc, a faint glow took shape and coalesced into a long sword hovering before him. The hilt was in front of his face, while the blade itself reached almost to the floor. A golden light ran the length of the blade. Maelstrom leapt in my hands, anxious to attack.

"Unleash it, Dante, I know you want to attack, let it." In an instant I was on him, driving Maelstrom in what I thought was surely a killing blow: an overhead strike descending directly on his head. His sword angled just enough to deflect the strike. A shield! Owl looked at me and a smile danced in his eyes.

"Good I see you are serious. Let's see if we can harness that weapon, Dante." I had no idea what he was talking about; it was all I could do to not lose rational thought to this thing in my hands. Owl brought his hands together in a universal form of prayer and closed his eyes. Too late for prayer, I thought. Slowly I stepped around him, looking for an opening. Every time I shifted, the sword protecting him shifted. Slowly, imperceptibly, the air quality shifted. The hair on my arms stood on end and the tré felt charged with energy. Owl remained motionless and then I saw them. The orbs. At first it was two slowly rotating around Owl, then four, then eight. each time dividing and multiplying, until Owl was the center of a small universe. They had started out large and gradually gotten smaller with each split and now were the size of small grapes. I couldn't count how many floated lazily around him. Then he opened his eyes and they stopped moving.

"These orbs are not explosive; they are what I would call percussive. I suggest you avoid them, if you can."

It was like saying I should dodge a bullet.

A swarm of the small orbs raced towards me as I held Maelstrom before me. This was not going to end well. The first one hit me with the force of a truck. Immediately I was glad the orbs were the size of grapes. It knocked the wind out of me and doubled me over.

"Dante, you must see with your entire being. Stop relying on your eyes." Easy for him to say, he didn't have a mob of mini explosive grapes – sorry non explosive – percussive, grapes flying at him.

"You're getting hit because you still haven't surrendered to the weapon. You are fighting on two fronts, internal and external and it's costing you," he said as more orbs came my way.

The orbs buzzed by my head like angry bees. I was getting a solid peppering and the bruises were starting to show. He wanted me to surrender to Maelstrom but not lose control. How was I supposed to do that?

"Thinking too much, Dante," Owl said as a group of five orbs smacked into my left side. It felt like my ribs were cracked as I brought Maelstrom too late, to defend myself. I was getting angry. Angry for being in this situation. Angry at my Sensei for sending me to this school and crazy promotion. What was Sensei Wei thinking? Angry at being hunted like some animal. Angry at the constant tests. I was done. Something in me let go and released.

"Finally, child," said the voice in my head.

I ran to the edge of the tré, orbs in hot pursuit. I stopped short of the edge and turned. Maelstrom glowed in my hand.

"Cesare," I heard my voice overlaid by another. Everything stopped. The orbs floated a few inches from me, pregnant with the promise of pain. I walked past, careful not to touch any. As I stopped past the last of the group, they sped up and slammed into the edge of the tré. I had dodged them!

"Very good, Dante."

I knew it wasn't me, but Maelstrom.

"I know you think that you had nothing to do with that. Remember your weapon can only function within the context of you as its vessel. This is its greatest strength and greatest weakness. It is only as powerful as you allow it to be."

I was beginning to understand. Even though the energy of what was Maelstrom existed independently of me, it required my energy, my chi, to manifest. Without me as a conduit, there was no way it could manifest. Once manifest, its expression, power and intent were subject to my level of control. As this realization dawned on me, I felt a shift occur within. Maelstrom glowed and all the red symbols transformed to a deep gold. The anger was gone. In its place there was stillness, a peace.

"Now you are ready, Dante." Owl grabbed his sword and stepped towards me, a cloud of orbs trailing him. He was grinning fiercely and I found much to my surprise that so was I. He was a blur. As his sword sliced through the air, I could swear the air itself split and made room for the blade. It was that sharp.

Barely blocking his first lateral slice, I felt incredibly outclassed.

"Excellent!" he roared. With a thought, another swarm of orbs raced to pummel me, followed close behind by Owl. How would I evade both?

"Stop thinking, Dante! Let yourself feel what your weapon wants to do. Listen to it."

Easy to say when you aren't the one being attacked. Wait, he could be. I could use the orbs as a distraction. Rather than run from them, I could run towards them and Owl! I changed tactics and direction and headed towards the impending swarm of pain. At the last second, I rolled forward to come face to face with Owl, who was still smiling. He lunged with his sword and I, with Maelstrom's help, parried sending him slightly off balance. As we locked weapons, I was conscious of the orbs coming at my back. As I shifted right, I allowed him to step forward into the swarm. He released his sword, which immediately reverted to shield duty and deflected the orbs. That gave me about two seconds.

It was all I needed. I lunged forward with Maelstrom, hitting Owl in his ribs. For a split second, the thought of consuming him crossed my mind, and then it was gone.

The word *vortejodairo* that escaped my lips was unintelligible to me but Owl's eyes opened wide. He encased himself in what appeared to be a golden sphere and then pulled me in with him. Then he looked up expectantly, sweat beading on his forehead. The orbs all vanished.

"Owl, what—"

He silenced me with his hand and began creating symbols in the air that glowed then faded.

"You summoned a vortex that will devastate this area very shortly." He shook his head. "You are full of surprises!" I didn't see anything out of the ordinary and told him so.

"We are in its eye. Would you like to see what's happening?"

"Yes, I would."

I was about to step out of the sphere, when the first large block flew by me and slammed into and opposite wall disintegrating into dust.

"Still want to see?"

"No," I said, visibly shaken. "I think it's safer in here."

"In that assessment, you are correct."

"What is going on out there? You said there was a vortex."

"Yes, but what you created, is something I have not seen in many years, since I was learning my basic skills and my master summoned this. I still don't know how you knew – Ah yes, it makes sense, your weapon. It is called Maelstrom, is it not?"

I remained silent; stunned that he had guessed its name.

"How did you - ?"

"Dante, never reveal that name to anyone."

He looked so serious I took a step back and almost stepped out of sphere.

"Promise me, Dante, on your life."

"On my life?"

"Yes, you must never reveal this weapon's name to anyone, ally or enemy."

"But some of them know it already."

"I will take care of that. Can you give me your word? I realized what he was asking, he was asking for a word of bond."

"I promise, Owl, to never reveal the name of this weapon even if it means my life."

He visibly relaxed the slightest bit.

"Okay, so what's going on? What's out there and how is this vortex with no air?"

"What you see, or rather don't see, is an energy vortex swirling around made up of chi that would shred us completely."

"But the tré –"

"Cannot withstand that kind of power, look." He pointed to the floor and I saw the symbols of the tré were getting dimmer by the second.

"In seconds, the tré will fail and then we only have this," he said as he pointed to the sphere.

I looked around; all of the symbols were not only going out but slowly being erased.

"Will it hold?"

"I don't intend on finding out. Come, help me."
He placed both his hands on the floor beneath us.

"Focus your chi downwards, through the floor.
When I tell you, release it. Understand?" I nodded.
With the tré failing, a hum was growing louder and
louder outside the sphere.

"Now!"

I unleashed my chi that had been gathering like
a coiled spring, towards the floor. Owl seemed to
have caught it, amplified it and directed it, creating
an opening in the center of the tré.

"In you go." He pushed me in and I fell for
what felt like ten to fifteen feet before landing in
something soft. Owl landed beside me and I saw we
were in the sunken circle he first greeted us in. I
noticed it was roughly the same size as the tré above
us.

"Now what?"

"Now we wait. That type of vortex is
notoriously hard to stop, since it feeds on energy,
much like a hurricane needs warm water. Once it
exhausts the latent energy in the tré, it should
dissipate."

"How long will that be?"

Owl thought for a moment. "Well, it's a practice tré, so not too much energy is stored in it. So I would guess four or five."

"Hours?" I asked hopeful.

Owl looked at me and then sealed the opening we had created through six feet of concrete with what looked like a golden bubble.

"Days."

I sat on the floor – stunned.

"How? I'm sorry."

"Nonsense!" He sat down next to me and got comfortable. "You have been given a great gift, or curse. It all depends on your point of view. Your weapon is one of the weapons thought lost, one of the three wielded by Lucius and his two guardians."

I didn't want to ask, but I had to, even though I knew the answer before I asked the question.

"Which weapon did Lucius wield?"

Owl looked at me and the staff in my hand. "Well, in his day it had a blade on the end and it was considerably longer, but I will never forget that vortex. The name of his weapon was Maelstrom."

CHAPTER TWENTY-BIRD IN HAND

The days passed and the vortex dissipated. Owl, to facilitate my control of Maelstrom, trained me in chi control.

"You won't be able to stay here long, Dante. Eventually they will come here for you. You pose too great a threat."

I knew he was referring to the Black Lotus.

"At some point, you will take a life." He raised his hand as I started to protest.

"It will happen and when it does, you will need this." Suspended on a silver and gold chain hung what looked like a mini tré.

"What is it?"

"It's called a soul catcher. If you are wearing this when you take a life, the essence flows into this."

I looked at the pendant. The outer ring was red, the middle ring, a deep blue, the center ring was a deep gold and in the center was a clear gem like quartz. They seemed to hang suspended without any form of attachment or structure to hold them in place.

"If the center ring ever turns black, touch it to Maelstrom. It will do the rest."

"What happens if I take a life—"

"Not if, but when, Dante."

"Okay, what happens when I take a life and I don't have this on?"

"Then you must decide what kind of bond you will have with your weapon. This will allow you some time before having to make that choice. Mind you, the choice will have to be made, Dante, eventually. Do you understand this?"

"I do."

"You must travel to the Akashic records to find a syllabist. You need one to help you master the words of power so you don't repeat the vortex, unintentionally."

"Where do I find the records?"

"The entrance is rumored to be on the lowest level of the South Watch." Owl was nodding his head. It was Meja.

"So it would seem, but first you must navigate the defenses there and I only know of one warrior who has been able to bypass them and survive."

Meja turned away, her jaw clenched. By this time, Zen had joined us. I looked from Owl to Meja.

"Who?"

Owl sighed. "It was one of my brightest and most promising students. He was manipulated and twisted."

I didn't like the sound of this. "And we want this person to help us, really?"

"It is not a matter of want, Dante. You need a syllabist. The records are the only way to find one, which means you need him to get you to the records."

"Fine, who is it, then?"

Meja turned to face me, anger and something else —fear, bright in her eyes,

"Only one person can navigate the watch because it was abandoned then sealed over 150 years ago. The defenses were left in place to present anyone from being too curious."

"Only one person I know is old enough to be around that long ago," I whispered to myself.

Meja turned away "Sylk."

"Are you kidding me?" I said, barely able to contain the surprise.

"Not only is he the only one that can put you past the defenses, he was part of the team that installed them," said Owl.

"This is just great. I don't need to tell you how bad an idea I think this is."

Meja looked at me, resigned. "We don't have a choice in this, Dante."

"There is always a choice in this! Someone else must know how to get around these defenses. Hell, I'm willing to try it without him."

Owl stared hard at me. "Are you sure you're willing to take that risk? Not just for you, you now speak for three. These two," he said pointing at Meja and Zen, are sworn to you. They will advise you but ultimately you have the last word."

When had this happened? I turned to face both Meja and Zen.

"He's right, D. You're the warrior. We can advise you but you have to make the choice."

"The hell he does!" burst Meja. "As a warrior, he has no experience; he is going to get us killed." She turned to Owl, "You know I'm right, Samadhi!"

Owl remained silent.

"Meja, I don't pretend to know what I'm doing. I know I have no experience. But I have you and Zen. I'm not so full of myself that I can't admit I need help, but if that help has to come from Sylk, I'll take my chances on my own."

"You wouldn't last five minutes out there on your own," she said.

"I know. Will you help me?"

She exhaled sharply. Turning to Owl. "We are going to need plans of the Watch."

Owl smiled. "I think I may have an old set you can take with you. You should be leaving soon. The Lotus will be here within a day or so."

"I'll get our things," said Zen.

"Okay, do what you need to do and meet back here in an hour," said Meja.

"Got it. See you two later." Zen headed off. Meja accompanied by one of Owl's men went off to get the plans of the watch. Owl sat down and for a brief moment looked very old.

"Are you okay, Samadhi?" He waved away my hand and smiled.

"Don't let her rub off on you too much, Dante," he chuckled. "I have never seen anyone turn her mind so quickly; she is usually as stubborn as a mule."

"Yes… she usually is."

"Do you know why she agreed to your idea?"

"She said it was suicide, and then agreed to go with me." It was suddenly clear. "Sylk."

Owl nodded. "She hopes he will be after the same information."

"You must remain in control when you face him next. He has his own twisted ideas about our fate and what needs to be done." I recalled the conversations I had with him.

"Twisted is right."

"When it comes to him, she only sees revenge; this is her blind spot and a weakness he will exploit. He will attempt to divide you, turn you against each other. Do not let this happen or everything is lost."

"How do I prevent that from happening? She sees red even at the mention of his name."

"When you think she is on the verge of losing her reason, remind her that a bird in the hand must be released in order to fly free."

Cryptic much? I thought to myself.

"And this means?"

"She will know what it means, you must say this to her only when you have exhausted every other argument."

"Why?"

"If you don't, then she will deceive you. You must be certain she is heading towards irrational behavior, that her anger, fury and rage have her under control. Only then can you tell her the words I have given you. Under no circumstances can you say those words, in any other context. Is that understood?"

I wanted to know what would happen, but I knew he wouldn't tell me. "I understand."

"You should help Zen pack your things."

I was about to answer when the world exploded.

CHAPTER TWENTY ONE-HOUSECALL

The blast doors that were the entrance to Owl's compound flew off their hinges and tumbled inwards. Each door was two feet thick. The power required to unhinge the doors with that much force was staggering. As the smoke cleared, a figure appeared in the opening.

"Hello, Samadhi." It was Diana. Flanking her were Rory and Andres.

"Oh shit," escaped before I even realized the words had left my mouth.

"It would seem the Black Lotus is here sooner than I anticipated," said Owl as if nothing had occurred.

"And my sentinels, Diana?"

"I spared a few, Samadhi, but some actually thought to detain and question me – me, can you believe the arrogance? Naturally I taught those their last lesson."

She picked up a body and flung it towards Owl. It was the sentinel who met us initially in the subway tunnels. His body was broken, bleeding from the eyes, ears and mouth. Both arms and legs were shattered and in several places the bone protruded through the skin. The fact that he was still alive was a testament to his force of will and strength.

"We tried to—" he gasped.

"Be still, child," said Owl. His hands glowed for a moment and he placed them on the sentinel's chest. The sentinel became still but was still breathing. Two other sentinels silently took his body away.

"That was unnecessary but you never did know restraint, even as a child."

Diana placed a hand on her hip.

"That was long ago, Samadhi and I exercised restraint. Isn't he alive?" She smiled an icy smile and strode into the compound.

"Our orders have been modified, Samadhi. We are to execute Dante Black upon sight, as a person of utmost threat. Any who aid or in any way protect and or defend said person will be considered a threat, and in violation of the decree to carry out this judgment. Thus they are subject to the same penalty —death."

Owl's jaw hardened.

"What will be your course of action, Samadhi?" Behind the Lotus, other figures emerged dressed in the same black clothing.

"Before you reply, I want you to understand that we are merely carrying out our orders," more figures emerged from behind the Lotus, "and that this time we are prepared to carry them out." A total of thirty figures stood behind the Lotus and began to divide into three groups of ten.

"You may have him, Diana—." I turned, shock registering on my face— "as soon as I breathe my last breath." he finished. I exhaled not knowing I was holding my breath.

"I see, very well, Samadhi. So be it."

Was she strong enough to fight Owl? Did she have that kind of power?

"This is not a battle you can win, Dante. Go find Meja and Zen. I will keep them occupied here."

As I turned to move to an exit, I saw Zen carrying Meja, running towards us.

"There was an explosion. She was caught in the blast as we were heading to another part of the compound."

This was getting worse by the second. Zen put Meja down on one of the cushions. My heart lurched to see the cuts and bruises on her face. She was hurt because of me. They would kill her, kill Zen, and kill Owl and anyone else who helped me.

"Dante, no—" I could hear Owl far away. I heard the thump of energy as a circle closed around us. I forgot the sunken chamber was really just another tré, disguised as a reception area. I walked to the edge of the tré and stepped through barely feeling a tingle. I turned and saw a grim look on Owl's face but it was too late. Maelstrom was in my hands, its symbols black on black. Around me, the air was charged. Maelstrom throbbed in my hands. "You want me," my other voice said, and I could see the surprise register on Diana's face. "Come get me."

CHAPTER TWENTY TWO-CARNAGE

"Diana! No! Do not approach him!" I heard Owl yell. I laughed, or was it Maelstrom? I couldn't be sure. I walked slowly to where Rory and his group of ten stood. Death was on my mind and in my hands.

"Diana, if you value your life and those of your brothers in the Lotus, you would keep away from him!" yelled Owl.

I stood on the edge of the sphere Owl had created, the anger in me coursing through my veins growing, expanding.

"What's going on, Owl?" It was Zen.

"It's the rage. It triggers a darker, powerful weapon. Manifested like this, he won't be in control."

I turned to face Owl but it was Maelstrom who spoke.

"He doesn't need to be in control, Owl of the House of Gana, now long since gone." Surprise, then anger filled Owl's face. "You have no right to do this."

"No? You who were still a babe when I was beyond years know that as I chose him, he chose me."

"This is truth, but he is the Master of the weapon not the opposite."

"Let me pose a question, young Owl: Who is the weapon?"

I felt myself slipping, giving in to the rage, feeding Maelstrom.

"Enough talk, there are lives to be taken." I turned to face the Lotus.

Owl approached me and spoke softly. "Remember, Dante, you know your greatest strength and your greatest weakness. You are not just a vessel; you are the conduit through which the energy flows. Do not lose yourself," he whispered.

"Do not worry, he is not lost. I know exactly where he is," answered Maelstrom.

"You know you want this. We can end this here and now. This is the only way if you kill them you

send a clear message that you are not to be trifled with." Maelstrom spoke within my mind.

"Not like this, not with death, there has to be another way."

"Of course, perhaps you can convince them with reason? The female looks especially open to conversation. Let's say we go over there and find out?"

I/we walked closer to Diana, turning from Owl and Rory's group. We stopped thirty feet from Diana and her group. Maelstrom cleared my throat. "It would seem this pup, this vessel, thinks you can be reasoned with. I explained to him that the only language you understood was that of blood, pain and death."

Diana's eyes opened briefly, surprise showing on her face, then vanishing just as fast, replaced with grim determination.

"I have my orders. You are to be executed," she answered.

"You cannot say I did not try," said Maelstrom.

"Can we do this without killing them?"

"I don't think they will show you the same courtesy, vessel. They will attack you and your friends with the intent to end your existence. This is not acceptable. What shall it be—you or them?"

I hesitated for the briefest of moments, "Them."

"Splendid, then you must truly unleash me or you and your comrades are lost."

I removed any restraint, however small I had on Maelstrom.

"Yes," he sighed.

"We won't need this." I felt my hand go to the soul catcher and rip it off my neck, tossing it to one side.

"No!" yelled Owl.

Maelstrom laughed and I laughed with him feeling free, primal and powerful.

"Take him." Diana signaled to her group. They advanced as one unit. I could tell they were highly trained. I also knew they were all dead. It was only moments away. From the group, three separated and came right at me. They each had short swords with black blades. I guessed this was the signature weapon of the black Lotus. I felt my hands move along the symbols etched into the shaft of the staff. For a moment, nothing happened then I noticed the balance began to shift slightly as Maelstrom grew to six feet. On each end, a foot long blade protruded making it eight feet in total. All three attacked at once, I ducked under the first slice, sidestepped a second slice and leapt above the third slice. I whirled Maelstrom around, waiting for the next attack.

"Enough, you will not be able to avoid their attacks indefinitely."

"I know."

"Then why play at this exercise in futility?"

"Because killing is not always the answer."

"We shall see which of us is right, in the end, my vessel."

Another group of three attacked. I blocked or parried each attack. As each attack came, I knew that I would need to attack or I would be overrun. The leader of the group advanced wielding a much longer sword. As he advanced, the other groups of three closed in. Maelstrom almost leapt out of my hands as I maneuvered around thrusts, cuts and slices.

"You have to cut, before you are cut."

"No."

"You must or you will die."

"No."

The leader with the longer sword had moved within range to attack. As he cut downwards, I lifted Maelstrom to block. He changed direction at the last second. I turned with Maelstrom and buried the blade in his throat.

"It begins." The voice was satisfied and smug.

The other nine stepped back, wary of Maelstrom, as their leader lay dying on the floor before me.

Beside my foot was the soul catcher. I grabbed it and put it on.

"Confound you boy. You are only prolonging the inevitable."

"I know, but I would rather not make that choice right now."

"You are a most difficult vessel."

I smiled a truly genuine smile of my own.

"You said cut, then let's cut, but not kill. No carnage, just chop them."

"Very well, vessel. Let's cut."

Maelstrom in my hands, I became as precise as a surgeon wielding a scalpel. All nine suffered injuries that ended their ability to fight but not their lives. Diana looked on with growing consternation on her face.

"Enough of this play. I will end this here and now." In her hands materialized her sai.

"Diana, listen to me. You must not engage him!" It was Owl.

"Surely you see the threat he poses, Samadhi. He must be put down like the rabid dog he is."

Owl turned to Zen and whispered something to him I couldn't hear then I saw him approach.

"If you attempt it, Diana, you will die as surely as this one here." Owl pointed to the now dead leader of the small group.

"What would you have me do, Samadhi? I have my orders. If I don't carry them out, you know the consequences."

"I expect you to honor my home and my position as Samadhi. I will deal with him. If I fail, you may do as you are ordered. If I succeed, you will honor his status as my charge and I will bring him before your Master."

Diana lowered her sai and stepped back.

"Very well, Samadhi. It shall be as you have said." In a louder voice, "Everyone stand down!"

From every doorway emerged figures clad in black. As I looked around a rough estimate was about one hundred members of the Black Lotus and those were the ones I could see.

Owl turned to face me, whispering. "It is time for you to finish your training."

I looked at him, part of me confused, most of me enraged that he would get in my way from finishing Diana. As much as I didn't want to kill, my hold on Maelstrom —what little there was— was slipping. I sensed it and I know he did too. The air around us grew thick with energy. I ran at Owl with Maelstrom a blur in my hands. I lunged and Owl sidestepped. I thrust and he would be a fraction of an inch out of reach. Each time Maelstrom's blades just missed him.

"You are going to die here, vessel, unless you surrender to me. You cannot even touch him much less dispatch him."

"What? I can't kill Owl!"

"Finally you understand me. Of course you can't. But I can if you let me. What do you think he is doing out here anyway? He has come to give you his knowledge. The only way possible now."

"I can't believe he would do that."

"I have spoken truth, vessel. Look into his eyes and see for yourself."

I looked across at Owl as we circled each other. In his eyes, I saw the truth.

"There is no other way now, Dante. You must surrender."

Anyone overhearing would only think he was trying to convince me to surrender but we both knew he meant surrendering to Maelstrom.

"I can't, Samadhi."

"You must if you wish to leave here alive. Do not forget those who have pledged themselves to you."

It happened suddenly like a rush. One moment I was in the forefront of my mind, the next I was a spectator in my own body.

Owl's sword materialized barely in time to parry a thrust. I followed with a kick that connected to his left side. The compound was silent but for the slicing of blades through the air and our footfalls as we danced a dance of death. Owl whirled his blade and stepped in with a feint. Disregarding the distraction of the feint, I took the opening and sliced with Maelstrom. He stepped back with unnatural speed. It wasn't until I saw the blood soak his top that I realized it wasn't fast enough. As he bled, I saw the blood coalesce into orbs around him

"Blood orbs!" I heard Diana hiss. "Everyone back!"

The orbs swirled around Owl.

"An act of desperation Owl, one you will never see fulfilled," said Maelstrom.

My hands began to touch symbols on Maelstrom and the energy shifted again. It felt like a blow to the chest, and then I saw the orbs fly off in every direction. All around us people were exploding and dying. Anywhere an orb touched, there was an explosion. In the midst of these explosions and confusion, Owl attacked. I sidestepped his lunge and buried Maelstrom in his stomach. He smiled and reached for my neck.. In his hand, as he lay dying on my weapon, was the soul catcher. He crushed it with what strength he had left.

"Make sure you choose wisely, Dante," he said and crumpled forward.

Simultaneous screams echoed from Diana and Maelstrom.

"That old bastard, that old and crafty bastard, he knew, he knew!"

Even as Maelstrom spoke, knowledge poured into me, threatening to drive me insane. Slowly I felt the rage subside. Owl's essence was with me, a part of me. Maelstrom's symbols began to change to a deep gold. My control returned and I felt the comforting presence of Owl. A hand clamped on my shoulder. It was Zen.

"We need to go! This place is coming down around us!"

"Zen, Owl—" My voice caught in my throat.

"I know, D. But we have to go now!"

Tears streamed down my face as we ran through corridors. I followed Zen reflexively as he carried Meja. In that moment I realized I could never know love or friendship: the risk was too great. As we headed back into the subway system, I promised myself I would make those responsible for this pay. Deep within, I could sense Maelstrom waiting, eager for release.

CHAPTER TWENTY THREE-TWINS

"We surfaced near 42nd Street and Times Square, which was perfect for us to blend in. We still had to be careful about not being followed by Sylk's people. I tried not to be overly paranoid and didn't look over my shoulder every three seconds; I kept it more to every five seconds. As I turned around to check for a tail, I felt a sharp object pressed against my side. I looked down to see a slip of a woman look up at me and smile.

"If you want to survive the night, you'd better come with us." The smile never left her face.

"Uh, Zen?"

"What D.? We have to keep moving—Kal!"

"You know this girl?"

"That's no girl. That's Kalysta. Kal, where's Val?" I didn't recognize the twin through her disguise.

"We have a place but we have to get there, now," Kalysta said.

"You knew about this?" I asked, amazed.

"Kal and Val are Meja's. This is her doing." The woman never ceased to amaze me.

"Is Val close?" asked Zen.

"She's running interference: you have some nasty tails."

"Okay, we need to get off the streets. Even in New York, my carrying Meja around is raising some eyebrows."

"Follow me," said Kal.

"Hey, was a weapon really necessary?"

Kal pulled out her empty hand. "What weapon?" she said and smiled.

We stepped off Broadway at 47th Street and walked into the Macklowe Hotel. Kal led us past the front desk without as much as a raised eyebrow, so I guessed she had paid the front desk reception to look the other way. The lobby was marble and gave me a feeling of being inside some ancient Greek palace. In the center of the lobby floor was a symbol that looked vaguely familiar. It took a moment to register, and then it hit me. It was a variation on the symbol of monitors. Then it became apparent and I saw motifs of it everywhere. Was this a trap? Did Zen know? I decided to wait and see how this would play out. I would be ready if this was a trap and Kal and Val were betraying us.

We got off on the third floor and walked over to room 300. Kal produced a key card and opened the door. She entered the room first.

"All clear. Come on in. All my seals are intact."

The room was spacious without being too large. I noticed the lack of mirrors anywhere as I examined the room. Even in the bathroom, not a mirror was to be found.

"No mirrors," I said almost off-handedly.

"None. Meja was clear about that and about this place. This building is owned by the Warriors."

Zen and I both said, "What?"

Zen put Meja down in the bedroom where she stirred but still lay asleep. I turned to Kal.

"What? Why would she want us here?"

Kal shrugged. "Those were her instructions. Do you question her?"

I had to admit Meja was not the type to take questioning well.

"She is sleeping. Whatever Owl gave her was pretty powerful to keep her out this long," Zen said as he entered the room.

The mention of Owl brought back a flood of memories. Suddenly I was exhausted. As I sat in one of the wingback chairs, there was a knock on the door. The door opened and I saw the threshold glow blue for a split second. It was Val.

She looked tired. There were cuts and scratches on her hands and face. She was wearing a matching leather outfit with Kal, and it was torn in some places with a gash along the outside length of her left leg. She limped slightly towards the bathroom.

"You guys have pissed off some very nasty people," she said looking at me then she smiled.

"Are you okay?" Zen asked.

"This?" she said pointing at the gash. "This is just a scratch. You should see *them*."

"Valeria, this is not a game," said Zen. He looked at Kal, an unspoken message in his eyes.

Kal's face was serious. "Let me take a look at that," Kal said as she pushed Val into the bathroom.

"We have a day, two, tops, before they find us here," said Val from the bathroom.

I don't know how she managed it and I was too exhausted to ask at the moment.

"We'd better get some rest, Dante. I'll crash out here. Kal will keep watch. Why don't you go in and crash on one of the beds?"

"You sure?" I asked.

"Yes, plus I have to figure out how we get to the Watch and not get killed in the process. You heard Val. We have at least a day. Meja picked this place so I'm guessing she has a reason for it. She will be waking up soon, I hope."

I headed to the bedroom. Could we trust the twins? Though at this point we had no choice. If Meja trusted them, so would I for the time being. I left Zen looking over maps. Kal was bandaging Valeria's leg in the bathroom and I could hear them arguing lightheartedly, Val finally giving in to the older sister's attention. As I entered the bedroom, I could see Meja's figure on one of the beds. She looked peaceful. As I made my way to the other bed, she stirred.

"Ugh, where are we?" she said groggily.

"A hotel on 47th. Kal brought us here."

She sat on the edge of her bed. Even in the dark, her beauty radiated. Her long black hair framed her face, and her lithe dancer's body masked her true strength. In that moment she looked small and vulnerable.

"Kal. That means her sister is not far away."

I nodded. "Val was getting rid of some people following us. I didn't ask for details."

"Why not? It doesn't matter that they may be monitors. You cannot trust implicitly, Dante. What if they are really part of the Lotus?" She got up and would have fallen to the floor had I not caught her.

"I must still be recovering from the explosion. Oh no! Owl!"

"Why don't you try and get some more sleep? Zen told me Owl gave you something to help speed recovery."

"That would explain this feeling," she said as she lay back down. She was unconscious seconds later.

I didn't look forward to telling her that Owl sacrificed himself for us, for me. That would have to wait, though. I was exhausted and needed sleep. I laid down fully appreciating that I may not have another opportunity like that for a long time.

CHAPTER TWENTY FOUR-EXIT

I woke up unaware of how much time had passed. Meja still lay sleeping. As I got up, I made my way quietly to the living room.

"The safest way to the South Watch is through the Mirror," one of the twins said.

I couldn't tell if it was Kal or Val – they sounded so alike. I heard Zen grunt in response.

"I don't like it. The Mirror is a tricky place and time is quirky there."

"I know. You have a better idea?"

I stepped into the living room and saw Kal and Zen pouring over maps and routes.

"Why can't we just drive out of here? New York is a big city."

"The funny thing about this big city is that it has few points of egress, easily covered by the Lotus, Sylk and the Monitors," said Kal.

"If it were any one of those groups, maybe—" said Zen.

"But not all three. We will be stopped at some point because we are heading south," said Kal.

"Then there is the matter of you being a beacon." The voice came from behind me, Meja.

I turned to face her.

"Not another word. I need tea, strong tea."

"Brewed and kept hot, just like you like it, Senpai. I'll get you a cup," said Kal.

Meja looked at Zen when Kal entered the kitchen area. "As far as I can tell, they are clean," he said.

Meja nodded, "Agreed, for now. Keep an eye out for anything that seems out of place," said Meja as she sat in a large chair.

"What do you mean about me being a beacon?" I asked.

"It's your weapon. Every time you manifest it, it's like sending a flare into the sky and broadcasting your location," said Meja.

"What? How?"

Meja sighed when Kal returned with a steaming mug of green tea. She took a sip. "Thank you, Kalysta," the pleasure evident in her voice. Kal stood behind Meja and placed her arms behind her back, in a smooth practiced motion. The scent of the tea filled the room.

"Every chi weapon resonates with its own frequency, just like we all do. Over time, the frequencies merge and become one. Usually this process takes months, sometimes years."

"But that's not the case here, right?"

Meja looked at me with a serious expression. "No, in your case it was almost simultaneous, which creates a dissonance. You and your weapon clash which creates a type of 'noise'. It leads me to believe that this is not your true chi weapon, but was somehow imposed on you by Sylk."

"I see."

"This means that every time you manifest your weapon, we will have company."

"How far can they track me? Is there any way to mask it?"

Zen turned to face me from the maps. "From what I've been studying, if the person looking for you is of a high enough skill level, then you're looking at about a two-mile radius. There is one exception, though."

"What?" I asked, figuring that putting as much distance as possible between me and the city seemed like a good idea that got better by the second.

"Well, if you are dealing with a very high level ability, then the range is unknown."

"You mean the Kriyas?" said Meja.

"Or groups like them. The leaders of the Lotus are a close second."

"Kriyas?"

"Nasty pieces of work. They get to higher spiritual levels by devouring chi. They've been around forever —the closest thing to a vampire you will come up against. I wouldn't be surprised if they were the reason the vampire mythos was created," said Zen.

"They are no mythos," said Kal.

"Well, my information says they are extinct," said Zen.

"Your information is wrong," said Meja. "They are dwindled in number but some still remain."

"So what now? It's one more group after us?" I said.

"No. think of them as bloodhounds who can attune to chi. Chances are they are being used by the Lotus to track us," said Kal.

"So how do we avoid them when we don't even know how far we need to be?" I asked.

"We don't avoid them. We use misdirection and make them think we are going somewhere else," said Meja.

"How do we manage that?" asked Zen.

"We need an exit strategy," said Meja.

"What about the mirror?" I couldn't believe I was suggesting the last place I wanted to go into. Everyone remained silent, and I could hear the thoughts going through our brains. The rich leather creaked as we shifted in the large sofa.

"It's risky but no less risky than any other option," said Meja.

"I don't like it. Time isn't linear in the mirror and we can end up any when," said Zen.

"I agree, Senpai," said Kal, "The mirror could put us at the mercy of other eyes, that we would prefer to avoid."

Meja was pensive. "It's the fastest way to the South Watch and if we don't get there as soon as we can, I fear we will not find the information we are seeking," said Meja.

"When I was with Sylk —in the mirror," I corrected quickly, "one of his followers was able to replicate herself using chi. I think I can do that now," I said.

Kal's eyes were open in surprise. Meja looked at me darkly.

"Zen, Kal, can you excuse us for a moment?" she said, her voice carrying an edge that would not tolerate argument.

"I'll go check on Val," said Kal quickly when she saw Meja's expression.

"I'm going to make a supply run," said Zen. "There are a few things we are going to need before we attempt this. I'll be back in an hour."

Meja sat across from me, looking as if she could incinerate me on the spot.

"Before you say anything more, I know you didn't spend enough time with Owl to learn such a technique. For you to even suggest you can attempt chi clones, means you will use that abomination of a weapon, which if you have forgotten, will let everyone who is after us know exactly where you are." She was seething, her cheeks were slightly flushed and she looked as beautiful as ever. I checked those feelings immediately, knowing I could never let anyone that close or risk losing them to Maelstrom. Still, her bronze skin and exotic features stirred something in me I couldn't explain. I also realized I was sitting in front of a woman who was as deadly as any of the assassins after us, probably more so. I chose my next words carefully.

"I think I can do it," I said softly.

"Oh, the arrogance! What makes you think you can execute a technique that takes years to learn, much less master!" she said in a rush, as she stood. "Do you plan on going back to Owl and dragging him here, because that would be one short trip to death!"

"We can't go back to Owl's compound," I said. "Obviously, the explosions took care of that."

"What aren't you telling me, Dante?"

I took a deep breath, "Meja, Owl is dead. Kind of."

She sat back down.

"What! What do you mean kind of?"

I explained what happened and how he had sacrificed himself so that I could have access to his vast knowledge. That it was the only way he saw that would give me what I needed to be prepared for what was coming. She sat still, silent, looking at me.

"Did you kill him, Dante?" she said after a few minutes had passed.

"No, —yes, I mean his body is dead but a part of him is part of me. I don't know how to explain it!" I said, frustrated, angry and exasperated.

"I believe you," she said after some time had passed. "If it were otherwise, you would be dead by now." She was eerily calm, which made her seem even more dangerous. "This means that your abilities in controlling chi have increased at least tenfold. I daresay you may surpass most of us now."

I remained silent.

"However, having access to Owl's experience does not make you a proficient practitioner of chi techniques. You are still a novice."

"Tell me something I don't know. It's like having an encyclopedia in your hands but you can't open it, except randomly or—"

"While your weapon is manifested," she finished.

"Exactly. When it's in my hands, everything is clear, but I know it's not just me."

"We need to find a syllabist and fast."

"The door burst open and Zen ran in slamming it behind him. His clothes were torn and his face was bruised and cut.

"We have trouble," he said, his expression serious.

CHAPTER TWENTY FIVE-ROGUE

"And you led them here?" I asked.

He gave me a withering look. "Give me a little more credit than that, D. Really?"

Embarrassed, I changed the subject, "What happened to you?"

"What does it look like, Dante? He was attacked," said Meja her voice on edge. "Where, how and how many?"

"Five, well two now. They were shifting in and out so I couldn't touch them. About ten blocks from here due north. On the plus side, I manifested my weapon. Something like an axe/mace."

"Excellent, Zen. You didn't think it was relevant to tell me what happened to Owl?"

Zen looked at me with a pained expression. "You were hurt, Meja."

"Excuses, from him," she said as she pointed at me, "I expect, but not from you."

Zen looked away. "It won't happen again," he said.

"Make sure it doesn't, Zen." Meja turned to me. "Everything I said about you being a beacon no longer applies. If you absorbed Owl's essence, you may as well be standing on the highest mountain screaming at the top of your lungs. There is no way to handle this until his energy has merged with yours and that will take time."

"Which we don't have," I added as I looked at Zen. He nodded, silent.

"It will take them some time to find us. I made sure they have a few dead ends to follow," said Zen.

"How long do we have?" said Meja.

Zen looked in his knapsack. "I was able to get most of the supplies we need before they attacked me. We have about five hours if they have a good tracker, less if these Kriyas exist," said Zen.

"Pack your things, get Kalysta and her sister ready to move," said Meja.

"Are we taking the Mirror?" I asked.

"We don't have much of a choice. We will try to go in through one of the lesser known areas and not alert any of the Watchers," said Meja.

"Watchers?" I asked as we assembled the bags.

"Hopefully we won't see one," said Kal, but her voice told me that the chances of running into a watcher were high.

"Are we ready?" asked Meja. We all nodded with identical bags slung over one shoulder.

"If we get separated, we will meet at this location." She pointed to Grand Central terminal on the map. "You wait at the information clock at exactly one o'clock day or night. If no one shows, assume we are captured or dead and head to the Watch," said Meja.

"I can't navigate the Mirror or know how to get to the Watch," I said.

Meja turned to me. "Then it would be a good idea if we stayed together, don't you think?"

I nodded as we headed out of the room, thinking this was a plan that was shaky at best, but knowing it was the only plan we had at the moment.

CHAPTER TWENTY SIX-CRACKED

We walked as a tight group, with Kal and Meja leading. Val and Zen brought up the rear with me sandwiched in the middle.

"We are heading to Grand Central to find a specific entrance," said Kal.

"Why?" I asked, feeling like the only one who didn't know.

"This entrance will allow us to skirt the edge of the Mirror and then arrive at the Watch. Think of it as a crack in the Mirror. This way we avoid Watchers," said Meja.

"What's the downside? I know there is some catch," I said.

"The only problem," said Val from behind, "is that it is very likely that the monitors, Sylk and the Lotus know of this unofficial entrance, which means any one or all three groups can be there waiting for us to use it."

"Which is exactly why we are going to use it, to draw them out," said Meja.

"We want to face them —why?"

"This way we know who is where and we don't have to guess about who is after us."

"I thought we had that established," I said.

The walking traffic along 42nd was congested as usual. At any moment, I expected some kind of attack. As we walked east on 42nd St, I was acutely aware of mirrors and window panes, realizing how any of these could serve as a point of attack from Sylk and his group. As we entered the terminal, I was impressed as usual by its size and scope. It was clearly a functional work of art.

It had undergone extensive restoration a few years earlier and a large quantity of brand name stores had been enticed to take up residency on the concourse level. It made the terminal feel modern and sleek with a touch of old world architecture. We walked past the stores on the concourse level and headed to the track level. That was when I sensed the first tail. I looked back to see a tall man with olive skin, his black hair combed back, sunglasses covering his eyes. He was dressed in a dark blue suit that contrasted the crisp white shirt. He looked like a power broker more at home on Wall Street.

"Meja—," I began.

"I know. Don't let him distract you. He is the one they want you to see, to force you into running. It's a monitor tactic. Let's head to track nine," she said calmly.

As we made our way down the stairs, I felt the shift in pressure. Too late I realized what it was as I saw Kal get slammed into a column. She crumpled to the floor unconscious, the wind knocked out of her. Val ran to her side as Zen moved next to Meja, who had drawn her ice blue sword. As we looked down the platform, I saw Rory standing with what seemed to be a whirling mass of energy in his hands.

"Rory, still using amateurish tricks?"

Rory's face reddened. "Hello, Meja. You would be surprised at the tricks I know now."

I wondered where the rest of the Lotus was, since I didn't think Rory would be there alone.

"Where is your mistress, Rory? Did she let you off your leash?"

"Bitch."

"Still eloquent as ever. I wondered why Diana kept a useless lapdog like you around but I'm beginning to understand now. Someone has to run errands and do the menial tasks, right?"

Rory's face grew dark and I could see anger twist his features.

"I'm going to show you who the lapdog is. Then I'm going to kill you and your excuses for warriors."

I noticed that the platform was strangely empty of people. When I looked around, I noticed all of the adjacent platforms were empty as well. How was this possible? Then I saw the suits on every stairwell entrance.

"If Diana sent you here, she must have considered this the lowest priority." Meja laughed then, and something snapped in Rory. The energy coalescing in his hands went from a pale blue to deep ochre, bristling with the promise of pain.

"Move to the end of the platform. Keep an eye on Dante," Meja said to Zen.

"You don't need us here to deal with him? He looked a little—"

"Imbalanced?"

"I was going to say crazy, but imbalanced fits," said Zen.

"That's exactly how I want him. Go to the end of the platform and look for a door hidden in an alcove that has a monitor symbol over it. Do not try to open the door. Take the twins with you. Go, now, we don't have much time."

"Got it." Zen moved over to where Kal lay and picked her up effortlessly. Her shallow breath was ragged and I was pretty sure she had some broken ribs from the impact she withstood. I could see the worry and anger on Val's face. She wanted to attack Rory. It was in every gesture, in every fiber of her being.

"Val, no, don't. Let Meja handle this. She can take him," said Zen as he put a hand on her shoulder.

"I swear, Zen, if she doesn't, I will," she answered through clenched teeth.

"Let's go and find this door. I have a feeling we are going to need it," Zen said as he ran to the other end of the platform.

I stood where I was, riveted to the spot. Something was off. I felt it all around me.

The energy Rory was manipulating was different, somehow familiar. As Meja raced towards him, I knew something was wrong. It was a trap and she had fallen into it. I had to stop her, but I was too far away. I knew she was running to her death. Rory being here was no accident or coincidence. They expected us. They knew the history Meja and Rory had, they knew she would taunt him, we had been played the moment we set foot on the platform.

"Meja! No! It's what he wants!" But my voice felt muffled and dim even though I was yelling at the top of my voice. Something or someone was dampening the sound and energy on the platform. I looked up the stairs to see Mr. Blue Suit in what appeared to be a trance. I raced up the stairs, Maelstrom in my hand, glistening like a strand of night.

"Dante, don't! It's too dangerous!" Zen's words came to me like a whisper.

The energy around the rogue monitor was a deep violet with shards of red flashing. I didn't want to kill him but I needed to stop him.

"Consume the energy, my vessel," Maelstrom's voice echoed in my head.

"Assimilare," I whispered as I placed my staff against the monitor. In a rush, the aura of energy surrounding him entered the staff, taking my breath away and sending me to my knees. No longer in a trance, the monitor recovered faster than I would have liked.

"What the hell —you!" he said as he lunged at me. The energy was still there, under the surface. I felt like a balloon at the bursting point. I barely ducked under the blade swipe as I placed my hand on his chest. Immediately I knew this was a bad idea. All the pent up energy rushed through my arm and slammed into him with percussive force. I saw him lift into the air and slam into a wall with a sick crunching sound. He fell to the floor in a heap. I was certain he was dead. Somewhere in the back of my mind, I heard laughter. It took a moment to realize it was my own. I ran down the stairs to see Meja suspended in a cylinder of amber light. From her expression and flailing I could see she was being strangled slowly.

"It's too late for her," said Rory as he grinned a smile full of malevolence. "She is going to die a slow and painful death, but you, your death can be swift if you surrender now."

The anger had reached a fever pitch in my head. My vision became crystal clear. I don't know if it was Owl's abilities or the effect of Maelstrom but I could see the weak links in Rory's defenses as I sank into my inner sight. I walked over to where Meja was trapped.

"Dante, don't come close! Head for the door and forget me," she gasped with what little air she had left.

"I can't do that."

"It was a trick. He is much more powerful than he used to be and I walked right—" she gasped as the circle drew tighter around her. I could see that it took all she had just to say those few words.

I looked down and saw the markings that had created the trap. They shimmered in and out, there but not. Rory was coalescing energy in his hand again. I didn't want to find out if I could withstand his attack. I slammed Maelstrom into the circle, that was trapping Meja.

"Dante! No!" but it only came out as a strangled whisper.

"*Desolver*!" I shouted and the circle collapsed. I didn't know where these words were coming from. On some level I knew this was Maelstrom but it was also heightened by Owl or rather Owl's essence. I didn't feel the energy rush into me like with the monitor. It had simply ceased to exist; there one moment and gone the next. Meja fell to one knee, murder in her eyes.

"I'll deal with him, Dante. Get to the door."

Rory took a defensive stance. "Come on."

"No!" Don't you see that's the point? He's a diversion to keep us here until the rest arrive."

Realization raced across Meja's features. "You bastard," Meja spat as she began to back up.

I really hoped Zen found the door. I had a feeling we were going to have a lot more Lotus on the platform very soon.

"We need to go now," I said as Rory headed to us. I touched Maelstrom to the platform and whispered, "*Mura*." A shimmering blue wall of energy sliced across the platform cutting Rory off from us. He was punching holes in it as we turned to run to the far end of the platform.

"How did you —? Never mind," she said as we made it to the end of the platform and to the others. Zen still held Kal and she wasn't looking good.

"Is he dead, Meja?"

"No, Val, he isn't. Please don't distract me. We don't have much time. It was a trap."

"What?! What do you mean —?"

Val grew suddenly quiet as Zen gave her a look, silencing her. Meja faced the door and placed her hand on the monitor symbol that I hadn't noticed earlier. The door frame glowed with a soft blue light and the door opened with a quiet rush of air.

As I looked around and out of the alcove, I saw that Rory was almost through the energy barrier.

"We should get moving," I said as I saw more and more of the barrier disappear. On the other side, I could see the rage in Rory's face.

"We will. I just have to set this entrance to destroy itself once we are through," said Meja as she touched some symbols on the inside of the door.

"You what?"

"It's the only way we can be sure they won't follow us."

"Let's go!" I said as I saw that Rory had made his way through. We ran into the doorway and pulled it shut behind us. A few seconds later we heard a muffled thump and the screams of an angry and hopefully hurt Rory. I turned around to take in

217

our surroundings. It looked like our plane with the exception of a silver patina if I moved my head too fast.

We were in the Mirror.

CHAPTER TWENTY SEVEN- REFLECTION

"We need to get moving," said Meja. "Even though this is the outskirts of the Mirror, given enough time, we will attract attention." "Watchers?" I asked.

Meja nodded. I looked around and except for the surreal aspect, it felt just like where we had come from.

"What are all these people? Are they dead?"

"No more dead than you or I. I am certain Sylk explained the workings of the Mirror to you?"

"Some things he did but I never went out and so I never met any people from this side."

"Don't think of it as this side. There are several planes of existence."

"So this is just another plane of existence or an alternate version of ours?"

We walked down the street and I had to keep reminding myself that this wasn't my plane of existence.

"No, you aren't going to run into yourself on this plane. It's not an alternate plane. It's an entirely different plane. One in which time flows differently," said Zen. "For us, because we are not native to this plane, time can be… strange."

"Yes this much I know from my time with Sylk."

"Yes, I recall," said Meja.

I didn't want to think about my time of incarceration at Sylk's place in the Mirror. The thought soured my mood. Changing the subject I asked, "Where are we going?"

"We need to avoid the Watchers and find an exit near the Watch. There is a nexus not far from here. That should lead us to the Watch entrance," said Meja.

"I have a question, Meja," said Zen.

"Ask it."

I looked at the people and noticed that no one was really paying us any attention, which I thought odd, since they had a distinctly different colored aura to the rest of us. I guessed not everyone possessed the ability to use their inner sight.

"Where was the rest of the Lotus? I mean they knew of the entrance. Why weren't they there in force? It's what I would do. Overcome us with superior numbers."

Meja stopped walking and thought aloud, "Something that Dante said has been with me for a while. About Rory being a diversion. What if his role was not to stop us, but to force us into the mirror, into the real trap?"

"That sounds like something the Lotus would do. Is there another way we can go to avoid the nexus?" I asked. I was getting a little self-conscious just standing on the sidewalk.

"No, not without alerting the Watchers."

"So it seems we have to take this risk. Let's minimize it as much as possible."

"Good idea, Dante. Let's find a place we can scout out the location," said Zen.

"How far to the nexus?"

"A few blocks south. It's a plain building on the south-west corner. In our plane this building is a FedEx office. Here it may be something else," said Meja.

"What about Kal? We can't get into a fight with her like this."

"That is why we need the nexus. I can get her some place safe where she will be seen to."

"I'm going with her," said Val.

"I wouldn't expect any less from you, Valeria," said Meja.

"Fine, it's settled. Dante and I will scout the building and see if we have the Lotus waiting for us." Meja nodded. "Be careful, Zen. Remember that they have the ability to sense us from quite a distance."

"I didn't plan on getting too close. Just close enough." With that we headed off.

"No chi use, Dante, or else we're done." she said.

"Understood."

As we made our way to the location of the nexus, I began to sense a growing electric charge in the air.

"Zen, something's wrong. This feels familiar."

"What do you mean?"

"Can't you feel it in the air, like being too close to power cables?

"No, what are you talking—"

The air shimmered and a blinding light obscured everything. It was like being in front of the largest camera flash in existence. When I was finally able to see, Zen was gone.

"Hello, Dante." I recognized the voice and realized that things had gotten exponentially worse. I turned around as my vision grew clearer. Clad in brown skin-tight leathers, a large knife in one hand, another strapped to her thigh, her hair in a long ponytail and wearing dark glasses, stood Mara.

"Hello, Mara," I said knowing that Sylk was not too far away.

"If you go any closer to the nexus, you will meet your death. It is in your best interests to come with me."

"Where is Zen?" I asked, not moving a muscle, controlling the flow of chi so as not to alert the Lotus.

"He is safe, for now. If you wish him to remain that way, come with me."

I had no choice, it seemed.

CHAPTER TWENTY EIGHT-GAMBIT

She led me through some back alleys and cross streets. I kept track in case I needed to make a hasty retreat back to Meja and the others. I knew Sylk had several locations in the Mirror. How he went undetected by the Watchers was something that I wanted to know. How did he avoid them for so long? Mara led me into a nondescript office building, with a lobby that was all glass and marble and looked very modern. Some abstract paintings hung on the wall, bringing the only jolt of color to an otherwise bland space of blacks and greys. As we walked to the elevator bank, Mara produced a key card, a silver rectangle that seemed to have circuitry embedded in it. She slid it into a slot beside the elevator call buttons.

One of the elevator doors quietly slid open in silent invitation. As we stepped in, I noticed the lack of floor buttons. In fact there were no buttons at all. The elevator itself was brushed silver and nondescript. The floor was the same marble as the lobby. The doors closed as we waited. I barely felt the motion and couldn't tell if we were ascending or descending into the building. After about two minutes, we came to a stop and the doors sighed as they opened onto a dimly lit corridor. Mara stepped into the hallway and the elevator closed behind us. I examined the hallway for a stairwell and found none. The hallway was painted a sky blue with a dark blue accent running the length of the wall. At even intervals hung a decorative mirror, directly across from its twin. The floor was covered in a slate grey carpet that complemented the blue on the wall. The lack of light was due to the fixtures, which weren't the usual fluorescents but decorative track lighting which snaked across the ceiling. It was the mirrors that caught my attention.

"We must step through this hallway quickly or risk triggering the Detention system," Mara said.

She pulled out the silver card she used to call the elevator and paused as she turned to me.

"Look straight ahead and do not stop to admire yourself in any of the mirrors. If you do, you risk being trapped in an infinite loop and it will be very difficult to extract you from it."

I understood. The mirrors created a kind of holding cell if you were curious or vain enough to look into them while they were active. The door at the end of the corridor was similar to the elevator doors. As I looked closely, I realized the doors, like the mirrors, were a mirror image of each other.

"Remember —stay close and keep your eyes fixed on the doors, no matter what you hear or see in your peripheral vision."

She slid the card into the slot that was meant for it and started walking. Initially I didn't hear anything, then the voices started. It was a whisper at first, gradually increasing into a cacophony of voices. I couldn't make out most of it but I caught snippets here and there: "let me out!" or "help me!" would quickly be drowned out by the din. I made sure to look straight ahead not realizing how difficult that simple action would be. As we approached the doors, Mara stopped.

"He is waiting for you," she said.

"Sylk?"

She gave the slightest of nods.

"Listen to him before discounting what he says. You may actually learn something of use." She turned to enter another door that was receded. "Don't attempt the corridor. You won't make it to the elevator, and even if you did, you couldn't it without this."

Walking away, she held up the metallic card I had seen earlier and entered the smaller door. I faced the brushed steel doors that led to Sylk and I hoped some answers. I placed my hand on the doors and they slid apart like an elevator. The room inside was cool. I had the distinct feeling this wasn't the Mirror and yet it was. One wall of the room was covered in floor to ceiling windows that let natural light in. The sunlight slanted in and shone on the black marble floor, making it seem like a bottomless lake. The opposite wall was covered in bookcases, each shelf full of books. At the far end of the room were several wingback chairs, four in a cross configuration and four more in no apparent order. In the center of the first set of chairs sat an ornate table with four dragons acting as legs. The top of the table itself was inlaid with symbols that I couldn't make out from where I stood. The shades were partially drawn and the light filtering in gave the room a timeless quality. Sitting in one of the center chairs, facing me, was Sylk. Along the windowed wall was a long sofa-style bench and in a corner of the sofa, still as a statue sat, Anna. I walked towards where Sylk sat. He was currently reading a sheet of paper in his hands.

"Welcome back, Dante. Please be seated. I'll be right with you."

I sat in the chair on his right.

"Anna, please take this message to its intended recipient."

Anna seemed to glide over as she removed the paper from Sylk's hand. "Yes, Karashihan," she said as she bowed.

Sylk then turned to face me. "It would seem you are in need of some assistance." His deep baritone words filled the air.

Not one to give away any information, I skirted the situation. "What makes you say that?" I asked.

Sylk smiled. "Aside from the fact that your guardian is, let's say, indisposed, you have one of your party gravely injured. The Black Lotus is currently searching for you, quite vigorously I might add and it's only a matter of time before the Watchers are alerted to your presence here. Does that sum it up for you?"

I looked down at the table and recognized the symbols; the table was a replica of tré. I said nothing. "I will take your silence as an affirmation that I have correctly assessed your situation."

"Yes, you have," I said.

"As I stated earlier, you need help, specifically my help."

"Where is Zen?"

"Don't be trite or cliché, Dante. It is beneath you. You know I haven't harmed him or we wouldn't be here speaking. He is merely a way to get you still enough to listen."

"Fine, I'm listening." I didn't really have a choice.

"Very well, I can help you achieve your goals provided I join you in your attempt to enter the South Watch."

"Excuse me? You want to come with us?" Obviously I was losing my mind because I thought I heard that he wanted to come with us.

"You heard correctly, Dante. I want to join your little group. In turn I will get you past the defenses of the Watch."

It didn't add up. "Why? What do you get out of this?"

"I get some information I require and to resolve some unfinished affairs."

"You realize that I can't trust you and certain members of my group would rather see you dead, right?"

"Yes, the monitor, Meja, is it?"

There was something I wasn't seeing, something that was nagging at me. "Wait a minute, I don't understand. Why do you need us to get to the Watch? You can easily get there on your own without us."

"Normally you would be correct, but in this case, there are extenuating circumstances, namely the Watch has been moved to an undisclosed location and no one thought to tell me. Can you imagine?" he said, the smile masking the steel in his voice.

A whole Watch moved? Now I was beginning to see: he didn't know where the Watch was and we didn't know how to get past the defenses he helped create.

"First show me Zen is safe."

"Of course." He touched one of the symbols on the table and one of the bookcases shifted and slid to the side. Anna stepped forward with Zen behind her.

"Zen!" I stopped when I saw him unresponsive.

"He can't hear or see you in this state."

It was then that I noticed that he was walking strangely, taking stilted steps. His face was impassive. Around his arm I saw a metal band that gave off a soft green glow. Anna wore a matching band.

"As you can see, he is perfectly safe. Those bands compel him and bind his mind. If the link is shattered or disrupted incorrectly, he will remain trapped in a world of his making in his own mind. As we both know, the imagination is a powerful thing."

"I understand." I was in a position without leverage. If I said no to Sylk, I lost Zen. If I said yes, then Meja would kill me right after she was done with Sylk.

"I need to speak to Meja and the others," I said, trying to buy myself some time.

"Perfectly understandable. I will give you two hours to arrive at a decision. If after that time I don't hear from you, I will assume our agreement is void and I will eliminate your guardian. You can contact me with this." He handed me a card similar to the one Mara had. "I suggest you make your decision quickly. Two hours is about how much time you have before Watchers close in on your position as well."

I put the card in a pocket.

"Mara will take you back to your people."

He pressed another symbol on the table and Mara appeared at the door. "Please escort Dante back to his group. He has pressing business and little time to resolve it in."

Mara bowed, "Yes, Karashihan."

I headed back to the doors, looking back at Zen.

"I'll be back for you, Zen," I whispered as I exited the room.

CHAPTER TWENTY NINE-ALLIANCE

We walked through the streets, Mara beside me.. I felt like I had been gut checked. I kept my anger in check, though, realizing that giving in to the frustration would only bring the Lotus closer to me. She must have sensed my anger and turned to look at me as we walked by to the surreal Grand Central terminal.

"Focus that emotion, Dante. It can be a great asset," she said.

I looked at her, realizing that being angry at her served no purpose. It was Sylk I needed to direct my anger at. Reacting to this situation was going to get me nowhere. I had to be proactive. I looked at her and took a breath. "I understand, Mara that you serve Sylk. I also understand that he is the cause of what happened to Zen. I don't blame you."

Surprise briefly crossed her face. "You have matured much in a short time, Dante. Do not underestimate him. He will kill your guardian as easily as you and I take a breath." She looked around and stopped walking. "I must leave you here."

I recognized the street as the corner we were standing on when Zen disappeared. We were a block away from the terminal.

"Your people are there," she said as she pointed to the terminal. "The Lotus is there," she said, pointing to the nondescript building Zen and I were to scout. "Make your decision with haste; you do not want to face the Watchers."

"Why not?"

"You don't know of them?"

"Only that I should avoid them."

"Perhaps that is best. Know that you cannot reason with them. They exist for one purpose only and that is to purge this plane of everything that does not belong."

"Wouldn't that include you, Sylk and all his people?"

She smiled then, a sad smile. "It may include his people but it does not apply to Sylk. Choose wisely and quickly, Dante. I hope to see you again for your guardian's sake."

Before I could say anything else, she walked away. Standing on the corner of 42nd and Park Avenue, I was left with more questions than answers. I crossed the street fully conscious of the fact that time was against Zen, against Kal, against us all. As I made my way through the terminal, its vastness slowly snuck up on me. I walked to the information kiosk and saw Meja standing there with a strained look on her face. Clearly she didn't like being this exposed. When she saw I was alone, her expression shifted and became darker.

"Are you okay" I asked.

"Not here, it's too exposed. Let's go." She headed off to one of the side passageways that ran through the terminal, like a series of catacombs.

"Where are Kal and Val?"

"They're safe. I don't want to risk that you were followed," she said as we stopped in one of the many corridors.

"Where is Zen?" she asked, her face neutral.

"Sylk has him."

"Sylk? I thought for sure the Lotus—"

"No, it's Sylk," I said as I shook my head.

"What does he want?"

I told her. and she grew pensive a moment. "This can work to our benefit. We can't trust him but we can surely use his knowledge. Also, we have no choice. We can't rescue Zen without tipping our hand or our location to the Watchers."

"I agree, but I don't like it."

"I like it less, Dante, but if we don't get Kal some help and get Zen back, they will both die. We will make this uneasy alliance and work it to our benefit. Contact him and tell him we will agree to his terms, provided Zen is set free and Kal is attended to."

"Don't we need a nexus for Kal?"

"No, Sylk should have someone who can treat her at his location."

"Are you sure of this?" I asked, hating the feeling of being backed into a corner.

"No. I'm not but right now, I don't see an alternative, do you?"

I took out the silver card because, like Meja, I didn't see any other choice.

CHAPTER THIRTY-WATCHERS

I pressed the silver card with my thumb. Immediately an image of Sylk appeared before me.

"You have come to a decision, then?"

"We have, with some conditions."

His image seemed to be solid. If I had not known this was some kind of hologram I would have sworn he was there.

"You are not exactly in a position to make demands but I will hear your 'conditions'."

"We have a member of our group that needs medical attention, and Zen needs to be free from whatever hold you have on him."

He turned to look at Meja, and then faced me again.

"Done. Mara and Anna will be there shortly to help with your injured associate. The guardian will be released when you arrive here. Now a condition of my own."

It felt like dealing with the devil, somehow. I knew his condition would end up backfiring on me.

"What is it?" Meja looked upset but said nothing, clearly not wanting to escalate the exchange.

"Your word, that neither you nor any of your party will attack or betray me in this alliance of ours."

I thought about it a moment. If I agreed, it meant no one from my group could attack Sylk while we worked together, especially Meja. Sylk was ensuring his safely from attack at least an attack from us. I looked at Meja but she gave me no indication, meaning I was on my own.

"We will agree to those terms, provided you and your group adhere to the same condition."

Out of the corner of my eye, I saw Meja nod just slightly. Sylk paused a moment before responding. Unclasping his hands from behind his back, he spread his arms wide.

"Very well, I agree." As he said the words, he traced some symbols in the air that glowed crimson and faded away slowly. As the symbols faded, I felt a tug in my lower abdomen.

"Mara and Anna will be there shortly. Be prepared to move." And with that, the image disappeared.

"What was that, with the symbols and the feeling in my gut?" I asked Meja.

"He created a bond with your words. If you or he violates the conditions you agreed on, there will be a blood debt."

"Which would be collected how?" Something told me I didn't want to hear the answer.

"It's pretty self-explanatory, Dante. You violate your word, your blood is spilled. That is the essence of a blood debt. I didn't know he knew how to invoke one or that it was possible without being actually present."

"But this goes both ways, right?"

"Yes, but you have to be careful. If you violate your word, the debt will most likely kill you." Her words hung in the air, their implied meaning filling the silence. If he broke the agreement, chances are the debt wouldn't kill Sylk.

"We will deal with this as it progresses. For now, let's get to Kal and Val and get ready to move."

We headed to another part of the terminal. As we walked among the people, we started getting more and more looks.

"This is not good," Meja said under her breath as she picked up the pace. Before I knew it, we were running.

"What's going on?" I said as I ran beside her. She stepped to a secluded corner of the terminal.

I turned around to see a dead end. "Where are they? Why are we running?"

Meja dashed to the end of the hallway and pressed her hand to a section of the wall. A section of it recessed and moved to the left, revealing a small alcove. Inside were Val & Kal. Kal looked pale, ragged breaths escaping her. Val sat beside her, face drawn with worry.

"She's not doing well," said Val.

"We are getting help but we may have a bigger problem," said Meja. "Watchers."

Val cursed under her breath then looked up. "What do we do?"

"We need to stay on the move. No place is safe from them. They can see into the fabric of this place. We have nowhere to hide."

"If we can get to Sylk's building, we can."

"Sylk? You're joking, right?" said Val.

"No time to explain. Dante, contact Sylk," said Meja.

I took out the card and pressed the raised surface. Sylk's image appeared but not entirely solid. It was as if the transmission was weak or the signal was being jammed.

"We have a problem –" I started.

"I am aware of your predicament. Watchers are closing in on your location. You must leave now and come to my location. Mara and Anna will meet you en route. Do whatever you can to avoid the Watchers, Dante. They are not to be trifled with."

"Can we fight them in any way?"

"No, not even your weapon would help you in this case. Avoid them."

"How – if they can track us everywhere?"

"Think of them as white blood cells, this plane as a body and your group as a virus. We will fool them into thinking you are a part of this body or convince them you have left the body, but that can only happen here, you must come to me. If I leave here, the Watchers will be the least of our concerns."

What could be worse than Watchers? I wondered to myself.

"How soon before Mara and Anna arrive?"

"Three minutes. The moment you open that door, you cannot stop for any reason. Do you understand?"

"We got it."

His image flickered and faded out.

"Three minutes. Can we wait that long?"

"These walls appear to hide us partially," said Meja. "I think we can. Let's get Kal ready to move." The seconds ticked by interminably as we waited. Any second I expected Watchers to show up and eliminate us. Not knowing what they looked like or what they were capable of was the worst of the wait.

"Do we know what they look like?" I said.

"I have never seen them. I have been told they are formless, which I find difficult to believe, since they would require some form to effect a change on this plane."

"Good point."

"The records I have read —and they are few — say mostly hooded figures dressed in grey."

"Well, let's not be too specific."

"Remember those who do run into Watchers are usually eliminated or purged from this plane, which means inaccurate accounts. Those who do survive are usually fleeing for their life, which makes eye witness accounts unreliable."

"I understand," I said, understanding nothing.

After a moment there was a knock on the wall.

"That would be our escort. Dante, you take Kal. I will take the lead. I don't trust them for a moment."

I picked up Kal in the makeshift harness Meja created. Val stayed close to me while Meja opened the door. Mara and Anna stepped inside. Meja looked at the women with thinly veiled disgust, looking especially hard at Anna. Mara and Anna were both dressed in casual clothing – dark pantsuits with white shirts, and around their necks hung identical pendants. On each pendant was the symbol of a monitor overlaid with something else I couldn't decipher. They handed each of us a pendant – all except me.

"As a warrior," Mara began, "this would not work for you. Your weapon is manifested."

"And it would only bring us more attention," said Anna.

"You are the reason we must move swiftly or rather your weapon is."

"We must go now. Are we ready?" said Mara.

It seemed we were ready to go. Meja opened the door and there was an immediate shift in the air pressure. Both of my ears popped as I looked at Meja. Her jaw clenched against the pressure, and then she nodded. This was not going to be good. Fear filled her eyes as she looked back at me. I looked past her and into the corridor. Beside me, Val cursed and pulled out her blades, and Meja's sword materialized into her hand. Anna held what appeared to be a metallic whip in her hand that glowed a faint green. Mara's hands took on a violet glow I was all too familiar with. I felt the fear course through my body but there was no way I could wield Maelstrom while carrying Kal.

Outside the door, as I followed Meja's gaze, I saw three figures. They were dressed in what seemed to be long grey cloaks. The figure in the center was taller than the other two. His cloak had a silver trim, which meant either he or she (were there female watchers?) had more fashion sense, or was a higher rank, which usually meant more dangerous than the other two. I was going with the latter. Their faces were hidden but I could sense they were looking directly at me.

"We cannot confront them in here," said Mara.

"I thought we couldn't confront them at all?" I said.

"It would seem we no longer have that option."

I put Kal down. Things were going to get ugly fast. I could hear Maelstrom laugh within, and fear, cold as ice, raced down my spine. When I looked down, I held Maelstrom in my hands, jet black with symbols a pulsing red.

CHAPTER THIRTY ONE-FUTILITY

We stepped out of the room, leaving Kal out of what may be the line of fire.

"You cannot defeat them, vessel. They are part of the fabric of this plane of existence. If you surrender to me, I may be able to contain them."

"You mean some things are even beyond your power?"

"Don't be foolish. I never claimed to be omnipotent, nor did I say I would make you a god."

"Why can't you defeat them?"

"I thought I explained myself on that matter."

"Pretend I didn't understand."

"Very well. The beings you know as Watchers are part of the fabric of this plane, which means it

would require more power than I possess to undo them. If it were possible to destroy them, a rift would be created in this plane that would have a cascading effect, the end result of which would be the undoing of this plane of existence. Was that clear enough for you, vessel?"

"Very well, so how do we stop them?"

"They can be contained for a very short amount of time, enough time for you and your friends to escape to the place of nothingness, near here."

He was referring to Sylk's location. The only question was getting there.

"How long can we hold them off?"

"At most, fifteen of your minutes and I will not be available to you for twenty-four of your hours hence."

So doing this would deplete Maelstrom to such a degree that it wouldn't be available for a day.

Tell your friends to step back or they too will be trapped, which would be most unfortunate for them.

I stepped forward in front of Meja. "I think you should all step back a bit," I heard myself say in a voice not quite mine.

Mara immediately stepped back. Meja was more reluctant. "Dante, these are Watchers, you can't pretend—"

"Child, if you value your life, you will step back." Meja joined Mara and the others. "When I am done, you will have fifteen of your minutes. Do not waste them," Maelstrom said.

I saw myself step closer to the Watchers. The center one stepped forward and pushed back its hood revealing an angelic face androgynous in its beauty. The features were soft with a hint of angularity. The skin was flawless, a porcelain white. The golden hair was long and fell to its shoulders. It was the eyes that threw me for a second. They weren't a fixed color, but rather shifted along the spectrum from black to white, slowly getting lighter until there appeared to be no iris and then getting darker again. He, it, looked directly at me. And then it spoke. It felt like being caught by an ocean wave unawares. The force buffeted me, sending me several steps back. Behind me, I could hear the screams of pain.

"You do not belong here," the Watcher continued. A look of disbelief briefly crossed its face when it saw I still remained standing. "You must be purged."

Once again I felt the force of its words rock my body. I knew that it was only because of Maelstrom that I wasn't deaf and curled up in a fetal position on the floor. Every fiber of my being wanted to run screaming from this place. As I walked closer, I heard Maelstrom speak.

Prepare yourself, vessel. This will be quite unpleasant for you.

When I reached about three feet from the Watcher, Maelstrom broke into four equal parts and embedded itself into the floor equidistant from the Watchers. As the last piece entered the floor, a circle of symbols materialized there. I recognized them as Maelstrom's symbols. The Watcher looked at me with distrust and began to reach for me, when a dome of energy materialized. I stepped back to the room, not taking my eyes off the Watchers. Every time the Watcher struck the dome, it exploded in a burst of bright orange and then faded back to clear. One of the other watchers dematerialized only to reappear again seconds later.

"That means that this is a sphere, not just a dome. How did you?" asked Anna. "Never mind, let's get moving. They can still contact other Watchers."

I moved to grab Kal. By the time I was ready to go, everyone was moving quickly past the Watchers. The one that spoke was sitting in a Lotus position, floating slightly off the floor, his eyes closed as if in deep meditation.

"We need to get to Sylk's now!" I yelled. That seemed to mobilize the group and we broke off in a run.

CHAPTER THIRTY TWO-SACRIFICE

We raced out of Grand Central, Mara taking point. My abdomen felt as if I had gotten punched repeatedly. I couldn't worry about that, though. Val was right beside me, with Meja behind us both. Behind her was Anna bringing up the rear. We drew looks as we ran onto the street, caution thrown to the wind. The harness, though effective, placed most of Kal's weight on my back, and still required arm strength. My shoulders, biceps and triceps screamed at me. All I could think about was that we were moving too slow. I didn't want to face Watchers, on any terms. How did you outrun a plane of existence? And how was a plane of existence sentient?

Questions best saved for another time as we avoided people and traffic. I flanked Val, her face drawn, her breath coming in short cycles. That was when I saw them. Out of the corner of my eye, I caught movement. The next moment something stood the hair on my neck on end. It was the lead Watcher, the one that looked like paintings of the Archangel Michael. I suppose it was fitting we were being hunted by 'angels'.

"Meja!" I pointed.

She didn't pause a second. "I saw them, Dante. It seems like an extension of the Watcher to keep track of us, or to—"

"Direct others to our location," said Anna. "Mara, continue to the master's location. I will deal with this."

Mara nodded as Anna ran over to face the specter of the lead Watcher. We were about five blocks away from Sylk's location. I felt the pressure in my abdomen ease, which could only mean one thing: we were out of time. I turned to call Anna back, but it was too late. Michael the Watcher was no longer ghostlike. He was very solid and was moving towards Anna. There was nothing I could do, nothing any of us could do, but run. Anna veered off and ran in a different direction, with Michael the Watcher in tow. He didn't run as much as appear to glide, which was eerie and disconcerting to watch. My heart was going into overdrive and fear was forcing adrenaline into my system. We headed for Sylk's building without pursuit. I was guessing that the proximity and the diminished presence of Maelstrom is what made Anna a target until I saw Mara wearing two pendants. Anna must have slipped her the one she had on. As we rounded the corner, Sylk's building came into view.

"We must hurry. The building is phase-shifting."

"It's what?!"

"It won't be there very soon, is what it means," said Meja.

We made it to the entrance of the building. I remembered the lobby, now empty. Mara stood outside.

"What is she doing?" asked Val. Around the perimeter of the building, symbols began to take form on the ground.

"This must be a failsafe system, which means it can only be activated from outside to protect someone inside."

Mara turned and held the pendant that was Anna's in her hand. It pulsed a deep orange, very similar to the sphere that contained the Watchers.

"She did this to protect us. Once I cross the threshold, we will be locked in."

"That means –"

"Yes, she will be locked out."

Anna turned the corner then, with Michael not far behind. The fear on her face transformed to anger when she saw Mara outside. She turned to face the Watcher, her whip in her hand. Michael stopped as if taking in the situation. When he saw the state of the building, he looked perplexed, a question on his face. It was then that Anna wrapped her whip around his neck.

"Mara!" she yelled. Get inside!"

"Anna! No!" Mara took a step to Anna but Meja held her.

"If he enters the building, all is lost!" Anna raised a hand as if telling Mara to stop, and released a burst of energy. "Get inside."

Mara flew inside the lobby, landing on her back. She had crossed the threshold. The symbols on the ground flared a deep red. Around the building, the air shimmered, like the horizon in desert heat.

Michael faced Anna fingering the whip around his neck. His face was impassive as he spoke.

"You do not belong."

A blast of energy washed over Anna. The glass in every pane of the lobby cracked, creating spider web designs. Somehow Anna was still standing even though I could see blood trickling from her ears. Michael looked at the whip as if seeing it for the first time. He put his hand on it and pulled, and Anna slid forward as if she were on ice. Her body was shaking uncontrollably and we could feel the vibration inside the building. Michael placed a hand around Anna's neck. For a moment, she became still. She turned to us, tears in her eyes.

"Go!" she was able to say before Michael lifted her into the air, preventing any more speech.

He looked at her, his eyes shifting color and whispered, "*Disipar*." What happened next couldn't register in my brain. Anna was simply undone. She disintegrated into nothingness.

Michael turned to face us and walked to the building, stopping at the symbols. He looked down and studied them and then stood very still with his eyes closed.

"What is he doing?" asked Val.

"Calling others to create a breach. We need to get upstairs now," said Mara.

CHAPTER THIRTY THREE- INTERSTICES

We ran to the same elevator I had taken earlier with Mara. It was waiting for us. As we got in, I looked at Kal who was looking worse.

"Meja, we need to get Kal some help."

"I know, Dante, but we have more pressing matters to attend to at the moment."

The doors opened a moment later. The hallway with mirrors was untouched, except for the mirrors; they each had a dim red glow to them, very similar to the symbols surrounding the building.

"Whatever you do, do not look directly into the mirrors, no matter what you hear or think you may see," said Mara.

"An infinite loop trap," whispered Meja. "I only heard of these. Are these –?"

"Functional?" finished Mara. "Frightfully so, yes. Let's go."

I remembered walking down that hallway and the eeriness of it. Now it was different though. I felt a tug, and was almost compelled to look into the mirror, if only for a second. An instant later my face stung.

"Don't look into the mirror, or you will be lost." It was Mara. We made it to the door without further incident. Inside, Sylk was packing what looked like a large knapsack.

As promised, he pointed to a side door.

"Your guardian."

I turned to see Zen standing there, realization slowly coming back.

"Zen! It's good to have you back."

"Dante, I didn't realize I had been gone."

"Yes, you were quite gone. Trust me."

Sylk looked over to Meja, and Meja looked at Sylk with impassive eyes.

"It would seem we need to work together to avoid those things out there."

Sylk nodded. "Watchers are quite formidable. I have yet to see one injured, much less destroyed." Sylk turned and picked up his knapsack.

"Sylk, she needs help," I said as I laid Kal down on the sofa. Sylk with an expression of impatience on his face, said. "This will take time you realize, which is a luxury we do not have. You could leave her here, where she should be safe."

"No deal," said Val before I could answer.

Sylk looked from Val to Kal. "Very well, I will honor my word."

"Thank you," I said.

Sylk bent over Kal and extended his hands over her body, and sweat began to form on his brow. Kal cried out in pain. Val moved forward. "He's killing her."

Meja held her back. "Be still, Val. If he is, his life is forfeit."

Sylk continued, oblivious to the activity behind him. The sweat was flowing freely now. I could hear Kal's bones knitting themselves together. After what seemed like an hour, but was probably closer to fifteen minutes, Sylk dropped his hands, and his palms looked as if they had been stripped of flesh. Sylk smiled ruefully as he looked down at them.

"Part of the cost of wielding that much energy without a channel is that the body must pay the price. It looks much worse than it really is."

Kal sat up and Val ran to her, tears in her eyes.

"Don't you ever do that again, Kal!" said Val, relief in her voice.

"I have kept my word, Dante. I trust that when the time comes, you do the same. Now please follow me, we are almost out of time."

He led us to an adjacent room that was completely bare except for a tré on the floor.

"This is a special room," he began when the building began to shake. "It would seem our visitors are growing impatient. Please enter the tré. It, like the building, is keyed to the interstices. Once active, we will cease to exist in this plane, having entered the space in between planes. A word of warning: do not step out of the tré."

We were all in the circle. Sylk bent down to touch the center and I felt the air pressure increase around us. Then everything went black.

CHAPTER THIRTY FOUR-NO TIME

When my eyes adjusted to the lack of light, I was able to discern a hallway of sorts, which appeared to have no end.

"What is this place?" I asked no one in particular.

"This is the space in between planes. If you can imagine the planes we inhabit as four dimensional constructs, this passage is the three dimensional connection between them."

"Three dimensions... You mean time—"

"Is not part of this particular place," said Sylk

I looked around again at the corridor we stood in and let it sink in. We were standing in a place of no time.

Sylk began walking ahead of us, with Mara behind him. "Once we re-enter the Mirror, the Watchers will find us now that they are keyed in to our—your— particular aura," said Sylk.

"Why me?"

"For the same reason the Lotus wants to erase you. The weapon you manifest is a threat not only to your plane, but to every plane of existence."

"I didn't ask for this," I said.

"Nevertheless, if Mara described your weapon accurately, there are some who believe it would be better if you and this manifestation of the weapon did not exist."

I looked at Meja, whose face was unreadable.

"Hey don't worry D.," said Zen. "There are a few of us that want you around."

"Indeed. It seems that while there are certainly formidable forces aligned against you, there is much to be said about a small force overcoming a much larger one."

We kept walking for what felt like thirty minutes when Sylk stopped and turned to face the wall.

"Once this connection is open, we will have no time to spare. We will arrive at another nexus that can lead us to the last known location of the South Watch. From there, it is in your hands, Head Monitor Aumera."

I had never heard anyone refer to Meja so formally but the title fit.

"I can locate the Watch," said Meja crisply.

"I have every confidence in your abilities. Just be aware we will not have the luxury of time as we enjoy here," he said, sweeping his arm around.

"I am well aware of that fact. There is no need to belabor the obvious. Let's get on with it."

Sylk nodded and began to trace symbols in the air before the wall. His hands shone a faint blue, leaving symbols as after-images in the air before him. I didn't recognize the symbols, but it seemed as if Meja was familiar with them. When Sylk had finished, he placed his hand on the wall and a faint blue line crept up from the floor. Meja turned to him.

"Where did you learn these symbols?" she asked. The line kept creeping up.

"Before the monitors were created to be the bearers of balance, there were others who held that same office. The monitors did not arise out of a vacuum. Granted, this may be a slower method, but more secure, a lower expenditure of energy means less chance of detection."

The line had crept up about seven feet and was now travelling horizontally. Sylk stood, watching its progress. For a moment he looked tired and old. Then he quickly recovered and began to look through his bag. The line had crept along about four feet and was now headed towards the floor. Sylk pulled out several small coins from the bag and handed one to each person except me.

Meja looked at the coin in her hand, testing its weight.

"Are these –?"

"Retrievers? Yes, in case anyone gets lost. They won't work with you now, Dante, because of your weapon. My advice is not to get separated from us."

The thin line had touched the base of the wall and now was making its way to connect the rectangle. As the lines met, the wall section took on a glassy composition. As I looked closer I realized it was –

"A mirror, but not just any kind of mirror. This one will allow us to travel through a passageway unused by most."

"This can't be—" started Meja.

"Yes it is. I'm afraid it is."

"This is Aurora's passage?" asked Meja.

"Yes it is, although most have forgotten the way to creating it. As you can see, some still recall the method," said Sylk.

"This is impossible," said Meja.

"No, it is improbable, not impossible," said Sylk as he drew closer to the wall.

CHAPTER THIRTY FIVE-THE WATCH

I had no idea what Aurora's passage was but it seemed to make Meja pause. If it made her pause, I paused as well.

"What is Aurora's passage?"

Sylk turned to me and pointed at the now-mirrored surface of the wall.

"This is Aurora's passage."

"Let me ask the next obvious question. Who was or is Aurora?"

"She was one of the first to navigate the mirror. She documented the passages and where they led. The rumor is that her travels drove her insane. No one knows for sure. Her body has never been found and I daresay she has chosen to remain hidden from all except the most daring, insane or persevering. Perhaps we are a bit of all."

Symbols had formed around the mirrored area on the wall shifting a faint yellow to red. They looked vaguely familiar.

"So what, she's dangerous? Is this another threat to worry about? We don't have enough people chasing us? Now, we are going to use some insane woman's passage?"

"Not dangerous, elusive," said Sylk. "She was one of the first to travel the mirror, documenting what existed where. She was also a wavedancer."

"Wait a minute, she was related to Lucius?" Sylk raised an eyebrow and nodded. "His sister, although between the two of them, I would say her skill surpassed his."

"Wasn't she killed when they eliminated the bloodline?"

I was fully aware that Sylk may have been the last living relative or member of that bloodline. The fact that I stood before Aurora's portal only lent credence to that.

"By the time the elders," he said the word with disgust, "decided to wipe out the entire Iman bloodline, Aurora was already presumed lost."

"And no one was going to go looking for her, I'm guessing?" I said.

"Aurora's passage is not like this place. The closest approximation you would understand would be a maze or labyrinth, made of mirrors."

I let that sink in a moment and looked at Meja. "Are you kidding me?"

Sylk stood in front of the entrance to the passage. He lightly touched the symbols along the edge, which became violet.

"Did I mention that she was also thought to be quite insane by the time she disappeared?"

"Yes you did," I said

"Insane with a vicious sense of humor or so I am told, since I have never met her." As I followed his hands, slowly touching symbols, it came back to me where I had seen those symbols before. Many of them were the same symbols along the shaft of Maelstrom. This was getting better by the second.

CHAPTER THIRTY SIX-AURORA'S PASSAGE

Sylk put his hands on the wall. The symbols flared for a second and then returned to their dull violet pulsing. The wall was not an entrance. I knew there were rules to mazes and labyrinths. The story of Theseus came back to me, and somehow I felt that a minotaur would be the least of our worries. As I looked in, I could see the reflective surfaces of the mirrors—even the floor and the ceiling were mirrored. Prolonged exposure was a guaranteed trip to madness. I wondered if Aurora went crazy because she had to walk this labyrinth. It seemed plausible. I didn't like this idea for a second.

"Is this the only way we can make the run to the Watch?" I asked.

Sylk turned to face me, his face serious.

"It's the only way to ensure that we are not followed, especially by your Black Lotus. There is not one among them that can open this passage," Sylk said as he pointed to the mirrored hallway.

"We have to take it, Dante," said Meja.

I realized that on some level they were waiting for me, that I was influencing their decision. Sylk looked at me knowingly.

"It hinges on you, warrior. I can open the door but I cannot force you through it." I knew I was going to regret it.

"Let's go, then," I said as I stepped into the mirrored passage. The effect was immediate. Once the last of the group stepped in, Sylk turned to seal the entrance. Once done, it was reflection upon reflection.

"Stay close," said Sylk, "and focus only on the person in front of you. I will try to lead us out of here as swiftly as possible."

"What do you mean try?" said Meja.

"As I said, Aurora was considered unbalanced, and this labyrinth changes every time it is entered, making it impossible to map. Those that have tried have ended up dead or worse, roaming these passages endlessly. Trust no one you may see."

Nice of Sylk to omit that little detail of a shifting labyrinth. We continued single file with Sylk taking point, and the rest of followed.

"Can the Watchers enter here?" Zen asked.

"In theory, yes, but since we are not a threat to anything here and this is not an area that requires watching it is unlikely we would encounter them in this place."

Somehow his answer was less than reassuring. He must have seen the look on my face.

"There are no guarantees, save that one day we will die. Embrace that fact and life will be worth living."

We spoke as we walked, our voices hollow and muffled as if in a padded room. Sylk stopped at an intersection, extending his hands into each corridor and choosing the right one.

"Why not the other passage?" I asked as we walked the corridor.

"I'm surprised you can't sense it, warrior. That corridor held certain death. This one, on the other hand, provides us with an opportunity at survival." We made our way to a fairly large room.

I don't know how he sensed certain death, since it felt that way the moment we entered. In the back of my mind, Maelstrom whispered something indiscernible, and I felt his presence increase. Before I realized it, Sylk was beside me. "Keep your power in check and do not lose yourself or you doom us all," he whispered.

Ahead of us was a figure, and even from this distance I could tell it was female.

"Is that –?"

"No, it's not Aurora. Just one of the lost who cannot find their way out of this place. If she is still alive, it means she is quite formidable in power.

"Do you know the way out?" the woman asked.

"I can lead you out if you let me," said Sylk.

"Really, you know the way?" she asked almost childlike. She was young, around mid-twenties and very attractive. Her waist long hair fell loosely, framing her face. She wore a loose-fitting robe, covered in some kind of emblem I couldn't make out.

"But if you know the way out, why are you here?"

"We are merely journeying to another place."

"Those symbols," whispered Meja, "I recognize them, they are ancient monitor symbols."

"How old?" I asked.

"About 100 years ago, but that can't be. It would mean she is—"

"Very old," I finished.

"Where are you going? Can you take me?" she asked.

"We can lead you out but we cannot take you with us," said Sylk.

"I want to go with you. Take me with you," she said a little more earnestly.

"You can come with us and we will lead you out," said Sylk evenly.

"You are a liar!" she suddenly screamed.

All the while during the short conversation I noticed Sylk tracing something with his foot on the floor. When she screamed, he stomped his foot down, creating a wall of orange energy just in time to catch the blast that was launched at us. Even with the barrier, it sent us flying back.

"Now you will all die," she said.

Her robes flowed and fluttered as if caught in a strong wind. I realized that it was her power that was creating the change in air flow around her, like a wind tunnel.

"Stay back, all of you," said Sylk. He approached the ancient monitor with measured steps.

"You don't want to do this. We are no threat to you," he said easily with his arms outstretched.

"You lie! We came in here because you sent us. They all died horribly. I'm the last one left." She hugged herself as she whispered those last words. I had no doubt now that she was clearly operating in a very different reality. Sylk's hands were glowing white. When she saw his hands, she seemed to snap back to the present. Sylk clapped his hands together and a white band of energy enveloped the ancient monitor. It looked like she was subdued, at least I thought so, until she started laughing hysterically.

"Fool! You think you can hold me with this?" she screamed. With a flick of her wrist, she bisected the energy holding her and stepped toward Sylk, who was clearly surprised.

"Do you know who I am? I am Mariko the last." Meja gave a sharp intake of breath.

"It can't be, —not her," said Meja.

"Sylk! You cannot let her touch you," said Meja.

"I am aware of the rumors surrounding the infamous Mariko," said Sylk. As he spoke, a blade materialized in his hands. It appeared to be a slice of emptiness. It was a black so intense that it seemed to absorb light. It emanated darkness and a feeling of unease crept into my abdomen. As I looked closer, I could now see the slight Asian features in Mariko's face. Her hair flowed with the energy she expended, creating a black halo around her head. Her almond shaped eyes glistened with madness.

"Who is she?" asked Zen. I was still transfixed by Sylk's blade to ask the obvious. Meja answered without taking her eyes off Mariko.

"It's in all the historical texts. She was one of the first monitors. Her ability was to siphon energy by touch. She was known as the monitor of Death.

In her time, she was without peer in ability. Most believe the Mikai are her descendants."

Even I knew who the Mikai were. A covert group of assassins that made the story of ninjas seem like a welcome nightmare. I wouldn't be surprised if ninjas were an expression of the Mikai. From the look on Meja's face, we were in serious danger.

CHAPTER THIRTY SEVEN-MARIKO

Mariko stood still, facing Sylk. A red sickly glow enveloped her hands.

"Let me put you out of your misery. I promise it will be delicious," she purred.

"I have grown rather fond of my misery, but thank you for the offer. You won't be terribly offended if I refuse?" answered Sylk.

She moved like a blur of energy. Her attack a lethal dance. We were in a fairly large room, mirrors all around replicating our images over and over. Mariko was graceful and lethal. She lunged forward, attacking with a velocity that made it near impossible to see her hands. All I could follow was the red energy trail. Each attack was parried or avoided entirely by Sylk. Every time Sylk attacked, his blade would miss by a fraction of an inch. After about ten minutes, sweat began to bead on Sylk's forehead. Mariko began to laugh.

"I can see your demise. Can you see it?" she purred.

Sylk remained silent, realizing the taunt for what it was, a distraction. The energy in her hands grew slightly and disconnected, floating around her. Sporadically a smaller sphere of energy would detach and launch itself at Sylk with blinding speed. Things were not looking good. Mariko continued to evade every attack as she drew closer to Sylk. The color in her hands shifted from red to black. As she drew closer, Sylk launched an attack of energy spheres. Mariko reached into her belt and pulled out a long rectangular object. She flicked her wrist and the rectangle in her hand opened into a fan. As Sylk's spheres bore down on her, she stood perfectly still in a crouched position. On the fan was an image of a dragon devouring a tiger. As each sphere was about to impact she would step slightly to the side and allow the fan to take the impact. Each time the fan was hit, a small shockwave would emanate from Mariko. Just enough to cause a stirring of air.

"The fan is absorbing the energy of the spheres, which means at some point she will release all that trapped energy," said Meja.

"We need to move, now!" said Mara.

"Are you quite finished?" said Mariko, growing serious. Sylk looked tired but ready for anything. Sylk again did not answer.

"Very well, I tire of this game, let us end now."

We were moving away from them when I felt a thump in my lower abdomen followed by a shockwave that sent us all flying across the floor. Only Sylk stood his ground, his sword cutting through the shockwave. His face, arms and any exposed skin was lacerated, as if he had been dragged across a rough surface. Mariko raised an eyebrow in surprise.

"Very well, then. I have yet to meet a warrior worthy of my weapon. Perhaps you will fare better than those who have fallen before you."

Sylk, clearly in pain, clenched his jaw. We all stood up slowly. Mariko placed the fan in her belt and placed her hands together as if in prayer. As she separated her hands, a sword hilt appeared in her left hand. The rest of the blade appeared to be withdrawn from the palm of her right hand. The blade wasn't long—maybe thirty inches. It was a straight sword coming to a point, and the edges looked razor sharp. Each side of the blade was covered in symbols but unlike Maelstrom, the symbols on Mariko's blade shifted and moved, travelling up and down the length of the sword.

"What the hell is that? I've never seen a weapon with moving symbols, "said Zen.

We were backing up as a group. Clearly, the blade Mariko wielded made Meja and Mara uneasy.

"No one knows its name, just what it's been called," said Meja.

"What?"

"If that blade touches any live flesh, it immediately kills it, not just the area it touches. There is a delayed effect, after some time, days, weeks, months in some cases, the person dies as death courses through the body. No one has been able to defeat that weapon, that's why it's called Death's Finger."

Mariko now had the fan in her right hand, open, and Death's Finger in her left. She was a blur as she approached Sylk. For the first time, I realized that

Sylk was outmatched. As he parried and evaded, I think Sylk realized it as well. Mariko advanced, lunging with Death's Finger as Sylk raised his own blade to deflect the lunge. Mariko turned in a circle, bringing the fan around in a deadly arc cutting Sylk across the right cheek. The fan was so sharp that the wound across Sylk's face didn't bleed for the first twenty seconds. Sylk didn't have a moment to think about the cut since Mariko kept attacking.

"It is only a matter of time, warrior. You will fatigue and commit an error —your last."

Mariko was right. It was only a matter of getting Sylk tired. Then she would find an opening and exploit it. Sylk was going to die unless I could stop Mariko. Against my better judgment and every instinct, which screamed at me to run in the opposite direction, I headed towards Mariko and Sylk.

"Dante, no!" It was Zen. "That's suicide. If Sylk can't handle her, you sure as hell can't."

I grew angry and quickly channeled it. There was no purpose in getting angry at Zen. I quickly ran towards Sylk and Mariko. In my head, Maelstrom stirred and whispered.

"Are you rushing to your death, vessel?"

273

"No. I have to keep Sylk alive."

"You do not possess the skill to defeat his opponent. In addition, she wields an envenomed blade."

"I realize I don't possess the skill but you do."

"I do."

I opened up and let Maelstrom take over, he/it rushed in and I had the sensation of being inside and outside of my body at the same time. As I approached, I saw Mariko slice Sylk just below his right shoulder. She ducked a lateral swipe and was about to cut Sylk again when her blade was blocked by Maelstrom. Sylk was pale. His right arm hung at his side lifeless.

"Go with the others, boy," I heard Maelstrom say.

Sylk retreated quietly, holding his arm in obvious pain. Mara rushed to his side to see what she could do. I sensed rather than saw these things. My awareness was nowhere and everywhere at once.

CHAPTER THIRTY EIGHT-FRIENDS

"Let us dance," I heard myself say. It was my voice and wasn't at the same time.

"It has been some time since we last danced, widow," I said.

Mariko's eyes opened in surprise.

"How do you know that name?"

I heard myself laughing.

"You are a grain in the sands of time compared to me, little girl."

Mariko's eyes narrowed and she took a step back. "Tell me who you are now!"

"You do not need to know that information."

Mariko lunged faster than I thought possible, stepping to the right. My left hand shot out and grabbed Mariko's sword hand.

"I was ancient when you were still being forged," I heard Maelstrom say. As I turned into Mariko, a blade appeared at the end of Maelstrom. I saw myself stab her once, twice and finally a third time. A look of peace came over her face as I gently eased her to the floor.

"Thank you, warrior. I have wandered these halls for far too long. Now finally, I can rest."

"I'm sorry," I whispered.

"Nonsense. I would have done the same to you, given the chance." I remained silent as she looked in my eyes as if searching for something. Her breathing was becoming labored and I could see she did not have much time left. She reached into her sash. For a moment I tensed, wary of some last attack. She laughed then began coughing. She motioned for me to draw closer, her voice barely above a whisper.

"Take this," she said, handing me her fan.

"It is quite valuable and will bring you respect among my children."

"Thank you."

"No, thank you, warrior. The journey that lies before you is filled with death and sadness."

I turned away to look at my friends, people who had sworn to protect me with their lives.

"You will lose them all one day." I turned to her, shock and anger on my face.

She smiled knowingly. "When that happens, and it will, do not surrender to the weapon, do not become like me. Find another answer."

She closed her eyes and died, her body lifeless.

CHAPTER THIRTY NINE-TIME

The situation was bad. Mariko's broken body lay at my feet. As I turned to look at the group, I saw in their eyes something that chilled me to the bone —fear. The only exception was Meja, who looked at me with concern. I turned back to look at Mariko. She seemed smaller now, the energy that was her life, now gone. The weight of her fan in my hand reminded me of her last words. Was she like me? Was I like her? Was this my destiny, to become insane, wrapped up in some reality created by my own imagination and the deaths caused by Maelstrom? I needed to become better. I needed to relegate Maelstrom to just a weapon; not a weapon that could wield me. At this point, I was the weapon. Looking down at Mariko, I could see how well that worked out for her. These weapons were cursed —at least I felt that way.

Owl showed me a different side, though. They could be harnessed, controlled to a degree. Of course that required skill and training, training I lacked. I'm not going to say I was a complete amateur or novice, only because there was no need to say it out loud. It was evident I was way out of my league. I'd survived on luck, lots of luck and the skill of those around me. The thing is, I knew that at some point I would have to confront something or someone on my own. I wasn't ready. I turned to walk back to the group. With Maelstrom gone, a weight was lifted. The air no longer held that charged feeling. The acrid smell of death hung in the air and I scrunched up my nose, turning away from the odor. It smelled like rotting flesh. I followed the odor to Sylk, who sat calmly with his back to the wall, Mara at his side tending to his wound. Her jaw was clenched; she knew there was nothing she could do. Sweat glistened on Sylk's face and I could see that he was in pain. Mara had cut his sleeve off to get to the wound. If I had eaten, I would have lost whatever food was in my stomach at that moment. As I drew closer to Sylk, the stench intensified. I didn't know how Mara was able to be so close without retching. The arm at the wound had turned black. Mara was removing maggots that were eating the dead flesh. As I watched, I could see the black area grow incrementally. It was moving up and down his arm, slowly but surely. I turned to Meja who was standing some distance away.

"Is there anything we can do?"

"Aside from letting him die, you mean? No. We could kill him quick, which would be better than the death that awaits him." Meja, a pillar of compassion.

"No other alternative?"

"There is no cure for a touch from Death's Finger, Dante."

"The arm, remove the arm." It was Sylk's voice, calm but laced with pain.

"There is no guarantee that will work." said Meja. "The venom has reached your blood. It is not confined to the arm."

"You would be amazed at what I could do with a small opportunity, Monitor. I prefer to have this slim chance than certain death."

"I will do it, Karashihan," said Mara with wet eyes.

"No, Mara, you cannot. It must be done with a weapon that will absorb the venom into it, along with any negative energy residue."

In other words, Maelstrom. Everyone remained still, the silence filling the space around us.

"You must do this, warrior," Sylk said through gritted teeth.

"I can't."

"If you don't, my death is certain." The implication in his voice was clear. I needed him alive to get into the Watch. I looked at the wound again, noticing how it had grown even in this short time.

"Don't be squeamish, boy. Besides, I'm certain you have ached for an opportunity like this."

"No, not like this." He smiled then and set his jaw.

I looked around at the group and saw that it was my choice alone to make.

"Fine."

"Make haste, warrior. We race against time. Sever the arm and I will deal with the wound."

Maelstrom appeared in my hands, hungry, eager. Mara laid Sylk down.

"A clean cut at the shoulder, right next to the deltoid. Make sure you don't miss." He tried to laugh but it came out as a raspy cough.

As I held Maelstrom in my hand, I could feel the weight shift as a blade extended from one end. It would be so easy, just a few inches to the right. No! I knew that was Maelstrom and I could hear a low laugh confirming my thoughts. *Coward.* I need him alive. *Do you? You can get into the Watch, you don't need him.* I need him alive.

You want him alive. It is a vast difference, vessel. A decision you may live to regret. Very well, let us remove his cursed flesh.

I brought the blade down, whistling through the air. I cut through flesh, muscle and bone, crashing into the floor beneath. It was as if the arm was not there. Sylk's right arm, now separated from the body began a rapid decomposition. Sylk, his left hand glowing a deep indigo, pressed the deep blue energy into the wound. The smell of charred skin wafted into the air. The left arm had gone completely black now, the flesh rotting.

"Thank you," said Sylk with genuine gratitude in his voice. I looked once more at the arm now turning to dust. I turned back to Sylk who had become unconscious and I hoped I wasn't prolonging the inevitable.

CHAPTER FORTY-ENTER THE WATCH

We needed to get to the Watch as quickly as possible. Zen picked up the now unconscious Sylk.

"Can you get a way to the Watch open?" I asked Meja.

"From this place it will be a challenge but it shouldn't be impossible."

"Let's try it. I'm getting sick of this place." Zen grunted in agreement.

Meja stepped to a mirrored wall and placed her hands on the surface. Her reflection fell away from the wall, replaced by blurring images. It was like looking at a movie in fast forward. Except in this case none of the images seemed related. Sweat beaded on her forehead from the effort, then the images stopped blurring and a large castle-like building came into focus.

"I can't find any points inside the Watch. This is the closest I can get us. I can't hold this open long. Go!"

I was already moving, the sensation of being pulled against my will and stretched, screamed across my senses. We all materialized at pretty much the same moment, which gave me pause. Meja was last and then I saw the shimmering rift seal itself and vanish. We were in a desert plain. Everywhere I looked, I saw sand. Sitting in the middle of this plain, loomed the Watch. It was a squat, rectangular structure, the walls the color of sand. The air was dry and I felt the change in temperature immediately. I started walking towards the Watch, sweat forming on my brow. Spaced around the Watch were trees. Large palms which provided some shade from the blistering sun. I headed to the closest tree —trees meant water. I estimated that the closest tree was about five hundred meters away. That was when I heard the howls.

"Wolves? In the desert?"

"No, not wolves, you have never seen an animal like this. This is the first defense of the Watch."

"What are they?"

We had started moving towards the Watch much faster now.

It was Mara who spoke. "They are called the Rah Ven. They make full grown wolves look like a child's pet." The howls were still in the distance.

"I'm sure between all of us, we can fend these Rah Ven off, right?"

Mara looked at me as if I could not truly be that stupid.

"You have never faced a Rah Ven or such foolishness would not escape your lips," said Mara. "Aside from being ferocious hunters, they have the ability to camouflage. They are also near impossible to dispatch because they serve as Watch guardians, which lends them even more power."

"So we have no chance?"

"We do." It was Sylk. He still looked weak. His face was pale. "Put me down, guardian. We must approach the west wall."

The howling was getting closer. Zen put him down. "The howling is a good sign, as long as they howl, we have a chance. Once they stop, the attacks begin," whispered Sylk.

The west wall? I had no clue where we were much less where the west wall was. The howling continued, creating an expectation of impending attack. It was surreal, hearing the chorus of animals no longer so distant.

"Over here," said Meja. "This should be the west wall according to the sun."

The squat building had no apparent entrance. Each corner held a turret-like structure and the blocks that made up the wall were immense. In between each block, the seams appeared air tight.

Whoever constructed this Watch had longevity in mind. It reminded me of the Great Pyramids.

"Where are we?" I asked.

"Right now somewhere in the African Sahara," Meja answered.

"What do you mean right now?" I knew I wasn't going to like the answer.

Sylk answered, his voice a rasp. "What the monitor means is that in a few hours, this entire structure will relocate to another desert on the earth. It could be the Gobi, Death Valley, the Arctic or Antarctic."

"Those last two aren't deserts."

"But they are deserted."

"True."

"I believe they were going for desolate wasteland, frozen or boiling doesn't seem to make a difference. The emphasis was desolate."

"So how were we able to find it, if it's shifting so often?"

"The answer to that question lies with the monitor. If you'll excuse me, I have a door to find before we get ripped to shreds and we don't have much time."

The howling had stopped.

"Shit," said Mara.

"Zen, stay with Sylk," said Meja. "Make sure nothing interrupts him." Zen nodded and stepped closer to Sylk, turning to face away from the Watch wall.

"The rest of you, fan out. Rah Ven attack in packs, so give them a wide target to disperse the pack." Meja had her weapon in her hand. It radiated a blue light that enveloped her in the midst of all the brown surrounding us. Kal and Val were on my left. Meja was close to me on my right and Mara was a few feet away from Meja. I felt a tug on my lower abdomen, and I knew what it was. In my hands materialized Maelstrom. It was getting easier and easier each time. I had a feeling that was not a good thing.

The sun beat down upon the sand, sending waves of heat, shimmering in the distance. Sweat began forming on my brow. I looked back to see Sylk working some intricate sequence of designs on the blocks. Zen, jaw clenched, held his axe/staff loosely in his hands, across his body. I turned back to look into the distance.

"*Vessel,*" he said and chuckled. "*You do find yourself in the most interesting positions. If I didn't know different, I would say you are deliberately looking for ways to end your existence.*"

I remained silent while I studied the horizon. It was always unsettling when it spoke and I could understand how wielders of these weapons went crazy: constantly hearing a voice that isn't yours doesn't contribute to long term sanity.

"It isn't funny. I've never faced a Rah Ven before or ever."

"*Rah Ven hmm. Are you prepared to die?*"

"Not today."

"*Will you release me to do as I must?*"

"No. Each time it seems like I lose a small part of myself to you."

"*I see, one of your comrades must have a plan, the monitor perhaps?*"

"I don't know. We just hold them back until Sylk can get the door open."

"*Outstanding plan, no more than two or three of you should perish then.*"

"Tell me about the Rah Ven."

"*Certainly, my soon to be dead vessel. The Rah Ven exists as an extension of a Watch. They cannot be killed conventionally, since there is nothing conventional about them. As long as the defenses of*

the watch are intact, the Rah Ven will give pursuit.
Their appearance is that of a very large, ferocious
wolf, standing four feet at the shoulder. They have
the ability to camouflage perfectly with their
surroundings and in the heat of battle have been
known to exhibit some type of temporal
displacement."

"They can teleport."

"Not truly. What they do is exhibit a sphere or
area of space around them that distorts time."

"They can warp time?"

"Not deliberately. It seems to be a response to
a serious threat. Something akin to your little
group, which is formidably armed, should be just
the catalyst."

"How do we fight them?"

"Running is always a good option, providing
you can run fast enough."

"How fast? You know what, never mind. I
don't think running is going to be an option."

"Wise choice, since no one in your little group
is fast enough." A comedian staff, amazing.

"So how do we stop them, at least long enough
for Sylk to open the door?"

"While they can't be stopped, you can certainly slow them down."

Exasperated and scared, I asked again. "How. Do. We. Stop. Them?" in my most serious "get to it" voice.

Maelstrom paused and instructed me to draw a circle. This should keep you safe at least from the Rah Ven for a few moments. *"You must attack them from a distance. That should allow you to escape the effects of the temporal shift. When they get close, remain in the circle and give me free reign."*

"No. No way."

"Well it's either that, or swift death for your friends. Your choice."

"Have any of you faced a Rah Ven, ever?" I asked the group.

No one answered, which I took to mean seriously bad news. I turned to see Sylk still tracing designs in the air. Every time he finished with a design, it imprinted itself into the wall, forming part of a larger design, it seemed. I didn't dare to ask how much longer when Meja did.

Sylk, without turning or stopping his hand movements, answered. "If I had another hand and maybe weren't poisoned, I could move faster."

Meja clenched her jaw. That's when I saw the first one. Off in the distance a patch of the horizon shimmered and solidified. To say that they looked like large wolves was a gross simplification. These looked like wolves the same way a dachshund looked like a wolf. Both have four legs, a set of teeth and are canine. The similarities pretty much end there. These creatures, yes that was the word for them, trust me on this, were the type of things that made your legs go weak. My body instinctively only wanted to flee as fast as possible.

They were large —huge by any canine standard. Their coat was short and brown, which allowed them to blend in well with the sand. Their teeth, if you could call them that, more like fangs, were a brilliant white. The most unsettling part was their eyes. They were a deep yellow. It wasn't the color but the intelligence that lay within. Two more appeared beside the first one and they were walking slowly towards us. Two more materialized as they drew within thirty feet. The lead Rah Ven continued walking towards us, while the others remained where they were.

"State your purpose," it/he growled. Meja stepped slightly forward.

"We seek safe passage into the Watch."

I couldn't believe they spoke. I must have had a shocked look on my face because Meja looked at me sharply, which meant get it together.

"On whose authority?" he growled in answer.

"I am Meja of the House of Aumera. First among the monitors of the Way." The Rah Ven paused and looked at Meja as if weighing her words or credentials.

"There was a time long ago when that would have been enough, but no longer. Are you prepared to die, Meja, of the House of Aumera?"

Maelstrom flared to life in my hands and the Rah Ven' hackles went up.

"The one beside you carries a cursed weapon, monitor. How did it come to be in his possession?"

"I am the one responsible, Ancient One." It was Sylk who had stepped forward. I really hoped he had that door open at this point. The Rah Ven turned its head slightly. In my periphery, I noticed several more Rah Ven materialized. I realized then that fighting them was not going to be an option. A quick glance let me count about fifteen and those were just the ones I could see.

"A Karashihan. Are you aware of the destruction that vessel can unleash, not only on this plane but on countless others?" asked the Rah Ven.

"I am aware and it was necessary to take the risk."

The Rah Ven scrutinized Sylk, smelling the air around him as he circled Sylk. "You are not long for this world, Karashihan. Poison courses through your body this very moment."

Sylk only nodded.

"Do you seek to destroy this poison?" The Rah Ven stopped circling Sylk and peered at him.

"I have lived a long time, Ancient One. It would appear that my time draws to an end."

"Contained within these walls, lies a cure if you are willing to pay the price it demands."

"I would be grateful for the opportunity," said Sylk.

"One of my pack shall lead you to the entrance of the Watch proper. Have you prepared the door?"

"I have."

"Very well, Karashihan, may you find what you seek."

"Run long, run fast, Ancient One."

"Long days to you, Karashihan."

The Rah Ven turned away and faced me. It took all I had to stay still as it drew closer.

"Discover who is the vessel and who is the weapon before it becomes your undoing." I could only swallow hard. I did however notice that it had easily crossed over the circle I had traced into the sand and made a mental note to ask my homicidal weapon about that when I got a chance.

The ancient one turned and started to shimmer. As if on cue, every other Rah Ven turned and merged into the background, effectively disappearing, except one

The Rah Ven that remained was smaller than the rest of the pack, which led me to believe it was younger. It stepped towards Sylk and the symbols he had placed on the wall.

"Greetings, Karashihan," it growled. Its coat glistened a deep blue black and it looked like an oversized wolf with the exception of the deep yellow eyes. Oh, and the talking.

"Greetings, gatekeeper." It was obvious Sylk knew more about these creatures than any of us. It didn't seem like the time for a history lesson on talking wolf-like beings.

Sylk stepped to the side, allowing the Rah Ven access to the wall. The Rah Ven drew close, sniffed the air and seemed to inspect the symbols.

"This will suffice," it growled. The rest of the group drew close and unconsciously gave the Rah Ven space, forming a loose semi-circle around it. It sat back on its haunches and for a moment nothing occurred.

"What's going on?" I asked Meja under my breath.

"I think you're asking the wrong person, Dante," Meja whispered back.

After what seemed like five minutes of sitting completely still, the Rah Ven's eyes glowed, which seemed to activate the symbols on the wall. After all of the symbols were glowing, it let out a growl, more like a rumble that started low and began increasing in volume. It continued the growl/howl until I could see the ground start vibrating. Even with my hands on my ears, the sound was piercing. The only one that seemed unaffected was Sylk. In ten more seconds I was sure my eardrums would burst. That was when I noticed the wall, which had taken on a gelatinous quality. Sylk walked over to it and touched it. The wall raced away from his hand exposing an opening. The Rah Ven walked in first, followed by Sylk. We quickly followed. Past the wall awaited a stark contrast to the desert exterior. Lush grass surrounded the entrance to what only could be described as a keep. The entrance to the keep was a solid wood set of double doors that stood twenty feet high. The keep itself was comprised of huge blocks. There were no windows to speak of but I noticed several arrow loops. The roof of the keep was the true sight. It looked like a giant geodesic dome. The dome was enclosed on four sides by turrets that towered over the dome. Sylk turned to the Rah Ven.

"Thank you Gatekeeper. Will you wait for us?"

The Rah Ven sat facing the entrance of the keep. "I shall await your return here. My position does not allow me entrance to the Watch."

Sylk nodded. "I understand."

"A word, Karashihan. There are several dangers within. The greatest of these lies within each of you." The Rah Ven ended his last sentence looking at me. A cold sensation gripped my abdomen.

"Understood," said Sylk and he made his way to the entrance. The Rah Ven remained so still I wondered if it had reverted to a statue. The only thing that moved was his eyes. As I walked by it, I drew closer to see if it was breathing.

"Do you have a name?" I whispered more to myself than to the Rah Ven. It turned its head then, with a suddenness, and I could almost swear, a grin.

"If you return alive, warrior, perhaps you will learn it," it said as I made my way to the huge double doors.

CHAPTER FORTY ONE-DISCOVERY

As we drew close to the door, I noticed the emblem of the monitors on it. I remembered that the Watches were run and populated by monitors. Sylk, who looked pretty bad at this point, turned to Meja.

"Monitor, I have done my part, you must now do yours."

"What do you mean your part? What about the inner defenses?"

"They won't mean anything if we cannot get past this door."

He had a point. It seemed that Meja came to the same conclusion and went to inspect the door. I turned back and looked at the Rah Ven, which sat motionless. The scent of fresh cut grass permeated the air and the day felt cool —quite the change from sitting in a desert. Meja drew close to the symbol with a confused look, then she started to look around the doorway.

"What's the matter?" I asked. I had never seen her anything less than secure and confident. "The symbol, it's correct, but the lock is missing there." She pointed to the symbol and I saw what she meant. It looked as if the lower third of the symbol had been erased.

"It's usually close by somewhere nondescript and usually inverted to hide its meaning."

I looked around and couldn't find anything that remotely resembled the emblem.

"Here!" she exclaimed. I couldn't see it but I took her word for it. She was crouched on the lower right hand side of the doorway. "Inverted and mirrored, I have never seen this before."

"Can you open it?" It was Mara. She had a worried expression on her face. I looked at Sylk and saw why. He looked paler than before, if that was possible. He was no longer sweating but if I looked carefully I could see him trembling slightly. He didn't look like he would last much longer. I turned to Meja. If he died out here, we had no chance to get to the records, which meant this entire trip was in vain. We had to move fast.

"Meja—"I began.

"I'm on it." She had seen me look at Sylk. "It just means I need to reverse and flip the order of the sequence."

"Are you sure? What happens if you're wrong?"

I had this image of some failsafe falling into place flash in my head. Something like an extra door or some kind of fence sealing the door.

She answered without turning to me. "You see the gatekeeper?"

"Yes, he hasn't moved from that spot. May as well be a statue."

"If I fail, that will be the last thing any of us will ever see. They are the failsafe of the Watch. To this day, no one has ever defeated a Rah Ven, this close to a watch." Now it was my turn to sweat.

Meja began to draw symbols in the air. Her hands moved slowly at first and then increased in velocity, until they were a blur. Blue trails followed her fingertips as she outlined the entrance symbol in the air. It seemed to require more than one application as I saw her repeat a sequence several times. I would ask her about that later. After the last sequence, she placed her hand on the emblem of the monitors. A blue glow suffused the emblem momentarily as if being absorbed. Nothing happened. I kept my eyes on the Rah Ven who was slowly disappearing. "No!" I yelled. Everyone was focused on the door as the Rah Ven seemed to evaporate.

"It's okay, Dante. If I had failed, I would have been the first attacked," said Meja with audible relief.

What sounded like counterweights and a very large locking mechanism began to move and shudder in the wall beside the entrance. Slowly the doors began to open. The stench hit me first. It was horrible—burnt flesh and something else, something rotting. The doors opened more rapidly presenting a view of the interior of the Watch. Inside the entrance was a courtyard, with an obelisk in the center of it. At the apex was a crescent moon with what appeared to be a silver owl in the center. The obelisk stood thirty feet high. Its sides, the ones that I could see, were covered in some brown liquid. As I followed the liquid up, I saw the bodies.

Impaled on either end of the crescent moon was a body. The points of the crescent protruded through the abdomen of each.

"Who could have done such a thing? Why?" The keep doors closed behind us with a slow sigh as if weeping for the victims.

I was still looking up when I heard a sharp intake of breath from around me.

"You," said Meja through gritted teeth.

Stepping around the obelisk, clad all in black a sai in each hand stood Diana.

"Yes, me. Their deaths will seem like mercy when I finish with your group," she said softly, her words carrying in the still courtyard. Around us, from the shadows emerged figures. The Black Lotus.

"Time to die," she said as she leapt towards Meja.

CHAPTER FORTY TWO-COST

Time seemed to stop. I saw Diana leap and wondered how anyone could ever leap so high. The figures around us stood motionless, apparently under orders not to interfere. It felt like time itself was holding its breath. Meja drew her sword just in time to deflect a double sai attack. The deep violet of Diana's sai vibrated in the air, seeming alive. Meja's sword flashed with a blue glow.

"You will not be able to draw another skein, Meja."

Meja didn't answer but circled around her opponent. Kal and Val made a move to enter. Diana looked at them, rooting them where they stood.

"Explain to them, Meja, how quickly they will cease breathing if they take one more step."

Meja looked at them, signaling them to back up. I wondered what she meant when I looked down at the ground around us. What appeared to be a lattice work of violet energy surrounded us. Now I understood what she meant about Meja not being able to draw another skein: we were in the middle of one. As I looked around, I saw that we were roughly in a large circle of energy. The figures in black surrounded the circle. We were trapped for the time being. Meja and Diana stood in what seemed to be a clearing, a circle within the circle, which was devoid of the energy lattice. We had walked right into this, like amateurs.

"This is simple, Meja. You kill me; you may enter the Watch proper. You fail, I kill them all. Either way, you must fight, my dear."

"I will not kill you, Diana," said Meja.

"Do you really think you even have the skill to face me? Compared to me, you are a neophyte, wet behind the ears. I have forgotten more than you will ever learn."

I could see the words stung; Meja's expression hardened.

"Very well, Sensei," whispered Meja. Diana smiled and threw a sai. Meja parried with her sword and deflected it, sending it on a trajectory to her left. The sai kept travelling and then stopped as if on a tether. It slowed and then snapped back into Diana's hand, barely missing Meja on the way back. As I looked carefully, I saw what appeared to be a filament running from the sai's handle to each of Diana's wrist guards. Diana lunged forward, sai in hand. Meja stepped to the side, blocking with her sword. Diana was fast; she almost stabbed Meja with that move. A flurry of attacks followed: lunges, slices, pommel attacks and throughout it all Meja managed to defend against each. Every attack missed her or was blocked and parried by a fraction of an inch.

"I know what you are doing, girl. And you can't keep defending forever. Sooner or later, you will tire and I guarantee it will be before I do." Diana was right. I could see the strain on Meja's face. Sweat ran freely down her face now.

"It seems you need incentive. I will provide it." Diana jumped into a forward roll and came out of it beside Valeria.

"You were eager to join us before," she said as she grabbed a handful of Valeria's hair.

"This is our fight; she has no part in it. Leave her alone!" said Meja.

"I disagree, Meja. They all have a part in this fight. Some are more pivotal than others, but all of them important. Take her, for example," she said as she slid a sai across Valeria's cheek. Her part is to make you realize your true potential." With that, she took her sai and buried it into Valeria's midsection. Valeria crumpled to the floor with a look of pain and surprise on her face. The grass beneath her began to turn crimson as blood rushed out of her wound. It had happened so fast no one reacted for a full second.

"No!" screamed Kal and Meja in unison. Kal launched herself at Diana, only to be flung back as if smashing into an invisible wall. She hit the ground hard. Meja ran towards Diana, anger transfixing her features.

"Now you are ready to fight? Good."

Diana joined her sai and they merged into a short sword. Meja was attacking, every thrust, cut, had the intention of removing Diana from existence.

"Your friend, your pupil, is dying, Meja. Is this the best you can do? Have you learned nothing? You cannot defeat me. Especially not in your state." That was when I felt the shift. The air around Meja shimmered briefly and her face changed. She no longer appeared angry. In fact, she appeared almost – peaceful?

Diana saw it and a flicker of worry crossed her expression. With each attack, Meja drew closer until their crossed swords were inches from each other's faces. I felt another shift and looked around; no one else seemed to have noticed it. Meja's left hand began to glow a deep indigo.

"You're right, Sensei. It may appear that I have not learned much," she said in a soft whisper, "but you were not my only teacher." Meja placed her palm on Diana's chest. The indigo from her hand spread across the width of Diana's chest almost instantly.

"What? No!" Diana staggered back.

"You should have left us alone, Diana," Meja said, sounding almost sad.

Diana fell to her knees. As she fell, the lattice work around us disappeared. Zen ran to Valeria.

"What have you done, you bitch!" Diana's voice sounded strangled as if she couldn't get enough air.

"I told you I would not kill you and I will keep my word. That –" she pointed to Diana's chest, "is a soul siphon."

Diana's eyes opened in fear. "How could you know… you are not skilled enough…" She fell back with her eyes open.

"I do know and it's evident I am skilled enough. I told you, you were not my only sensei. You will remain alive but without any power until the siphon has run its course." Meja looked genuinely sad.

"How long does a siphon last?" I asked her.

"It varies. Usually one or two," she said as she rushed over to Zen.

I ran behind her. "One or two days, months, hours, what?"

I did not want to run into Diana anytime soon. I was hoping for years. Actually I was thinking— driving a blade through her right now was not such a bad idea. Preemptive nightmare avoidance.

Meja was bent over Valeria. I touched her shoulder.

"How long?" She looked up at me, tears in her eyes.

"Centuries, Dante. One or two centuries, which is more mercy than she showed Valeria."

"No." I said looking down at Val.

Zen looked at me and nodded.

"She's gone," he whispered.

Meja stood and faced the circle of shadows. With steel in her voice, she spoke, "Go and tell your Masters what occurred this day. Tell them that if they want us, they will have to send someone much stronger or come themselves." The shadows faded into nothingness, leaving us alone. When I turned, Diana's body was gone as well.

"Kal, oh no. Zen, tend to her. This will be devastating for her. I fear for her survival," said Meja.

I looked over to where Kal lay. I was certain this was going to crush her; she just lost her sister to psycho bitch from hell. But her life was in danger? Meja must have read my face and turned away from Valeria's body.

"They were more than twins. They shared a life bond."

"Life bond...Their lives were joined?"

"In a loose sense, no. They did however share a chi bond which allowed them to be conscious of the other anywhere on the planet. They knew how the other felt without needing to express it in words. When that bond is severed, especially violently, the twin that survives is greatly affected. In rare occasions, the bond is so close that the death of one can signal the death of both. That is what we are making sure of in this case – that Kalysta survives."

We walked over to Kal's body, where she lay breathing. Zen was gently bringing her to.

"Ugh —what the hell. Val! Where is Val? Where is she?" She looked around frantically until her eyes landed on her sister's body.
"Nononononono it can't be. Val!" She stood up and nearly collapsed. Zen held her steady. "Take me to her." She looked up at Zen.

"Kal, are you sure?" Zen said, before he got a chance to look at her face.

"I said, Take. Me. To. Her." She was determined to see Val's body. She knelt beside her sister and took her hand into her own. "I'm sorry, I'm so sorry. I didn't protect you."

Tears flowed freely from her eyes. We all stood around Kal paying our last respects to our fallen comrade. I knelt down beside Kal. She stood shakily. I bent down and picked up Val's body. It was so light, as if life had lent it weight and now lifeless she would float away.

"Put her here, Dante." She stood before the monitor's obelisk. I gently placed her body at the obelisk. I stood back and gave her some space. "I promise you, Valeria, you will not have died in vain," she whispered softly. After a few moments, she stood with a new resolve on her face.

"Let's go, Dante, she is at peace now."

We made our way to the entrance of the Watch proper.

CHAPTER FORTY THREE-KEEPER

The first thing I noticed was the immensity of the Watch. Having never been in a Watch before, I didn't know if this was the typical design. It felt like being inside a giant cathedral. The ceiling was vaulted and ornate. Each of the walls depicted murals of large scale battles or vistas that seemed to go on forever. Many of the columns had statues carved into them. The floor was polished to a high gloss. The red marble, at least it resembled marble, was a rich, deep color. Our footsteps echoed in the atrium and I got the impression we weren't alone. At the end of the atrium was a pair of brass doors that were intricately designed. On each door, the monitor's emblem was etched in a deep blue, almost black. Sylk walked over to the doors and whispered some words I couldn't hear, causing the doors to begin to hum. I saw the crescents shift and turn to form a circle with interlocked owls. Looking nothing like the monitor's emblem, the circle shifted from blue to red, outlined in white.

"These doors predate monitors by about a hundred years. Beyond this point, touch nothing unless instructed," Sylk said, his voice raspy. A look of concern crossed Meja's face. Once we were inside, I could immediately sense the difference. The space was still cavernous but it felt lived in. We entered what appeared to be an antechamber. Around the room were spacious sofas or lounge chairs. In some areas were wooden benches. Sitting on one of the benches was a very old man. He appeared to be at least eighty or ninety years old. In his hands was a large mug of steaming liquid. It reminded me of how long it had been since I had eaten anything beyond our provisions of dried food and water. The old man didn't look up at us. He sat there with his eyes closed, as if savoring the aroma of the liquid. We drew closer and Sylk stopped before him. After some time the old man sighed, as if interrupting a reverie. He had been perfectly still up to that point. He opened his eyes, which to my surprise were pupil-less. His eyes were a deep blue. There was no discernible difference between what was usually the iris or the white of the eye. Everything was a deep blue. It was unsettling to say the least.

"Welcome," the old man said, his voice deep and robust. Sylk bowed as best as he could in his state. We took this as a cue to follow suit. The old man stood slowly as if feeling his years. He looked intently at Sylk as if gauging his words. He wore a simple blue robe that matched the color of his eyes, and in his left hand, he held a simple wooden staff that he used to stand. The staff also served as a walking stick as he stepped closer to Sylk. I could feel the power emanating from him. He placed his mug down on one of the tables and placed one hand on Sylk.

"One more sunset and one more sunrise, that is all that is left to you, Karashihan." Sylk remained silent. Judging from the way he looked, I guessed the old man was pretty accurate.

"Do you seek the end of your days? If so, then you need to do nothing. It will happen soon enough."

Sylk shook his head.

"Then you seek to remain here?"

"Yes, yes I do," whispered Sylk.

"Are you prepared for the cost?"

"Yes, I am."

"We shall see, walk with me." The old man turned to exit the room and walked down one of the dimly lit corridors. The corridor was one of four facing what I could only describe as a rock garden.

Within the garden were large boulders with lines of gravel and sand surrounding them. Trees grew throughout the space. At first it seemed the trees were placed randomly, but after a moment a pattern emerged, or so I thought. We wound our way around the garden as I wondered where everyone else was. Aside from the monitors killed by Diana, I saw no one else but our group and the old man. In the center of the garden ran a stream that deposited into a small lake that was crossed by several wooden bridges. At the edge of the lake were three stone benches side by side. The old man made his way to the center bench and beckoned Sylk to sit beside him. The rest of us filled the other benches, except Zen who remained standing.

"What will you do if I return your life to you, Karashihan?" asked the old man. A smile played upon his lips.

"I will prepare him," he said, gesturing to me, "for the threat that is coming," said Sylk. The old man turned to look at me as if for the first time. I couldn't tell if he saw me or not, but I got the distinct feeling nothing went unnoticed by him.

"I see he bears a named weapon, one of the three. Is this not preparation enough?"

"He has no skill in its use. He is not ready and we need a syllabist."

Well, thanks for the glowing review, Sylk.

"Do you realize the threat that this weapon presents, Karashihan? Do you remember the last time it was unleashed?"

"I do."

"And you still feel it is the answer to the upcoming threat?"

"Yes, we were fortunate to have one of the three." The old man nodded as if agreeing to something.

"Very well, then, the cost. What are you willing to give as payment?"

"I pledge my life to the Watch," said Sylk. Meja, who had been serious throughout this exchange, gave a sharp inhalation. The old man looked out over the lake, saying nothing.

"This is no small thing, Karashihan. Once pledged, you will be bound to the Watch. Are you certain?" The old man turned to face Sylk, his expression serious.

"Yes, I am."

"What does that mean?" I asked Meja, who was looking at Sylk in disbelief.

"It means that once he is done with what he considers preparing you, he must come back and live here, permanently."

"Is that a bad thing?"

"For someone like Sylk, it would be like putting you in a box or a cell. Yes, it is a bad thing."

"What if he doesn't do this?"

"Then he dies," she said.

Life imprisonment or death, didn't seem like either was a good choice. I stood and was about to head to Sylk but Meja grabbed me by the wrist. "Watch your words. That old man is an embodiment of the Watch. He could kill you with a blink."

That made me pause. I headed over slowly. Sylk and the old man turned to face me and I asked the most burning question first.

"Why?"

The old man answered. "The Karashihan feels you will be enough of a deterrent to the entity that seeks the destruction of all."

Sylk looked at me, with a lopsided grin and said, "Not much of a choice. If I don't do this, I have about a day left. At least this way, I can help prevent the imminent destruction of this and other planes of existence."

"But you will be a prisoner here, won't you?"

"That's a very strong term. I wouldn't say prisoner, more like caretaker or executor."

"Would you be able to leave this place?"

"Not in the conventional sense, no. This does not mean that I will be trapped."

I remained silent. It didn't seem like there were many options. He appeared to be getting weaker by the hour.

"It doesn't appear like I have much of a choice at this point," he said echoing my thoughts. Out of the corner of my eye, I saw Meja stand and walk over. This didn't look good.

"Why don't you just accept death?" she asked. Sylk looked at her and then turned to look at the lake the still surface reflecting the garden and trees.

"I still have a few things left to accomplish, things that I cannot do if I am dead. Rest assured, monitor, that when my time comes, I will face it as I am called upon to do so."

Meja didn't seem satisfied. She turned to the old man, a little less indignantly. "Why, why are you letting him do this? He deserves to die. He has slain many, whose only offense was to stand against him."

The old man stared at her with those bottomless eyes.

"Before monitors and warriors, I was. Before Karashihan past and present, I was. I have seen countless ages come and go. Your life is but a passing thought in the scheme of all things. If I allow this, it is because it serves a purpose you may not see, and may never be able to see. I sense that this is not enough to quell the rage within you, so perhaps another answer will suffice. Give me your hand." Meja slowly extended her hand to the old man. He clasped it in his gnarled hand and pulled Meja a little closer. As he pulled her hand, I noticed that his eyes shifted across the spectrum of color. "This is one of the most probable outcomes if the Karashihan is removed at this time." He looked into her face closely and I knew she was seeing something horrific from the way her face contorted in pain and disgust.

"No more, no more," she whispered, tears streaming down her face.

"Was that answer sufficient, monitor?" She nodded.

"Very well, let us do what must be done." The old man stood and began walking to the lake. Sylk followed him. When they were both at the edge, the old man pointed with his staff.

"In the center of the lake lies a chest. In the chest lies the medallion of Sacrifice. If you manage to locate the chest and if you are allowed to wear the medallion, then your offer will be accepted, your pledge will be valid and you will be restored." He swung the staff at all of us. "They cannot assist you in any way whatsoever."

He grasped the staff with both hands and stood facing Sylk. "If your offer is rejected, this will be your final resting place. Not bad as resting places go." And with that the old man disappeared.

Mara began walking towards Sylk but he stopped her with an upheld hand.

"No, I must do this alone."

"But you cannot! Not in your condition."

"I must. Sylk was intractable and his voice indicated that the conversation was over. He jumped head first into the lake.

CHAPTER FORTY FOUR-REBIRTH

We all stood beside the lake. All of us except Meja. She had moved over to stand beside one of the trees that encircled the lake. I walked over to her.

"Hey, you okay?"

"No, not really. The things I saw, the death and destruction," she choked up, her eyes watering anew. I had no way of knowing what she saw, but if she was this shaken up, it had to be bad.

"Dante, imagine the most horrific expression of Hell on Earth. Take that and magnify it one-hundred fold. That image will seem like a vacation compared to the visions shown to me."

I remained silent a moment, thinking.

"So what are our options?"

"If he doesn't return, we will have very few options," she said, looking at the lake.

At the edge of the lake stood Mara, silent and expectant. The day was starting to wind down and at least an hour had passed since Sylk entered the lake. From the other side of the garden approached a young man. He was dressed simply in a blue robe with white accents. His shaven head glistened in the afternoon light. He was of average height and wiry and his hands gave the impression of hidden strength. His tan skin contrasted well with the colors of the robe and I wondered how old he was, since he didn't look a day over twenty. As he made his way over to us, I noticed that he didn't so much step as glide to where we were. Everything about him indicated that he was considerably trained. I was suddenly glad we were not meeting as adversaries. He stopped a few paces from us, placed his hands together before him in prayer fashion and bowed.

"Hello, my name is Rin. I have been instructed to show you where you may lodge while the Karashihan undergoes his trial."

"Do you have anything to eat?" asked Zen. I'm starving."

Rin smiled and outstretched his arm. "If you follow me, I will show you where you can leave your things and eat." His voice gave no indication of his age.

Mara turned to Rin. "May I stay here?"

Rin bowed to her. Did he know her or was she someone special?

"You are welcome to keep a vigil if you desire," Rin said.

"How long do these trials take, usually?"

Rin shook his head as he turned to Zen. "That is impossible to say, Guardian. Each trial is unique. What appears as a lake on the surface is very different beneath it. I will say this: the only other attempt at the medallion lasted two days, but he did not return."

"How long ago was that?" I asked. He turned to me.

"That was fifty years ago." So he was much older than he seemed. Although his eyes were not completely filled in like the old man, I wondered if it was a gradual process.

"Are you like the old man?" I ventured.

"Do you mean the keeper of the Watch?" His eyes opened in surprise. "You have seen him?"

I nodded. Controlling his surprise, he answered. "No, I am not like him; I am very much like all of you, flesh and blood. You have indeed had a special privilege to meet the keeper. Some of us live out our entire lives here and only catch brief glimpses of him. He usually only appears to the most senior of us." He shook his head in genuine amazement and looked at us again, as if seeing us for the first time. "This way, please. I will take you to your rooms."

We followed him to a path in the garden that I had not noticed before. Mara remained behind and sat on one of the benches. I looked at the lake again and wondered what was happening to Sylk. Our rooms were palatial along the same line of the antechamber —each room cool but not uncomfortable. All of the rooms were adjoining. In the central room, which was a common meeting room, there was a table with a variety of bread, cheeses and fruits. I didn't realize how hungry I was until I saw the food. I noticed that each of the rooms was connected to this central room. The common room itself was a pentagon, each side being formed by one wall of our rooms. I realized that the pattern was a pentagon inside of a pentagon. Zen made a beeline for the food as I noticed the absence of any meat. Meja saw the question on my face. "Most monitors abstain from eating any kind of meat," she said.

"Really, why?"

"It was thought to enhance their abilities as monitors. It's no longer required to give up meat, but a place like this, I'm sure would adhere to the old ways."

I walked over to the table with the food, helping myself to ample amounts of bread, cheese and fruit. In pitchers around the table was what appeared to be water. I filled a large glass and was about to drink when Rin put his hand on my wrist. "You may want to drink that in small amounts. Think caffeine that's super concentrated without any of the ill side effects."

I noticed that the others were taking very small sips with their food. I took a small sip and instantly felt revitalized. I felt as if I had slept an entire night and was well rested. I was still hungry but only slightly so.

"What is this drink called?" I asked.

"The original name has been lost over time. Thankfully we still retain the means to make it. I fear we are the only Watch that still produces it. At one time this was present in every Watch. We call it manar and it is best taken in a small dose, that is if you want to sleep," he said and laughed. "We brought it out because we knew your path ahead will be long."

"Hmm, manar," said Zen as he sipped his glass. I took another sip and my hunger vanished. "You should still eat. You will need the nutrients. Manar is excellent but it will not replace food indefinitely," said Rin. I forced myself to eat and then made my way to where Meja was.

"What's wrong? Are you okay?"

"Not really. Part of me wishes he never gets out of that lake, but what I saw, Dante, the things I saw." It was rare for Meja to be so frank with me so I did the smartest thing I could think of – I remained silent. The silence stretched out between us. I tried to give her some small comfort.

"The keeper did say it was probable, not certain," I said quietly.

"If there is a slight chance of that ever coming to pass, I would rather die first." There was nothing I could say. I looked into her emerald eyes and saw fear, anger and determination in them. I noticed just how beautiful she was. I also recalled just how dangerous. I decided it would be wiser to keep my feelings to myself.

"We will be ready, don't worry," I tried to assure her. Too late I realized that I had allowed my testosterone to cloud my brain function. I could see the walls go up immediately as she pierced me with a look.

"I *am* concerned, as you should be. As for getting ready, I don't need to be ready —you do. I am going to bed."

She headed to her room and Kal followed her. I hadn't heard a word from Kalysta since her sister died earlier. I wondered how she was doing. What a group we were. Not for the first time I thought about how we were going to accomplish saving not only our plane but every one that was connected to ours. Zen headed to where I was sitting, food being his primary focus.

"I'm worried, Zen," I told him as he sat down with the largest piece of bread I had ever seen.

"About… what?" he said in between mouthfuls.

"If Sylk doesn't come back, if my weapon takes over, if Kal decides life isn't worth living without Val. What the threat I'm supposed to be ready for is? You know, little things like that."

He looked at me a long time without answering. So long in fact that I was beginning to think I stunned him into silence.

"Dante," he said after a while. "You are worrying about things and events you cannot control or influence, at least not yet. All this energy you are putting into worrying about this stuff, you can divert into learning about your weapon, and getting ready."

He had a point.

"Listen, why don't you sleep on all of that? I'm sure if Sylk decides to surface, while we are asleep, someone will come get us. Mara is at the lake and I'm sure she will be the first to say something when he comes back."

"You said when not if that time," I pointed out "You know something we don't?"

"The only thing I do know is that if he doesn't come back, this whole expedition just became much harder. He may be creepy but something tells me we need him on our side."

"I'm not sure he is on any side, but his own, Zen."

While we were speaking, he had finished his food.

"Why don't you go to bed? I think I'll be up a while longer, see if I can convince Rin about the importance of meat in a guardian's diet." I looked at him and we broke into laughter, his huge frame shaking.

"You should have seen your face! I'm kidding, D., really, so get some sleep. I'll see you in the morning." I headed off to my room, which was directly opposite Meja's. As I undressed and got ready for bed, I had serious doubts about actually getting any sleep, partly due to the manar. I lay on the bed wide awake, looking at the ceiling.

At some point, exhaustion must have taken over because I found myself in a large green field. Everywhere I could see there was grass. Somehow I knew this was a dream. Interspersed on this field were immense boulders the size of houses. I walked over to the nearest boulder and ran my hand over it. Parts were worn smooth while others had the rough texture of heavy grain sandpaper. On the boulder farthest from me sat a figure. I couldn't make out the face. As I drew closer a sense of familiarity washed over me. The figure leapt from the boulder and landed gracefully on one foot a short distance from me. He was dressed in black. —black leather pants topped off with a black silk shirt. A black long coat finished the ensemble. The coat itself had red brocade that ran the entire edge of it. His hair was salt and pepper and cut short. He looked to be in phenomenal shape. The most striking feature was his face. His piercing eyes looked into mine as he took me in. "You look like shit." And then he laughed. It wasn't a pleasant sound. His face was my face, aged several years.

"Hello, Maelstrom," I said as coldly as I could.

"*We really need to keep meeting like this, Dante. What's this place? Your field of dreams? It's quaint,*" he said as he looked around.

"What do you want?"

He turned to me. "*Now that is a most interesting question, don't you think?*"

"You almost got me killed with the Rah Ven," I stated matter of factly.

"*It would have merely precipitated the most probable outcome of our relationship. Face it, vessel, you can't handle this, can't handle me. The sooner we resolve this, the better it is for both of us.*"

"By resolve, you mean my death."

"*Well, yes. It's the fastest way to extricate myself from this uneven yoke. Truly I don't know how this occurred when I think of the warriors I have been joined with. You are but a pale shadow of them."*

"You are right. This was thrust upon me. I didn't ask for it," I said slowly.

"Exactly, you were not adequately prepared. You have very little training and next to no proficiency in the words of power."

I remained silent, looking at the older image of me, realizing for the first time that this was the true battle. Maelstrom's purpose was aligned to whoever wielded it. It was neither good nor evil; it was a weapon completely in the control of the person it was bonded to. This was why it was on this campaign to get me killed. It wasn't that I wasn't ready or couldn't control it —even though on many levels this was true, the real reason was that it chafed at being subjected to another will other than its own.

"When was the last time you were bonded to a vessel, that you deemed worthy?"

He glared at me for a moment then turned away and looked off into the distance.

"How long?" I asked again softly, knowing the answer.

He turned to face me again. I stood there feeling a soft breeze blow against us. The grass waved to and fro and I had to remind myself that this was a dream.

I felt a hand rest on my shoulder and looked to my right to see Owl standing there.

The shock must have registered on my face and Owl smiled. He was dressed in white robes with gold trim. He turned to face a snarling Maelstrom.

"You have no call to be here. This is between the vessel and I," said Maelstrom.

"I am as much a part of him as are you.*"*

"You are not the weapon and have no right to be heard."

"I have every right to be here. Why don't you answer his question?"

"Because it is of no consequence!" spat out Maelstrom.

Owl clasped his hands before him and looked to the sky. "I disagree. That question above all others is the most relevant. Normally you are quick to action and here you hesitate. Shall I answer the boy?"

"You pretend to know me? I who have existed for millennia? Who saw the birth and death of

countless stars? Who has seen the rise and fall of man as I have?"

"All that means is that you are old —very very old. Wisdom is not a condition of age, nor is age a prerequisite of wisdom," said Owl. Maelstrom crossed his arms and glared. I had gotten over my shock at seeing Owl here. Somehow it wasn't so surprising and made sense in a strange way.

"I will tell you the answer he cannot, because he knows it will be his undoing." Owl looked at Maelstrom with something like pity in his eyes. "Every vessel this weapon has possessed has died an untimely death shortly after bonding with it. Just as you would have had you attacked the Rah Ven, causing your death and the death of your comrades." Even in a dream I felt my throat close and my mouth go dry. I had been so close to total destruction.

"Why?" was all I could manage.

"This existence is a punishment for the being that he once was. He who controlled multitudes must now surrender to control. Throughout all this time that one trait was allowed to persist. And so although he may no longer have any recollection of what it was to be as he was, he still remembers what it is to be free. Being bonded robs him of that and so he plots and schemes his vessels death to be free once again."

"It's not so simple but I don't expect you to understand, vessel. Suffice it to say that your death eases this curse I call being. So what say you now Dante? Now that you know the answer to your question, what is your reply?"

Owl looked at me. The wind was blowing stronger now and clouds had gathered on the horizon. Somehow I knew this meant the dream was coming to an end.

"Maelstrom, I know you can't be free without my death and I have grown fond of living as of late. I can assure you that if there is a way to attain your freedom and my life, then I will find it. Until then, can we establish a truce?" I extended my hand towards him. *"Will you really do this, do I have your word as bond?"* he asked.

"If I do not honor my word, may my life be forfeit." Maelstrom smiled a smile that turned my stomach. *"This is agreeable."* he said above the ever-increasing wind. *"A truce for now and let us see where this takes us, vessel."* He clasped my hand and I awoke. From the light streaming in, I could tell it was morning. I felt refreshed but I attributed that to the manar, not my dream. I made my way to the common area. It must have been very early since the area was deserted. The others were probably sleeping still. As I sat down to think about the dream and what it meant, the old man appeared next to me. As much as I have seen and experienced, that still startled me and I jumped, my heart beating rapidly. I think he did it on purpose because he was chuckling at my reaction , at least I thought it was chuckling since it sounded like rubbing two stones together.

"My apologies. I did not mean to startle you." Yeah right. I could see the mischief in his eyes.

"It's fine, still getting used to everything."

"Sometimes our dreams can be quite unsettling, no?"

"How did you? – no, never mind." He waved his hand as if dismissing my words, then moved closer. "When Rin approaches you today," he angled his head and looked up, "and that should be shortly, tell him you need Samir to teach you."

"Who is Samir?"

"He is the worst syllabist we have in the Watch. Or so everyone thinks. He has talents that are not easily seen."

"How do I know Rin will honor my request?"

"At first, he will not and will try to push you off to accept one of the other syllabists. Do not let him dissuade you. Insist for Samir and you will attain what you need. Accept another and you will receive what you want."

"Do I tell him you told me to ask for Samir?"

"There will be no need if you remain firm. He will honor the request. If you refrain from mentioning my name, then he too can learn from the moment. That, I leave to you. The path you are upon will be altered if Samir is not your syllabist."

I let the words sit with me as I absorbed them. As I turned to ask the old man another question, I realized I was alone in the room. As I sat wondering how he disappeared so effortlessly, Mara came rushing in, her face flushed with excitement.

"He's back! He just surfaced!" she gasped, out of breath.

"What? Where?" I asked.

"The lake, he's there and he's been changed somehow. I don't know, something's not the same."

"Let's go." And we ran off to the lake, Mara and I, without alerting any of the others. As we approached the lake I saw a figure near one of the benches. It seemed to shimmer like heat in a desert. After a moment, it seemed to coalesce.

"Karashihan, is that you?" Mara asked.

It looked like Sylk, except now his hair was silver; his face looked the same, maybe a few more lines, as if he had aged. His right pectoral was covered in silver lines forming ornate symbols. The most surprising change was his missing arm. It wasn't missing any longer.

CHAPTER FORTY FIVE-SYLLABIST

"Yes Mara, it's me." She looked dubiously at him for a moment then bowed at his feet.

"Karashihan for a moment I wasn't sure, forgive my doubt."

"No forgiveness is required. I myself had a few moments to be concerned, but as you see, I have returned. Please stand."

"It would seem that you have."

I turned, startled, to see the old man leaning on his staff. He smiled at my expression and I swore he got some hidden enjoyment from making me jump.

"Well met, old one." Sylk bowed.

"Well met indeed. I see the medallion has accepted your pledge. What are the terms?"

"I will be granted leave until such a time as the warrior no longer requires my presence."

The keeper nodded as if considering the terms.

"Gifts bestowed?" The keeper drew close to Sylk and narrowed his eyes.

"Life, restoration of what was lost and wisdom."

"Very good," said the keeper. Mara and I stood to one side as this exchange took place. We were both unprepared for the keeper's next move. Standing three feet from Sylk, the keeper began to walk away leaning heavily on his staff. If I had blinked I would have missed the motion. Even as I saw it, I couldn't believe anyone could move that fast. As he took a step away from Sylk, he thrust the staff behind him. The weapon was a blur. Sylk must have sensed something or been on his guard because he stepped to the side in a fraction of a second, the staff missing him by a hairsbreadth. The keeper, who looked about a hundred years old seconds earlier suddenly began moving like a young man in his prime. He swung the staff around in a descending arc; Sylk leapt back at the last possible moment avoiding having his knee shattered. The keeper now facing Sylk began to close the distance, walking slowly. I looked around. No one was close. The lake was quiet, resembling glass. Around us everything was still, even the birds that were singing earlier had gone silent, as if watching in anticipation of the outcome. The sky was a clear blue with the sun rising on the far side of the lake. The setting could not have been more serene, except for the keeper intent on striking Sylk. It was almost perfect. Sylk who emerged topless from the lake, stood still as the keeper approached. The symbols on his body began to shift and run, like liquid mercury. They began to travel down his right arm, encasing his entire right side from the waist up in what looked like silver skin. The keeper drew close and thrust. Sylk parried with his right arm. I half expected to hear a metallic clang, but it was as if sound had been muffled. The keeper ducked and swept his right foot across to catch Sylk unaware. Sylk did a hop step, avoiding the sweep, ducking in time to miss the staff from crashing into his temple. The keeper leapt, much higher than I thought possible. Staff in both hands, held overhead, he reached at least twenty feet. As he came down, I saw that the staff was radiating a dull blue green. I began to back up, pulling Mara with me. She looked askance and I pulled her faster. Something told me we didn't want to be close when that staff connected with Sylk's enhanced arm. Maelstrom reflexively reacted to my heightened level of anxiety and appeared in my hand.

"*I see the Karashihan has returned with the medallion of sacrifice in place.*" It was always disconcerting to hear my voice being used by Maelstrom.

"*You are still too close. In fact even if you left the Watch you would be too close. Place me in the ground quickly.*" I did as he said "*Now focus on a sphere, an entire sphere surrounding you. Make it wide enough to encompass both of you, unless you no longer wish to see her among the living.*" I could almost see his smile. "*Vessel, I would do this quickly, or you will no longer be a vessel.*" I focused on a sphere surrounding us. In my mind's eye, I placed Mara and me inside a large ball. "*That should do, now hold that image, do not let it waver."* I took the suggestion seriously and found myself encased in a shimmering sphere of violet energy. *"Maintain your focus, it should be any moment now."* I felt the impact as I saw the keeper bring the staff crashing down into Sylk's arm. It felt like getting kicked in the stomach, hard. I almost lost the sphere but regained focus right away. The light was blinding. I heard the staff splinter and felt the ground shake. When I opened my eyes, it looked as if we had been transported to ground zero of an immense explosion. We were in an impact crater. The ground sloped up away from us at least four feet. I looked and saw Sylk and the keeper facing each other, smoke wafting from their bodies. It seemed like they were speaking, but my ears felt like they were full of cotton. Maelstrom was gone but Mara and I were intact and that's what mattered. We started to walk back cautiously and as we drew closer, the landscape behind us began to shift and alter, returning to a pristine state. By the time we were close enough to hear Sylk and the Keeper speaking, it was as if nothing had occurred.

"What just happened?" I asked.

"The Watch is self-regulating. Any damage done to it is immediately repaired," said the Keeper.

"Not that," – even though it was interesting to note that the Watch could do that. "I mean between you two."

"Oh that," the Keeper said dismissively. "A small test to measure the commitment of the pledge made. Had it been found wanting, the Karashihan would not be here to partake in this conversation on such a pleasant day."

Sylk bowed. The Keeper looked at me and chuckled.

"It's good to see you were aware enough to protect yourself. It would have been a shame to lose you."

I was speechless. I looked to Sylk but I couldn't read his face. Before I could say another word, the Keeper moved his hands and a new staff formed in them. "I believe you have more pressing matters to attend to, like procuring a syllabist? Ah, here comes Rin now, perfect."

I turned to see Rin walking to us. He bowed, and the Keeper returned the bow.

"Is everything well? We heard an awful sound," said Rin.

"Everything is as it should be," said the Keeper. Rin bowed in response. The Keeper looked at me pointedly, with a smile on his lips, as if waiting to see how it would all play out. I got the underlying feeling we were all just pieces on an immense chess board. I cleared my throat. "Good morning, Rin," I said and bowed. He bowed in return. "We need a syllabist."

"Ah! I have just the one! His name is Eric and he is our top syllabist. You will not—"

"How about Samir?"

I could swear the Keeper was enjoying this entirely too much. Rin, who had stopped mid-sentence while extolling the virtues of Eric, looked as if he had bitten into a lemon.

"Samir—" He drew out the name as if I had been mistaken. "How do you—"

"It's the syllabist I want," I said as I cut him off.

"Surely you realize this is no light task. The training of a warrior of your caliber requires, no, demands the very best. Are you certain you want him?"

The last word was uttered with such disdain that I almost reconsidered. I took a deep breath and exhaled, hoping I didn't regret listening to the Keeper.

"Yes, I am certain. Please have him meet us in the common room." Rin hesitated a while longer.

"Rin, you did say he is a syllabist, yes?"

"Well, yes, technically."

"Well, does he hold the title or not?"

Rin, defeated, sighed. "I suppose he does," he said dejectedly.

"Excellent. Please give him the news and have him meet us in the common area."

Rin headed off to get Samir. Mara looked at me with a question on her face. A question I didn't have the answer to. I looked at the Keeper, who I could say with near certainty was suppressing laughter. "I hope you're right about this."

Finally he let out the laughter, full of mirth. It was a pleasant sound, and even Sylk smiled, caught by its contagious nature.

"Me too!" he replied. Shocked, I looked at him.

"But this was your idea! You told me to pick Samir—"

The Keeper held up his hand. "I know my words, warrior and stand by them. Come let us see

341

to your syllabist." He headed off in the direction of the rooms.

I looked at Sylk who shrugged and followed the Keeper, trailed by Mara.

"I can't believe this," I muttered to myself. And I followed them.

CHAPTER FORTY SIX-BOOK AND COVER

We arrived at the common area as everyone was stirring. There was food arranged on one of the tables, plenty of everything, except meat, much to Zen's dismay.

"Really? Would a little meat kill them? I mean, come on."

"No, it wouldn't kill them but it would violate their way of life," said Kal quietly. Everyone turned in our direction as they heard us approach, most looked shocked to see Sylk again and whole. Only Meja remained reserved. She looked him over as if assessing the changes and then nodded, returning to her breakfast. Everyone began to fill their plates with breads and cheeses and other assorted cereals and fruits, of which there was an abundance.

"Good morning," I said as I sat next to Meja. She clearly didn't want to speak but I trudged on anyway.

"Morning," she said. An arctic winter was probably warmer than she was at this moment. Undaunted, I forged ahead.

"Did you see Sylk, and his arm?" Someone of course needed to state the obvious and of course that someone was me. She looked at me as if I had smacked my head against one of the marble floors, repeatedly.

"What do you want?" she asked tersely.

"I just wanted to know if you're doing better, than yesterday that is." I stood to walk away realizing that I was daring, but not insane. As I stood, she looked at me with a look I had never seen from her. Something close to concern crossed her face. "Dante?" I turned to look at her. Once again as it always did, her beauty threatened to make me say something I would definitely regret.

"Yes?" I said, hoping for a slight thaw in her reaction. I was disappointed.

"You need to stop worrying about me, about any of us, and focus on what you need to get done.

It's the only way we have a chance of coming out of this alive."

If she had put up walls the night before, they were now surrounded by an electrified fence, patrolled by guard dogs and covered in concertina wire.

"I got it, thanks." I turned to walk away to minimize the chance of frostbite from being in proximity to her.

"And Dante?" I turned again bracing myself for some other comment laced in pain and designed to embarrass me.

"Thanks for asking." She smiled, a real smile that reached her eyes. In that moment I knew without a doubt that I had given her my heart. My brain however didn't get that memo. As I was about to speak, Rin entered the area with a frail looking tan man in tow.

"Good morning." He bowed in our general direction. "I trust you all rested?" He didn't wait for a reply. "Before your journey to the Akashic Records, which are traversed through this Watch, I have been informed you required a syllabist. It was the warrior's request that this be your syllabist." He stepped aside and we were able to see the small man more clearly. He had jet black hair and looked fairly young. Even though I learned long ago not to judge books by their covers, he was rail thin with a muscular body. He seemed to be able to handle himself.

"I thought that is what we were heading to the Akashic Records for, to find the location of a syllabist?" Zen whispered to Meja.

He bowed to us. Then he spoke and the only word I could make out was his name. We all had the same look on our face. It was a collective "Huh?" moment.

"He says, it's a pleasure to meet you all and he hopes to be of service, his name is Samir," I turned to Rin. "He doesn't speak English?"

Rin bowed in answer. "This is the syllabist you requested, and there is only one Samir in this Watch in the capacity of syllabist." I looked at the Keeper who was conveniently looking away at that moment.

"You can't be serious. How are we supposed to communicate? Sign language?"

Somehow it felt like a cruel joke. Samir stood there as we spoke back and forth with an easy smile on his face. I could see he was paying attention, because his eyes were sharp, following each speaker in turn. I could tell Rin was rubbing it in for my not accepting his choice of Eric, the super syllabist. I walked over to the Keeper and with all the respect I could muster, I lost it. "What is this, some joke? Were you just trying to unload a defective syllabist on us? This is ridiculous!"

So sue me I have a death wish. Rin's mouth had dropped open at the way I was speaking to the Keeper. Sylk looked amused as did the Keeper, which only pissed me off more, because now I thought they are amused at my outburst and fail to see the gravity of the situation.

"He is always this way?" the Keeper asked Sylk.

Sylk looked at me and nodded. "He has a strong spirit, maybe it won't get him killed."

The Keeper turned to Samir and spoke to him in a language I couldn't grasp. Judging from the looks on everyone's faces, including Rin, no one else seemed to understand either. Except maybe Sylk, who smiled with Samir at whatever the Keeper said. "Samir has a very rare gift, one that has been overlooked in this Watch, partly because of our isolation, but more because of arrogance."

The Keeper looked at Rin who turned away, flushed. "What say you Samir?" the Keeper asked him and I prepared myself for another round of gibberish.

"My apologies," he said in halting English. "I must first be exposed to a language for some time before I can acquire correct speak? This is correct, yes?"

Rin's eyes were wide as saucers. Samir's diction was flawless and he had no trace of an accent. Except for his one mistake, he sounded like any of us.

"Correct speech," I say to him. He nodded and bowed.

"Thank you, I will remember." At this point I'm not far behind Rin in the amazement department.

"How is this possible? A few minutes ago, I couldn't understand a word he said and now he speaks as well as I do?"

Samir comes from a long line of syllabists. With each generation their gift gets stronger provided both mother and father are syllabists. As you can imagine this is a rare occurrence as the gift of tongues is rare. Samir's family however was an exception. They managed to continue the blood gift of tongues for seven generations."

Rin, still in shock, spoke. "He is a master syllabist," he said in awe.

"All this time and no one knew," Rin said quietly to himself.

The Keeper coughed. "I knew," the Keeper said quietly. "When I suggested he be evaluated, what did the Council declare?"

Council, I thought to myself. So there is a ruling body, here in the Watch.

"They decided to, umm, pursue other avenues and other candidates."

"Yes, they brushed off an old man in favor of counsel from newer, fresh blood." The Keeper was serious now.

"Surely we can't let him go with them. He is a treasure!"

The Keeper looked at him silently, sighed and put his hand on Rin's shoulder.

"A short time ago you were secretly relieved to get rid of what you considered a burden. Now you consider him a treasure. He is still the same man, is he not?" Rin was red-faced and bowed. The lesson was not lost on me since I shared in Rin's opinion of Samir and thought he could not possibly be of any help to me or to the group. In other words I judged this particular book by its cover and found it wanting. "Now go tend to the necessary preparations, they must leave for the Records as soon as possible, and as we both know it is no easy journey."

Rin bowed and left the common area trailed by at least five monitors much younger than he.

"Come, we must prepare, there are others who would see you fail and we must not give them the satisfaction."

The Keeper shuffled off through a doorway looking very much like an old man. I had many questions whirling in my head. Who wanted us to fail? Who was this Council? Why did we need to go to the Records if we had a syllabist? Zen thumped me on my arm.

"Wake up and focus, D. We need to get moving." I saw that we were the only two left in the common room. I had drifted off with my questions. Zen smirked at me. "Stop being a space cadet." I laughed to shake off the embarrassment. "Let's go."

CHAPTER FORTY SEVEN- THE AKASHIC

I had a lot of questions and few answers. The most important of them was, why go to the records if we had a syllabist and not only a syllabist but a master syllabist at that? As we headed down the brightly lit corridors, I glimpsed other monitors moving to and fro. It seemed we were approaching a more populated area of the Watch. Up ahead, I could overhear the Keeper and Sylk discussing something but I couldn't make out the details. Behind me Kal and Meja brought up the rear. I noticed once again how I seemed to be protected by placement in the group. We turned a few times more making lefts then rights, until I was convinced we were in some kind of maze. Finally we reached a door and the Keeper pushed it open to reveal a small courtyard dominated by what seemed to be an onyx obelisk. In the midst of the sunlight and bright colors, it appeared to be a sliver of night. No light reflected off of it. Each side was covered in symbols, some I thought I could make out, others were beyond me. Sylk and the Keeper reached it first. As the Keeper began walking around the obelisk, he started touching some of the symbols.

"This is an interstitial doorway. I'm assuming you are all familiar with what that is?" said the Keeper.

I raised my hand as if in school. "Not really."

The Keeper nodded at Sylk and I was almost certain that Sylk was some kind of public school educator at some point in his life. He turned to me and everything from his stance to his voice said Teacher.

"An interstitial doorway," he began and paused to see if I was paying attention and seeing that I was, he continued, "is a doorway that leads to specific places between the planes. The Records are priceless, so access to them is limited to this doorway and of course this Watch." I looked at the obelisk again. The air around it had begun to thrum in vibration.

"So you are saying the only way to get to the records is through this doorway?" I said pointing at the obelisk as the Keeper kept circling and pressing symbols. The vibration grew in intensity and I was feeling it in my lower abdomen. Sylk looked at me as if I just enjoyed stating the obvious.

"As I was saying, the Records are irreplaceable, and extremely valuable. We need to find a particular book," said Sylk

I looked at him, "You're kidding, right?"

"No, he is not. This book is instrumental for Samir to teach you to be an ascended warrior to meet the threat that seeks to engulf us all. To answer your question as to why the journey must be made if you have a syllabist, the book is as essential as the syllabist."

It was the Keeper, who it seemed had finished with the symbols on the obelisk.

"I do not subscribe to the notion that this is the only doorway to the records. I have lived too long and have seen too much for that to make sense," said the Keeper.

He looked at Sylk. "Karashihan, although the title no longer fits, eh?" Sylk nodded. "Do not believe the old wives tales or in this case the stories of old men. You do not know what awaits you in the Records, so you must be prepared." He turned to me. "You are the greatest threat, and so will be the greatest target. Keep your wits about you and remember, upon you much hinges. Each of you plays a part in what is to unfold— this is only the first step."

The Keeper stepped aside and struck his staff on the ground. The obelisk shimmered and shuddered. When it stopped it looked different. Sylk walked up to it, placed his hand on the surface and vanished. One by one, we each did the same and left the Keeper and the Watch behind.

CHAPTER FORTY EIGHT-SHERFYM

I floated weightlessly for what seemed like ten minutes. All of a sudden gravity re-established itself and I found myself in a very large corridor. I looked around and could have sworn I was in the New York Public Library. The walls were a white stone, it looked like marble. The floor was polished to a high sheen, the green stone highly reflective. The doors that were visible were of a deep brown oak, immense, and weathered with age. Each door was easily ten feet in height. This gave me pause since I have learned that large doors usually meant large beings to walk through them. Suddenly around me, I heard a series of low pops like bubble wrap being burst and found myself surrounded by children, at least I thought they were children, at least until they spoke.

"You, remain where you are!" said the one who appeared to be the leader. There were five of them and they stood phalanx style, the speaker in the center. They each had a rod in their hand, the ends of which had a dull red glow. Each of them was fair with blue eyes and long blond hair, even the males. They reminded me of a smaller version of the Watchers. Each was wearing a pair of rough leather pants and a crisp white top. The leader's pants had a gold stripe down each leg.

"State your purpose," the leader said as he took a step forward. I wondered where everyone else was, and how those rods looked painful.

"I asked you a question. Do you understand what I am saying?"

"I do," I said, trying to buy some time. Maybe the others would arrive any moment?

"Good, what are you doing here?"

I figured honesty would be the best way to approach this. "I'm looking for a book."

The leader narrowed his eyes. "Is this a jest?" He took another step forward, unsure of the threat I posed. He didn't seem the type to have a sense of humor and I wasn't about to start telling jokes.

"No, my group and I are looking for a specific book."

He looked around me for a few seconds then looked directly at me, clearly displeased. "What group?"

What group indeed, that was my last thought before he hit me with his rod. Then everything went black.

I woke up feeling pain, everything ached. Whatever that rod was, it was serious in the pain department. I looked around. I was in what appeared to be an infirmary of sorts. As I tried to sit up, I realized I was strapped in. This was not good. After a few futile attempts, I realized I wasn't going anywhere. I took in the room. There were ten beds—all of them empty, except mine. The room was bathed in natural light, or what I guessed passed as natural light. The design of the room, floor and door matched the corridor I was in earlier, so I assumed I was still in the same building. The room had a faint lavender smell to it and come to think of it, so did the hallway before I encountered what I decided to call the hallway monitors. Since I was strapped in with nowhere to go, I tried to connect with Maelstrom. There was nothing, just a large hole, a void where I always felt it to be. Had I rid myself of the weapon? Strangely, I missed its presence.

"What you are feeling is an effect of the auric flail," said a female voice. I turned to look and found her across from my bed. She was the same height as the hallway monitors, same blond hair, and same blue eyes. I wondered if they were all related. She was also strikingly beautiful. She was dressed in white and I guessed she was some kind of doctor. After my initial shock at seeing her by my side, I tried to get my mouth to work.

"The what?"

"The flail is designed to disrupt chi flow in a target. The effect is unpredictable. It can be hours or days before your flow is restored, without assistance."

"Who are you?"

"I am Mia and I am the director of this area." She spread her arms wide to indicate the infirmary.

"Maybe I should ask the most pressing question—where am I?" She looked at me seriously for a moment.

"Don't you know?" I gave her a blank look to indicate that at this point I didn't know much of anything. "This is most odd," she said. "You are in the medical facility of the complex that houses the Akashic Records. You are the first visitor we have had in one hundred years."

I let that sink in for a moment. At least now I understood the hostility. But where was everyone else, did something go wrong? Were they lost somewhere?

Thoughts raced through my head. "I have to go. I need to find the others." Though how I was going to do this escaped me. "You have been found trespassing. I can treat you but I cannot release you."

"Oh, I think you will find that his release will be very possible." It was a voice I recognized, but never expected to hear. I turned my head in the direction of the voice and there stood Devin.

For a moment, I swore I was imagining him. He strode over to the bed and made a quick gesture with his hand. I felt the straps undo themselves and Mia gasped. "You can't!" she said.

"I must," answered Devin. I was still in shock so I had no words to express my surprise. I'm pretty sure it was evident on my face though. "We need to go, now." And he grabbed me by the wrist. He was dressed all in black. It looked like silk. Every time the light hit his clothing, it danced and rippled as if on water. There were flecks of gold interwoven into the fabric that glittered every time he moved. He still looked the same and I mentally recalled the last time I saw him; he was fighting for his life.

"How did you -?" I managed, before the scent of lavender permeated the room.

"They're coming," he said and turned to face the door. He looked briefly at Mia, who held her hands up. "I had to. I would be tortured if I didn't."

Devin approached her then. "I understand."

He placed a hand on her forehead and she passed out. He placed her gently on a bed.

"She called them?"

He nodded. "All the Sherfym have the ability to communicate telepathically, it makes them very difficult to fight."

"Who are the Sherfym?" I asked.

"Later, right now we need to leave this area." He headed for the door as I stood there. Something seemed off. Why would Devin appear now, and how did I know this was really Devin?

358

"I know you have a lot of questions right now. I can assure you I'm here to help you. You can come with me or take your chances with the Black Lotus on your own. Its your choice." I figured it was better than being strapped to a bed, so I followed him.

"Stay close to me, we won't be invisible, but we will be very hard to see."

I stood next to him as he clasped his hands together and said something under his breath. As I looked at my hands, I saw they were transparent. I looked up to see, or in this instance to not see, Devin beside me. He was a vague outline, and I was able to see the wall behind him, well, through him.

"Let's go," he whispered. The smell of lavender filled the hallway and I thought I heard footsteps. We stopped suddenly at an intersection and hugged the wall. Two groups of five ran past us, headed I guessed to the infirmary. We went down several corridors that way, moving quickly at times and coming to dead stops at others. After a while I was completely disoriented and hoped that Devin knew where he was going. He stopped walking and looked around, placing his hand along the walls. "It should be here somewhere," I heard him mutter. Faintly I detected the smell of lavender.

"Devin?" I whispered.

"I smell them too, Dante. One moment." I didn't think we had many moments left.

"Ah! There it is!" He pressed on a wall and it slid in and to the side silently. "Come on!" He stepped in and I followed. The wall/door slid back into place silently. "We just bought ourselves some time. I don't think they will check the storage areas for a while, no one outside the Records really knows about these rooms." The words came rushing out. "How, what, how did you?" He held up his hand.

"First things first, we need to restore your balance, that is what Sherfym are tracking, the trace of the flail." He sat on the floor and motioned for me to do the same. He closed his eyes and placed his hands, palms in as if praying.

"Focus your chi, Dante." I tried. It felt like falling into a vast open area and said as much.

"Keep trying." I reached inward again for what seemed an eternity, I felt nothing and was about to give up, when something tugged at me.

"Yes! That's it, focus on that," he whispered.

I focused all my awareness on that sensation. The only way I could describe it is like finding an island after hours of swimming in the open ocean. It felt solid; it felt like peace, like home. I grabbed onto it with all my will and felt an explosion of energy within, unlike anything I had felt before. "That should do it." He smiled but he sounded exhausted. I felt different as well. I felt whole. When I reached in, I found the familiar sensation of Maelstrom deep within, stirring.

"We have some more time, now that you aren't a homing beacon," he said, the tiredness creeping in to his voice. I looked around. We were in what appeared to be a large closet. It was mostly empty, save except some carts and ladders I assumed were for the Records area proper.

"How did you find me?"

"What makes you think I ever lost you?"

"What do you mean?" He gave me a look as if I missed some important lesson at some point. "It means that outside of death, I will have knowledge of where you are, as your Senpai."

"But that means —" The realization dawned on me.

"Yes, I am being hunted as you are. Apparently you are too much of a threat to be allowed to live."

I tried to think of this logically and then another thought hammered into me. "Devin, don't you have a Senpai?"

His face darkened for a moment. "I did. He is no longer alive on this or any other plane." For a moment, he looked grim. Then his expression changed. "I sense your weapon has manifested. Have you learned to control it?"

I shook my head. "That was the whole purpose of coming here. Samir was looking for a book."

He looked at me and asked, "Who is Samir?"

"The others! Devin, we have to find the others! Meja, Zen, Kal, Samir, he's the syllabist, Sylk and Mara!"

"You found an actual syllabist? What kind of weapon did you manifest?" Then as if dawning slowly, he clenched his teeth and grabbed me by the shoulder. It felt like my arm was in a vise. "Did you say Sylk?" He must have seen me wince because he let up on my arm slightly.

"Yes, Sylk the Karashihan. Although he isn't that anymore," and I explained what had happened since I last saw him. He was sitting quietly as if analyzing all I had told him.

"Truly you have been in the midst of some very interesting circumstances. Someone went through great pains to separate you from the group."

"What do you mean? I got here to the Records. It's the group that never made it."

"Actually, have you considered that the Akashic Records would not have a need for an infirmary?" He let the question hang there until the realization hit me.

"But Mia, the doctor, she said —"

"They have a limited ability to read non-Sherfym minds, she merely picked up thoughts from your mind. Anything that would keep you docile. Her job was to keep you there until you were picked up. The question is, by whom?"

"So where are we?"

"This is a Sherfym stronghold. It's not even on your plane, at least not often. The Sherfym are distant relations to the Watchers you ran into, nowhere near as powerful but dangerous in their own right. Even more so in their own stronghold and plane, which I'm guessing we aren't in yet, or we would have been overrun."

"How do we get out of here?"

"We can't —that is, we can't just yet. We have to wait until whoever wants you comes and gets you. Then leave with them."

"But that means –"

"Yes, we need to wait. I will have to mask your flow so it seems as if it's still interrupted or else they will hit you again. Then we see who will visit you."

"Won't Mia remember?"

"She shouldn't, not if I did it right," he said more to himself than to me. We made our way back to the hallway that led to the infirmary, when the smell of lavender encircled us. We both looked at each other and ran. As we entered the infirmary, I noticed Mia was still in the bed where Devin had placed her.

"Quickly!" he whispered. I jumped into the bed and he readjusted the straps.

"Don't say anything," he cautioned, "and whatever you do, do not manifest your chi." I understood the implications. He turned and looked towards the door. "I'll be close, don't worry." Every time I heard those words they had the exact opposite effect.

CHAPTER FORTY NINE-CAPTURE

"My master will be most displeased if he is not here." I overheard the voices in the hall as I feigned sleep. Mia was stirring and I heard her get up.

"Oh my head," she moaned. She came over to my side and gently shook me.

As I opened my eyes I could see she was struggling with a headache.

"Wake up. They have come for you."

"Who? Who has come for me?"

"I do not know. I was only instructed to keep you here. Oh my head. Please excuse me a moment." I sensed rather than saw the group enter the room. A tall dark figure dominated the group. He stood at least six feet tall, which meant he dwarfed the Sherfym. His jet black hair hung straight and framed his face. He seemed to be of average build but his movements spoke of an underlying strength that rested beneath the surface. He wore a form fitting garment that was similar to what monitors wore, except his were black. Something about him reminded me of Sylk. It had to be his composure and carriage. If he wasn't royalty, he was the closest thing to it. He turned away from the Sherfym he was speaking to, the same one that hit me initially.

"Is this the one" the Sherfym asked. Tall, dark and scary looked me over, the same way a wolf might look at its next meal.

"Yes, yes I do believe it is." He handed over a small satchel to the Sherfym leader. The Sherfym bowed and left the room. The leader however turned at the door. "Be wary. Great power resides in that one." He bowed and left the room.

CHAPTER FIFTY-REASONS

"I can sense you're awake, so let's just stop the pretending." I opened my eyes fully.

"Let's keep the straps on for a moment, shall we?" He sat at the foot of my bed as if he were a relative visiting an ill member of the family.

"I'm certain you have many questions, yes?"

"You could say that."

He looked at me expectantly. "Well?" he said, fixing me with a look that meant I should be asking my questions.

"Who are you?" He waved his hand at me as if waving the question away. "Surely you can do better than that."

I remained still and thought. "Why me? Why are you chasing me?"

"Excellent! A much better question, don't you think? Why you, indeed. It had been the question I had been asking myself from the beginning. You were sent to the warriors because you are unique. So unique in fact that many prefer you dead than alive." He paused.

"Which group do you belong to?" I asked warily.

"Right now I belong to the group that prefers you breathing; the interesting part is that there are a few of that same group that would rather you stop."

"Stop what?"

"Breathing, am I not being clear? Never mind, suffice it to say you are to remain among us for the time being."

"So, what makes me so unique?" I asked, trying to stall the inevitable.

"You see, Dante, I may call you Dante? It's not just the fact that you can manifest a powerful weapon, one of the three foci. It's what you will be able to do with that weapon once you have ascended."

"Ascended, ascended to what?"

"Hmm, they didn't tell you? I swear, these warriors of the Way are getting sloppy."

"I didn't have much time for training, what with being hunted."

"Well, there is that. Very well, to truly master your weapon, you have to become completely merged with it, no barriers, and no compartments. You and your weapon are one, an extension of each other."

I didn't like where this was going but I remained silent. "So does this require some special training?"

"You could say that."

"What do you mean?" He stood up and started removing items from his pockets and placing them around me on the bed. They were small spheres, opaque and grey. "This should make your trip a bit easier and prevent any detours —know what I mean?"

"You didn't answer my question."

"I know, Dante, and frankly I'm not certain you are going to like the answer. Are you sure you want it?"

"Yes," I said without hesitation.

"Of course you would," he said. "Very well but before I continue, understand that this is what I have learned from research and not first hand. Be that as it may, it's very reliable."

I nodded. He sat on the bed directly across from me so I had to turn my head right to look at him.

"Long ago, and I mean hundreds of years ago, there were many Ascendants, both guardians and warriors. Over time, it was being noted that the number of Ascendants were diminishing, nothing great at first but after many years, it became more and more pronounced."

"What caused it?"

"No one knows for certain. Some say bloodlines were involved, others say it was a scheme of the first Karashihan. Whatever the cause, the end result was less and less Ascendants." I looked at him quizzically. "Oh yes, you wouldn't know —well without enough Ascendants the barriers of a plane, any plane, collapse. Which means easy access, no need for portals or mirrors, basically the front door is open, so is the back door, the side doors too."

"That can't be good."

"No it isn't, at least for the inhabitants of the plane in question. So a plan was formed to create ascendants, sort of breed them. Whenever a warrior or guardian exhibited the correct traits or abilities, he would be a candidate for Ascension. Many never overcame the first part of the process and after some time it was stopped once a stabilizing number of ascendants were created."

"Why start again?"

"Well, ascendants are notoriously hard to kill. They aren't immortal, just long lived, not to mention incredibly skilled fighters. Lately someone or something has found a way to kill Ascendants. This is not a good thing, considering the entities that would enjoy your plane."

"And that first part that many failed to overcome?"

"Oh that, yes, you have to die."

CHAPTER FIFTY ONE-ROMAN

"I have to what!?" Panic began a little dance in my stomach.

"Obviously it's not permanent. Think of it as a reset of sorts."

"A reset of sorts? You mean I have to die, be dead? And this is a reset of sorts?"

"Hey, you asked. I was quite content to just deliver you, ignorance intact."

"Deliver me where?" I asked off-handedly.

He smiled. "That's not for me to divulge at this moment, I'm afraid."

"Fine." I didn't think it would work but it was worth a try. "Let's get back to the dying part. Why do I need to die, and how is this done?"

He checked his watch and nodded to himself as if making certain of something. "Throughout time and cross culturally, this component of ritual death has existed. You are familiar with the concept, yes?"

I nodded, too stunned to even form words.

"Good, well it turns out they were on to something. The entire process of death and revival, under the right circumstances can create or at least trigger Ascension."

This had to be some twisted nightmare. "How many Ascendants are needed to keep the barriers intact?"

He narrowed his eyes and looked at me. "That is the best question you have asked so far."

"The answer being?"

"Well from what I have heard, it's 100 per plane, although I have other numbers, 100 comes up more often than not."

"What happens if it falls below that number?"

"Ah, this is the interesting part. After the threshold number is reduced, things go crazy. Instability becomes rampant and the plane barriers are diminished enough to allow unrestricted access. We start getting visitors we would rather not have, mostly unpleasant visitors."

"What does any of this have to do with me?"

"I was getting to that. Every so often the warrior or guardian being ushered into ascendancy develops a special quality. They are able to facilitate ascendancy in others. Those are called Core Ascendants. You could imagine how pivotal it would be to have an Ascendant of that caliber on your side."

"So a core Ascendant can basically create or help create other Ascendants?"

"Well that's a gross oversimplification, but something like that."

"So there you go I'm sure there are core Ascendants left, right?

"Of the hundred or so Ascendants on your plane, a number that I am certain has decreased, only five were Core Ascendants. Out of those five, three are dead; one is missing and is not even on the plane."

"What about the last one?"

"She is the one that sent me."

"Why?"

"Surely you aren't this obtuse. She thinks you could be an Ascendant, more importantly she thinks you may be a core."

"Me? A Core Ascendant? I don't think so."

"It's no longer up to you to decide. You have many people counting, depending on what you could become."

"I think you are leaving some things out, Roman." It was Devin. Was that his name or was he at some point an actual Roman?

Roman turned to where Devin stood at the rear of the room. "Devin, I was wondering when you would show."

"Tell him, Roman; tell him the part you left out."

Roman turned to face me. "It's inconsequential really, considering the greater good."

"Tell him or I will."

Roman sighed. "Very well, there is a small matter, actually a small chance that the Ascension will suppress your persona to the extent that your weapon, not you, will remain in control."

"And?" said Devin.

"And there are quite a few interested parties that would like this to occur."

"So aside from having to die and be brought back, somehow I also run the risk of completely being controlled by my weapon."

"See? He understands and I daresay he is facing it rather well," said Roman.

They both turned to look at me.

"No, I don't think that is something I am going to take rather well," I said

Roman stood and walked over to the doorway. He turned to face me. "I'm afraid I'm not offering you a choice. You will have to come with me."

"This is not going to happen," Devin said as he undid the straps holding me down.

Roman looked on with a pleased expression. "Are you saying that you are going to stop me?"

"Roman, that's exactly what I'm saying."

"You realize I'm here under Aurora's request and that if I fail it only means she will be angry and more determined."

Devin said nothing.

"You know you are no match for me. We have established this countless times."

"Maybe I'm just hard-headed."

Roman shook his head as he pulled his sleeves tight to his forearms. "Devin, Devin, Devin, you would throw your life away today? We aren't sparring, I will show you no quarter."

"None expected, Roman." Devin's face was grim.

"Let us see if you have improved from our last meeting."

Devin stepped into an open space on the other side of the room.

"I will finally put you out of your misery Devin, and I will enjoy this," whispered Roman.

"Roman, you talk too much," Devin said as his hands began to glow.

CHAPTER FIFTY TWO-FINAL GAMBIT

I made a move to get closer to Devin, but he stopped me with a stare downwards at the spheres on the bed surrounding me, and shook his head. As he drew closer to Devin, Roman removed his outer cloak, revealing a defined physique. It was obvious Roman trained, very hard. He paused a moment to speak to me. "I would suggest against any sudden movements. The spheres around you are keyed to your chi energy. They function as a type of retriever, in the extremely unlikely event of Devin defeating me, you will be sent to Aurora immediately. Just sit tight; this will be over soon enough." He turned to Devin, looking almost bored. "Are you ready?"

The glow that was around his hands now coursed over Devin's entire body. It looked as if he were in the middle of an electrical field.

"Is that new, Devin?" Devin remained silent and then disappeared. He reappeared slightly behind Roman as a blur, disappearing an instant later as Roman turned to swing his arm where Devin was only moments before. Devin reappeared again, slamming a palm into Roman's chest. Roman managed to get his arm up in time, but only barely. The blow sent Roman sliding back four feet. Roman shook his arm as if shaking off the strike.

"That was impressive. Seems you have been making good use of your time, Devin."

"I have," Devin said as he prepared to launch another series of attacks. This time Roman was prepared and evaded or blocked each of Devin's attacks, with a greater margin of ease. I could see Devin begin to sweat, while Roman looked as if he were engaging in some leisure activity. That was when I felt the shift. I sensed something subtle change within Devin. It seemed like Roman sensed it as well. He was no longer taking Devin's attacks lightly. The flow that surrounded Devin had disappeared but I could feel the energy roiling the air around him. His hands were glowing blue and Roman was having a difficult time staying out of range.

The first clean strike was a knife hand to Roman's inner thigh. He grunted in pain. Devin followed the strike with a percussive set of strikes to Roman's body. I could hear the ribs break as Devin struck Roman. He finished his attack, evading a lunging strike by ducking and spinning a back fist into the side of Roman's head, sending him across the floor to land sprawled on his back. Roman stood up. I could see the blood in the corners of his mouth, indicating internal damage. His face was bruising rapidly where Devin had struck. He spit on the floor, a mixture of blood and saliva. Then he started laughing.

"I haven't felt this good in years! This is excellent! Allow me to return the favor!" In his hands a double headed hammer coalesced. It looked like a long dumbbell but rather than the ends being round, each was a rectangular block. Symbols covered each of the hammer's heads. Each head was black and seemed to siphon the light around it. The symbols were a deep blue. The shaft between each of the hammers was silver and reflected the light as if it was glowing. Getting hit by that weapon did not seem like a good idea. Roman wiped the blood from his face and with a smile lunged at Devin. Devin clasped his hands together as Roman smashed into him. A bluish green light filled the room, blinding me. I turned my face to avoid the glare. When it subsided, I saw both Roman and Devin were sweating freely now. Devin however was breathing heavily as if he were exerting himself..

"A shield Devin, how quaint. You know this can't last," Roman said as he struck at Devin. Each time the hammer struck an invisible barrier, I noticed the light from each strike grew dimmer and it seemed Devin became weaker. When it seemed that Roman had broken through and his barrier was gone, Devin ran to where I sat.

"Time for you to go!" he said with difficulty, in between breaths.

"What about —" I turned to see Roman moving slower than normal.

"What he thought was a shield was really a temporal catalyst. Each time he hit it, it displaced time around him in very small increments. With each strike that amount grew exponentially."

"Is he stuck?"

"No, he will come out of the temporal trap in about sixty seconds or so. That's plenty of time to get you out of here."

"What about you? You're coming?"

"I can't. If I release the trap too early it will unravel and envelop me."

"How are you holding it intact?" He gave me a grim smile. "The temporal trap is a last ditch effort, Dante. Right now, my chi is what is keeping him in place. Once time runs out, I'm done. I'll be lucky if I could stand, much less fight him."

"There has to be a way, there is always a way."

"There is, the way is to get you back to Meja and the group. My journey along this path is complete, Dante. You on the other hand, have much to do."

I couldn't believe this. I refused to believe it. While speaking, Devin had disabled the spheres around me and had manipulated one so that it became a dull blue.

"This one will take you to Meja. The instant the trap winds down, you press here." He indicated a slight depression in the sphere. "I've already set the other spheres to destroy themselves. You must do this, Dante. Don't worry about me. I'll find a way out." We both knew it was a lie. He went back to where Roman stood and put both hands on the hammer. "Remember, Dante, as soon as the trap runs down, not a moment before."

I nodded my head, my voice caught in my throat.

"I'll see you soon, Dante." He didn't look at me as he spoke. I felt the air around us charge and then thump as Roman emerged from the temporal trap.

"Very elegant Devin, a temporal trap, disguised as a shield. Surely you didn't make that one on your own."

"Go to hell, Roman."

Roman chuckled. "Devin, it's where I vacation, didn't you know?"

Devin sagged against Roman. "Now you die." Roman pulled the hammer, and Devin, in a semi-circle. Twisting the hammer, he wrenched it free from Devin's grip. He rotated with blinding speed driving the hammer into Devin's midsection. I heard a sickening crunch as I knew several ribs were broken. Devin bent double as he coughed up blood. Roman slammed the hammer into his back, crushing it. Devin's legs crumpled beneath him. He looked up at me, fire burning in his eyes. "Now!"

As Roman brought the hammer down for the final blow, I pressed the sphere. I felt the air around me compress. I turned to see Roman, his face livid with rage. He brought the hammer down on Devin's broken body several times, and then he turned to me. He was becoming indistinct. "I will find you, Dante. On that you can rest assured." Then the spheres detonated and everything became white.

CHAPTER FIFTY THREE-REUNION

"He's coming to." For a moment all I could see was the hammer coming down over and over again. The image burned into my brain. A face came into focus: Meja.

"For a moment, I thought we lost you."

"Where are we?" Meja looked at me quizzically. "What do you mean, where are we? We have just arrived at the Akashic Records. Where did you think you were?"

"I saw Devin." I couldn't have dreamt that.

"Devin? How, when? You never left my side."

"I did. Some guy named Roman –"

"Did you say Roman?" It was Sylk.

"Yes, he…" I couldn't look at Meja. "He killed Devin, said something about some woman named Aurora and Ascendants. It's all jumbled at the moment."

Sylk looked apprehensive. "If Aurora is involved we have just attracted the wrong kind of attention."

"Is this the same one from the passage? Who is she?" I asked.

"I can't go into more detail. Not now, we really don't have time. Samir, did you find it?"

"I found it, extricating it will be another matter," said Samir, running his hands through his hair.

"Leave that to me. We must make haste. Time has become our enemy now. Guardian, gather up the Warrior. Everyone else stay close. The Akashic Records are more treacherous than what appears on the surface."

I tried to stand and found that my legs were no longer receiving signals from my brain, "What the hell?"

"It can be a side effect of wave ride, an unforeseen detour can sometimes cause shorts in the electrical system of the brain. Your body just needs some time to readjust. Unfortunately, time is the one thing we have precious little of." Sylk looked down at me, sadness in his eyes. He turned to Meja. "My sympathies, Monitor. If Devin was facing Aurora's enforcer, his was a path destined to end. No one has defeated Roman's infernal hammer."

Meja, tears in her eyes, turned away.

"We'd better get moving then," she said thickly.

Zen picked me up like a sack of potatoes. "You okay, D?" he whispered. I couldn't answer. How would I ever tell Meja that Devin sacrificed himself for me? Even now the truth of it pressed heavily on my chest. I had to tell them what was going on with the Ascendants, and what we were up against. How would I explain it all? More importantly how would I keep them safe, especially Meja? All these questions plagued me as we entered the hallway that led to the Akashic Records. I looked at Meja, my heart breaking with her pain. I knew I would die before I let anything cause her any more pain. I vowed to end this and get her away someplace safe. Deep within, I heard a laugh. It was Maelstrom.

"Let's see what it will take to keep that vow, vessel. I look forward to it."

The End

Thank you for joining me, please share with family and friends. It would be great if you could leave me a review wherever you purchased the story. Thank you, your reviews help!

Please visit my blog, leave a comment and join my email list.

I look forward to hearing from you.

Other titles by Orlando Sanchez

Blur-A John Kane Novel

The Deepest Cut-A Blur Short

The Last Dance A Sepia Blue Short

About the Author:

Orlando Sanchez has been writing ever since his teens when he was immersed in playing Dungeon and Dragons with his friends every weekend. An avid reader, his influences are too numerous to list here.

Aside from writing, his passion is the martial arts; he currently holds a 2nd Dan and 3rd Dan in two styles of Karate. If not training, he is studying some aspect of the martial arts or martial arts philosophy, or writing in his blog. For more information on the dojo he trains at, please visit www.mkdkarate.com

Connect with me online:

Blog: http://nascentnovel.com/

Facebook:
https://www.facebook.com/OSanchezAuthor

Twitter: https://twitter.com/SenseiOrlando